The
Anchor

Sam Bushala

ARCHWAY
PUBLISHING

Archway Publishing books may be ordered through booksellers or by contacting:

Archway Publishing
1663 Liberty Drive
Bloomington, IN 47403
www.archwaypublishing.com
1 (888) 242-5904

Because of the dynamic nature of the Internet, any web addresses or
links contained in this book may have changed since publication and
may no longer be valid. The views expressed in this work are solely those
of the author and do not necessarily reflect the views of the publisher,
and the publisher hereby disclaims any responsibility for them.

Any people depicted in stock imagery provided by Thinkstock are models,
and such images are being used for illustrative purposes only.
Certain stock imagery © Thinkstock.

ISBN: 978-1-4808-2347-1 (sc)
ISBN: 978-1-4808-2348-8 (e)

Library of Congress Control Number: 2015916879

Print information available on the last page.

Archway Publishing rev. date: 12/10/2015

To Marian

The Major Characters

Larry Lincoln - Television News Anchor

Burt Baywatch - Publicity Agent

Tomaso Vocino - Mayor of Castella, Sicily

Angelo Vocino - Mayor Vocino's brother

Steve Tanner - Vice President,News Programing

Alex LaRue - News Production Manager

Pearl Necklace – Television News Anchor

Paolo, Carlo, and Gianni Polucci - Black Hand Mob

Tom Dauber - News Director

Victorio Marcasi – Mafia Don

George Ingersoll - CEO, YOURchannel

Willian Saxton – President, News Division

Henry Handleman – President, Entertainment Division

Carl Macon – President, Public Relation Division

Philip Sanford – President, Legal Affairs

New York

"I'm tellin' you, Larry, if you go along with this once-in-a-lifetime opportunity, your television ratings will break off the chart and race up the wall. I'm talkin' whole points here, pal, and points mean money. Big money. Would you like to know how big? Close your eyes. Go ahead, close your eyes. That's it. Now picture a long line of numbers. Can you see them? Count them."

"I'm counting."

"There's more, Larry. You can open them now. I'm also talkin' hero worship. Everyone from CEO Ingersoll on down pushing each other out of the way to say good morning. Your face in the annual report, maybe the cover. That's what I'm talking. Open your eyes, Larry."

Burt Baywatch had spent twenty years as a Hollywood press agent, talking his short list of clients into situations that he always claimed would produce an avalanche of publicity while he dreamed of the day when he would hit it big, creating a public relations sensation that would bring him a reputation for transforming unknowns into celebrities. With this would come fame for himself, a Madison Avenue office, important clients, and prized contracts. After twenty years, it was still only a dream, but this time he was certain he had the big one, the bases loaded home run at the bottom of the ninth idea. He could feel it in his gut, and his client, Larry Lincoln, television news anchorman, would be his ticket to the big time.

In the beginning of his career, when things were slow, Baywatch tried acting but with little success beyond filling space as an extra. His opportunity in television came in a *Baywatch* television production in which he was to portray a drowning swimmer. Fearful of being denied the role, he avoided telling the casting director he couldn't swim, a career-ending decision, which nearly resulted in drowning both himself and the show's star actress, who had the lifeguard role of saving him. The moment he jumped into the water, panic struck, and he began thrashing about frantically, giving what the director felt at that moment was the most realistic performance he had ever witnessed. When the lifeguard swam to him, Baywatch lunged at her in desperation. Mistaking his struggle to survive for an opportunity to grope, the actress promptly drove her knee into his groin, putting an end to the scene and his movie career.

After being revived and fired, he decided to give his public relations agency his full attention and for the third time in his career changed his name. In a moment of self-described brilliance, he selected Baywatch, thinking that an association with one of the world's most popular television shows at the time would impress potential clients.

Now he was in Lincoln's office to once again review and persuade Lincoln to acquiesce to his plan for a blockbuster news story that he had uncovered, and which he felt certain was a fantastic opportunity for both his client and himself. To his disappointment, it was a plan Lincoln was hesitant to engage in.

"Maybe we should clear it upstairs first," Lincoln said, not wanting to take the chance of further weakening the precarious hold he had on his job anchoring the television evening news show on YOURchannel, a cable company. Lincoln had worked hard at the job, and though he performed to the best of his ability and felt his performance and his handsome appearance were as good as his competitors' on the networks, he was unable to build a wide audience. After two years with YOURchannel, he was losing both rating points and confidence in himself and his agent.

"Negative, Larry. No way." Baywatch advised. "You say one word about this breakthrough opportunity to those spineless suits, and in twenty minutes the whole world knows. Zap! We lose the exclusive! There's not a single person on that seventh floor with balls. I know how that scenario plays out. 'Gee, Larry, it sounds risky.' That's what you'd get. Then in come Moe and Curly. I can hear them now. 'Lincoln, do you want to offend our Italian viewers?' And finally, the old standby: 'It's not a bad idea, but let's think about it.'"

Baywatch began pacing the floor as he always did when excited by a promotional idea. This was the best he had ever come upon, and he didn't want it lost because of Lincoln's uncertainty and the weak hold he had on his job. Without a doubt in his mind, this was his one-way ticket to a Madison Avenue office.

"Larry, no one—absolutely no one—must know about this interview. You, me, and my Italian contact. I'm talkin' CIA–KGB stuff here, big guy. Top secret in big, block capital letters."

He walked up to face Lincoln and laid his hands on his client's shoulders. "It will be simple and fast, Larry. You fly to Sicily like on vacation, you rent a car, and drive to Monte Castella where I meet you. We pick up my guy, Angelo, and we drive to the don's villa. Once inside, you do the interviewing and I handle the video. We do three or four hours of his tell-all and then out the door, back to Palermo, and on the plane home. Think about it. Four hours, Larry, and you have the hottest Mafia story ever recorded."

Baywatch began pacing again. Using his arms for emphasis, he continued: "Picture this headline on the screen: 'Mafia Exposed … The Lowdown on the Lowlife'. Is that great or what?"

Lincoln frowned, raised a hand, and gave him a thumb down disapproval.

"Okay, not to worry. The writers will come up with something great. The important thing here is your story--your exclusive story, I must add—of the entire Sicilian and US mob operations exposed by an insider. Not just any insider but a top don. One of the original men of respect, my guy tells me. He's at that level, the guy who decides what and who goes down. Can't you just see it, Larry? There you are in millions of households, anchorman Larry Lincoln, the guy who told it all."

He stopped to face Lincoln again. "From that interview we'll get enough for a ten-minute segment every day for a week on your evening news show, and then we end with a wrap-up hour special Sunday night prime time. Jackpot, Larry, jackpot! Emmy time! I can't tell you how excited I am about this. This is it for you. I can feel it. I just know it's right."

Lincoln turned and walked across his office, stopping to stare into his full-length mirror, slowly turning his head from side to side to inspect his hair. "About your guy, Burt …

"Solid, Larry. He's your kind of guy. True blue, pure gold. You think I can't spot a phony? How long have I been your agent, your friend?"

"One year."

"Right, but like a lifetime. Listen, I told you from the start I would take you to the top, to that number one level ratings-wise before your contract runs out. Take you to the multi-million dollar rung. And remember, I said that while being fully aware of your hair problem."

"I don't have a hair problem."

"Yeah, okay. Whatever you say. Let's put it this way, we don't have a lot of time. You have eleven months left on your contract and by that time … Let's not give that another thought. By that time you'll be on top of the hill with everyone looking up at you and your hair won't matter."

Lincoln's shoulders sagged. Unconsciously, he raised his hand and gently ran his forefinger across the top of his hair. "I don't understand it. My father still has a full head of hair and he's six-ty-five. Dammit!"

"It's your grandfather, Larry. It always skips a generation."

"Where did you get that?"

"The Internet."

"Oh."

"Come on, pal. Don't go weak-kneed on me. With this coup we'll be talking instant contract restructuring. After that, let the hairs fall where they may."

"Can we get off that?"

"Can we do this deal, Larry? That's the question. A question we must answer now. I can't keep this guy hanging. This is serious stuff. The don won't wait. He's already told my guy he's taking a big chance doing this. He's putting his life on the line."

"What's he getting out of this?"

"He's evening the score. There's a contract out on him, and he wants to fight back. Plus some money. But not a lot. A measly three hundred grand, and you know YOURchannel will cover that easily. Hell, they paid that call girl fifty thousand just to nail a congressman, and that didn't do a damn thing for their ratings. Just a blip on the screen. We'll have to pay up front, of course."

"By 'of course,' you mean I'll have to pay up front."

"Well, you can't ask for three hundred thousand from the company without a reason. That would blow everything. Don't start counting pennies on me now, Larry. We're talking a major career move. You'll get that money back plus a new contract with seven figures plus." Baywatch followed Lincoln to the mirror and stood behind him, observing the area of thinning hair on the top of his head. "How about it, pal. Can we swing? Can we do it?"

Larry Lincoln spotted his agent in the mirror and moved away. He crossed the room to the window and looked out upon the park. Nothing seemed to have gone right for him over the past year. There were constant, embarrassing blunders on the show, and his ratings had continued to drop with each monthly report.

Now what was most disturbing, rumors were circulating around the office and in the press about major changes that were about to occur at YOURchannel. He had hired Baywatch, whom he met at a movie premiere, with the hope of turning his fortunes around, but the few ideas he dreamed up never worked as they were intended. Some had turned into disasters. However, his fee was low.

"I just don't understand," Lincoln said. "After years of working in every lousy small-time television newsroom. Years of reading every stupid story they threw up in front of me. Years of voice lessons, diction lessons, reading lessons, intonation and breathing lessons, geography lessons, and a fortune in clothes. Ten years of having really great hair, I might add."

"Forget about the hair. I'm sorry I brought it up. Just concentrate on this news story. This is the big score. It will be television history, a crime exposure that will make you top anchor. Then there's a definite book deal. Like Hemingway said, Larry, it's time to make the earth move. That's where we are right now—earth moving time."

Lincoln struggled with his feelings. There was something about his agent's big plan that made him uneasy. The fact that his ideas had not gone well in the past preyed on his mind. He remembered when on Burt's advice he had talked his boss into allowing him to do live interviews on the street. He called the segment, "Get It off Your Chest." It started out smoothly, but the third person he interviewed punched him. Baywatch thought it was successful because the story was covered on television and in all the newspapers.

"What's this mafia guy's name?" he asked.

"My contact is Angelo Vocino. His brother is the mayor of Monte Castella. He wouldn't give me the name of the don. He said it was too dangerous to give names in advance. That's what I keep telling you. We're in the danger zone here. We can't mess around."

"I just hope you're right this time, Burt. Not like the last one."

"Hey, that's not totally up and up. You never bothered to tell me that improvising was not your strength. Forget all that now. We learn by our mistakes and we go forward to success. That's what we're about to do now, if you just give me the word."

"Our mistakes?" Lincoln snapped back.

"Okay, I admit, I've not always been right. But this time I am. This time it'll work out, Larry. I'll be there every minute. I'll be right with you to make sure everything goes as planned. No chance for errors. Absolutely control-city all the way. You watch."

Monte Castella, Sicily

Ajubilant Angelo Victorio Vocino bounded up the stairs to the mayor's office while singing his favorite Verdi aria. He had finished his telephone call with Burt Baywatch less than fifteen minutes ago and was anxious to relay the good news to his brother, Tomaso Alberto Vocino, the mayor of Monte Castella for the past sixteen years, who had been waiting impatiently and welcomed him with a question the moment the door swung open.

"They're coming?"

Angelo smiled and swung his arms out to embrace his brother. "He went for it like a baby to his mother's teat. Everything we planned is underway. They will be here in just three weeks from Monday."

Mayor Vocino bounded from around his desk and threw himself into his brother's arms, an act made difficult by the enormous size of the two men. After kisses on both cheeks, they laughed loudly, then separated and finished the last of the aria together, holding the final note as long as their lungs permitted.

Breathing heavily from his climb up the stairs and the singing, Angelo sank into one of the office chairs and threw his feet up on the other.

"Tell me all the details, Angelo."

"They will be arriving in three weeks, landing in Palermo, and then driving here. They are traveling separately with the agent coming first and the newsman the following day. I told them to do that to add intrigue. I'm to meet the agent here for breakfast and the newsman will be meeting us the following day for lunch. This will be at my restaurant, of course. After feasting on the best meal ever placed before them, we will come here to talk to you. It will be as an interview, and they will tape it."

Mayor Vocino interrupted, breaking out in a laugh. "Good, good. I will turn Monte Castella into the jewel of Sicily. I will create an Eden."

"I'm sure you will, Tomaso. After that, we'll drive around town and the countryside for a couple of hours, and then we'll allow them to rest before dinner. This time at your hotel."

"It will be glorious," the mayor interrupted. "I will prepare it myself. Listen to this. We will begin with funghi marinati, followed by zuppa di pesce and just a small dish of fettuccine alla Vocino. Then my masterpiece, pollo con rosemarino e peperoncino. What do you think?"

"They will go mad," his brother shouted.

"After that, a little tartufi de cioccolato. But I interrupt. Continue with the plan."

"Actually, that will be it for the first day. Of course, we will spend the rest of the night sampling our wines. The next morning we will conduct the great mafia interview."

"You're sure Giuseppe is up to it?" the mayor asked.

His brother laughed. "Without question. He can't wait. He sees this as the start of an acting career. He's already talking about an agent. You should see him rehearsing. He tries to look like Brando. I've given him a dozen crime movie videos and four books about the mafia. He's writing his own script. He'll fill that TV man with stories Coppola would drool over. We have plenty of time to rehearse."

Angelo rose from his chair, walked to his brother's side and placed his arm around his shoulder. "This will go well, Tomaso, believe me. Everything is set and everyone is cooperating. We will have it all on tape. You, the town, the mountains, the food and wine, all of it. Of course, we will have exciting stories about the mafia. When this is shown on American television, it will put Monte Castella on the map. The Hollywood people will rush over here to do their pictures. Then the movie stars. And where the movie stars go, the tourists will follow. I guarantee it. Look what *La Dolce Vita* did for Rome and the Via Veneto."

Mayor Vocino hugged his brother again, and then walked across his office to the window. He looked down upon the sunny, empty streets.

"I pray you are right, Angelo," he said softly. "We need this. We need it badly." He shook his head slowly. "I remembered the day as a child when I watched the American army ride through this town on that very street. It is like it happened yesterday. They were on their way to Palermo, and it was the most exciting day in my life and in the lives of our people. Nothing had ever been like that day before or since. Nothing! The streets were filled with everyone in town and those who had come from the farms and neighboring villages to cheer the Americans. They danced, shouted, drank, and waved American flags, Italian flags. They jumped on the soldiers and on their tanks, hugging and kissing them, showering them with flowers and wine. They would not let them pass, wanting them to stay there forever."

Mayor Tomaso never forgot that scene. It was an explosive celebration of joy, love, music, wine, and liberation, an exhilarating madness that went on right through the night and well into the next day. He remembered every magical moment, and he longed for it again, wanting to see his town full of life, his people happy and celebrating. He wanted it all back again.

"Three weeks is a very short time, Angelo," he said. "Are you sure we can do it? Three short weeks to clean up the entire town, bring in people to fill up the streets, rehearse our musicians, hire some horse and carriage outfits, and hang flags. We must have flags everywhere. And remember, we must have pictures of the liberation of Monte Castella in every store window, in every restaurant, and, of course, in their rooms."

"It's all underway, Tomaso. Your granddaughter Nina is in charge of the musicians and the cleanup. Ferraro and his brother will arrange to bring in all the farmers. You will contact the mayors from every town around here to participate. Committees will be formed to paint, clean, hang flags … Everything is planned."

Angelo had been a child at the time of the great day of liberation, but he had heard every detail of that experience from his brother many times over the past five decades. The story had been related so often he had begun to feel that he had been witness to it himself. He also wanted those moments to return to his town.

Monte Castella had not grown much since those days, remaining frozen in time as a farming town in an agricultural region. The government had brought in a few small industrial plants, but the last new one to move in was over ten years ago, and it had closed. After that, nothing had changed. Time had passed the town.

"Have you talked to Father Autobelli about a religious festival?" Mayor Vocino asked. "A religious parade always looks good on television."

"Of course! He loves the idea. Naturally, I didn't tell him everything. I also talked to the Polucci brothers about providing a little mafia atmosphere."

Mayor Vocino grimaced and swung around. "You watch out for those three. They're all a little crazy. This is our big opportunity, and we don't need crazy. You know the trouble we had with them in the past. You never know what they might do. They could ruin us."

"I will watch them personally. They are to do nothing but sit around, stare, and smoke. I told them they are to look like mafiosi. They are to be the don's guards, but nothing more. I threatened all three of them with jail if they do anything crazy. They promised to behave."

"We have so much to do, Angelo, and it must be done right. No mistakes. Remember, the election is in three months, and the town is depending on us and this plan."

"It will go smoothly, brother. We will fill these news people with food and wine and music and crime. I'll even throw in love if I have to. When we're finished with them, they'll have more than enough film to keep the town of Monte Castella on American television for a month."

"Forget the love part, Angelo," Mayor Vocino said, waving his finger. "I don't want Father Autobelli running in here. Keep their minds on the mafia, the town, and the countryside. Especially the mafia. That's the key to this whole thing."

"I've already set that up. I told this Baywatch guy my life was on the line making the arrangements. You won't believe this, but he offered me an FBI witness protection program in Hollywood. He was salivating when I hung up the phone. He simply couldn't wait to get started. Relax, Tomaso. Everything will go smoothly."

New York

Steve Tanner, vice president of YOURchannel news pro-graming, lit his cigar and leaned back in his chair, re-laxed and happy about the way things were turning in his direction. Larry Lincoln's request for vacation time came as a surprise, but with it a grand opportunity to put into action a plan he had been thinking about for a long time. He knew immediately Lincoln's temporary departure from anchoring the failing daily evening news provided the opportunity for his grand venture. The news program had serious problems that needed to be solved, but even more important in his mind, television journalism and news reporting had to be saved. Even if it meant his job and career, this was the time to take a stand and he would do it.

Like a cat ready to pounce, he sat silently behind his desk and waited patiently while Alex LaRue, his production manager, rambled on about how much time and effort he had spent in finding just the right temporary replacement for Lincoln, some-one with enough talent who would hopefully not lose any more rating points.

Like Tanner, LaRue had also been preparing for changes in the YOURchannel evening news show. Immediately upon learning of Lincoln's vacation plans, he devoted as much time as possible viewing videos of television news readers. He was looking for someone new, a potential star, someone he could take credit for in hiring. His desire to please his boss was of great importance, second only to furthering his own career, and there was a wide gap in between. He never walked into Tanner's office without thinking about the furniture changes he would make once his inevitable day of promotion would come.

He began his presentation in a deep, earnest voice. "We have three top players who could fill in for Larry, but the one I would strongly recommend is Hadley. He's really good. Distinctive, serious voice, resonating with authority and substance, yet warm. Thirty in appearance, but he exudes broad experience. Blue eyes with 20-20 vision and a master-class reader. An imposing six-footer, yet not overpowering. A lady-killer face, yet athletic enough to appeal to men. He has great hair, outstanding hair! Practically down to his eyebrows. I've got videos, but look at these press photos. Look at that hair."

LaRue leaned across his superior's desk and spread out a series of head-and-shoulder photographs of his prospect, each taken from a different angle and offering different expressions. As a collection, they showed a wide range of emotions from joy to cheerfulness to compassion to tragedy.

"That's his end-of-humorous-story look," LaRue said, pointing to one of the photos. Look at that smile and those teeth, Steve. Have you ever seen that many teeth in a smile? What's more, he can smile and talk at the same time. Better than any evangelical preacher I've ever seen. Here's another one. It's his DCD face."

"DCD?"

"Death, crime, or disaster. He's also great at reading from the teleprompter without making it obvious. Not like our Larry, whose eyes always move back and forth."

Tanner leaned forward to scan the photographs. After a few moments, he backed away and reached into his top drawer to pull out a four-month-old magazine.

"Forget him. Here's our new anchor." He tossed the magazine across the desk.

LaRue froze, unsure of what his response should be. He was not good at handling the unexpected. He required time to find his position.

"The centerfold," Tanner told him. "Turn to the centerfold."

LaRue deliberately fumbled with the magazine, allowing it to drop to the floor. He slowly picked it up and worked his way to the center spread while trying to determine if Tanner was serious or simply playing with him. He needed to know how to react, how not to appear taken in if this were a joke, and what his reaction should be if it were serious.

"She's beautiful," he said, opening up the spread.

"Of course she is. More than beautiful, she's smart. Right now she's waiting for my call. All five foot ten of her, all voluptuous curve of her. Look at her. Look at the beauty of that face, the eyes, the hair, the body. Picture the news coming out of those lips five nights a week. Can you picture it? Can you feel the excitement?"

LaRue realized Tanner was serious and his demon nature took over. He was in control of himself again. He knew instantly he was in a win-win situation. Either this would be the biggest television disaster ever, in which case Tanner would be toast, or it would be a rating sensation and Tanner would be promoted. Either way he would replace him. He was sure of that. His thoughts turned quickly to his new furniture.

"Do you think she can handle it?" he cautioned, playing the adviser role, but not strongly enough to cast doubt on the plan.

"Handle it? Are you serious? Handle what? Listen, Alex, you know damn well how long anchors are actually on the screen in that half-hour of television evening news. Never over five minutes. They read a twenty-second story intro, and then it's cut away to the reporter or film. During the entire half-hour show, they're only on live a few minutes. And then reading from prompters, I might add."

Tanner took the magazine and placed it in a drawer. "Think about it. Are they there because they're more informed or have a profound grasp of national and world events? Hell, no! It's because of profile and feel-good and because TV made them celebrities. Well, believe me, we're going to create the biggest celebrity in the news business." He leaned forward and smiled. "Can she handle it? you ask. Can she read large letters on a prompter? Ha! She can handle it in spades. I've already met her. She's smart and talented. She'll melt that screen. She'll steam, and she'll send YOURchannel ratings up like a rocket!"

LaRue felt it was time to make his move. In his most re-hearsed sincere manner, he answered, "I have to tell you, Steve. This is a genius move. This is a shaker. This could do to TV news what Murrow's London broadcasts did for radio."

Tanner looked up at him over his glasses and frowned. LaRue stiffened, realizing he had overplayed it. "I was only kidding with that, Steve, but I just wanted you to know I think it's a great idea."

Quickly LaRue changed the subject. "What about Larry when he returns?"

"If this clicks like I know it will, we give him segments and other programs. That's our option. It's in his contract's ratings clause. Now let's move. You have three weeks to train her, to turn her into a professional news reader. But listen, Alex, I want all of this carried out in total secrecy. No one knows anything until just prior to show time. Have you got that? Absolute secrecy. Rent a small studio somewhere and you do the training yourself. I'll be checking in daily and I'll cover for you here. Here's her bio."

LaRue looked at the file Tanner handed him. "That's her name? Pearl Necklace?" he asked incredulously. "That's it?"

"That's just her stage name."

"Her stage name? Pearl Necklace?"

Tanner waved him off. "It's all in the file. Just read it."

As LaRue headed toward the door, Tanner added, "Anyway, it's a helluva lot better than Lawrence Lincoln."

LaRue felt the stab. It was a reminder that he had been the one who came up with Larry's new last name as a way of creating an aura about the news show. Names were always of great importance to him. Years earlier, before he was hired at YOURchannel, he had changed his own name to LaRue, hoping it would cover his weak character.

"I'll move on this immediately, Steve. You can depend on me to do the job and do it right." With the photos he collected from Tanner's desk, he walked quickly out of the office.

Once he was alone, Tanner envisioned the daily news show he was going to produce. *Oh yes, Pearl Necklace*, he thought. *You and I are going to do it right. There will be cleavage and legs … lots of legs. Miniskirts and short pants that barely extend below your hips. Lots of skin. What's more, you won't be stuck behind some phony news desk. When that screen opens, you'll be on a chair. Nothing on the set besides a chair. Maybe sometimes no chair at all, all by yourself with dramatic lighting, and the photos behind you will be huge and eye-popping. I'll handle that part of the production myself. We'll merchandise you like no other product has ever been merchandised. We'll make you a household name overnight. If it's high ratings they want, we'll give them ratings they never dreamed of. Believe me, Pearl Necklace, this is going to be terrific. Then let the chips fall where they may. We'll soon see how this affects television news.*

Monte Castella

Paolo, Carlo, and Gianni Polucci had dreamed living a life of crime for as long as they could remember. In their early school years, they had tried to set up a protection racket, but their classmates beat them up. Later in life they attempted to establish a brothel in town, but the priest pounded them senseless and promised them eternal damnation. Once they even tried robbing the town bank, but the other customers threw them out. Soon after that, they ran away to Palermo to join a mob, but they were robbed and beaten, and their father had to drive there to pick them up and take them back home to the farm. Then he used a belt on them.

The farm was their big problem. They hated it and they hated the work their father demanded. From the day they saw their first American crime film, they knew the life they wanted in order to escape the farm and their father. Their major obstacle was their size. At five foot, five inches, no one took them seriously as gangsters. Or they beat them up.

Now they saw their opportunity. They had spent hundreds of hours watching movies and videos, studying the Hollywood criminal minds of Al Capone, John Dillinger, Bonnie and Clyde, Lucky Luciano, and Dutch Schultz, plus the mythical criminals portrayed by Humphrey Bogart, Edward G. Robinson, Al Pacino, Marlon Brando, and Robert De Niro, all of whom had created an image of the future they wanted. The *Godfather* movie trilogy was their gold standard. They had watched it dozens of times, replaying certain scenes over and over while memorizing the dialogue.

Their father tried constantly to make them farmers. Before he died at a relatively young age, which everyone attributed to the unending stress of living with his sons, he enrolled them at the university in Palermo for a year to study the latest farming techniques. In addition, one summer he had sent all three off to Iowa in the United States as exchange students for a three-month farming seminar but to no avail. They would attend a few classes but their primary interest while they were there was the movies in which they invested every available hour in theaters or with DVDs, learning and loving the walks, stares, smiles, apparel, and most importantly, the language of the American master criminals.

After their father died, they saw an opportunity to escape farming. They enlarged and reconstructed the barn and turned it into a bed and breakfast with two large apartments. They lined the walls of each room with crime movie posters and provided tapes of crime movies. The enterprise failed, however, due to the lack of both their enthusiasm and tourists. That didn't matter to them because they didn't enjoy the work anyway.

Paolo was the acknowledged leader of the Polucci Black Hand Mob, the name they had decided upon for its hint of violence. With their movie experience background and mindset, they were more than ready when Angelo Vocino told them of his plan to place Monte Castile on the tourist map and asked them to play the part of the don's bodyguard and create a criminal atmosphere while his guests from American television would be in town.

Angelo Vocino knew the Poluccis well, and he immediately set the rules and a warning. "All you have to do is walk into my restaurant when they are there and pretend to be gangsters," he told them. "Just swagger in with your coats draped over your shoulders like your movie actors and stare at everyone with a mean look. Have a bulge under your jackets. Keep your backs against the wall. All that stuff you usually do when you're not with your mother."

Angelo laid both hands on Paolo's shoulders. "Let me make something very clear to you, young man. No funny business, you hear me? You do nothing more than I have told you. All I want from you three is acting. Do you understand?"

All the brothers agreed. However, Paolo's mindset sparked an idea immediately far different from Angelo's instructions. "This is what we've been waiting for," he told his brothers later. "This is our opportunity for the big time, the big score."

"We put our guns on the table?" asked Carlo Polucci.

"We whack someone?" asked Gianni Polucci.

Paolo responded with a slap across Gianni's head. "Idiots! I'm talking big caper here. No, we don't do any such foolishness. What we do is we change the plan. We change everything. Listen, this guy is a television star, a man of importance, a celebrity. This is what we are going to do."

He paused and looked back and forth at his brothers, hoping to establish an atmosphere that would allow for the most dramatic effect in his announcement of the plan he had been thinking about since his conversation with Angelo. Both men leaned forward in anticipation.

"We kidnap him."

Carlo leaped up and grabbed his brother in a bear hug. "That's beautiful, Paolo. Magnificent! We kidnap him! Then we bring him here and cut off his ear."

It was Carlo's turn to receive a slap.

"We don't cut off his ear, stupid," Paolo explained. "How in the world could he get back on television without an ear? Without an ear he's useless. No, we simply hold him for ransom."

"We cut off his hair?" Carlo timidly asked, stepping beyond Paolo's reach.

Paolo thought for a moment. "That's good, Carlo. Very good.

We cut off a little hair and send it to his boss for proof that we have him. From the back of his head, of course, or the side. We must not ruin his looks. He must be able to get back on TV and talk about us. In my telephone call I will demand the ransom money. Lots of money. Two million dollars, maybe five million. This is going to be a big score for the Black Hand Mob."

"Ten million! And no credit cards," Carlo shot back, regaining his confidence and remembering the problems they had with credit cards when managing the bed and breakfast.

"That must be twelve million lire," shouted Gianni, who considered himself the gang's money man. He had difficulty in this role because he always wanted to convert foreign currency into lire first to get to euros.

There were a few moments of silence while each of the brothers tried to figure the exchange rates, a difficulty they also encountered in their tourist business venture.

"Anyway," continued Paolo, giving up on the math, "here's my plan. The newsman lands in Palermo and is supposed to rent a car and drive to Monte Castile to meet Angelo. Instead, we meet him at the airport first and tell him everything has been changed and we are to drive him to Monte Castella. Then we bring him here."

"Will he go along with that?" asked Carlo.

"You fool! He won't have anything to say about it. Remember, we are kidnapping him! We will tie him up. Then when we bring him back here, I will start the negotiations."

"What about Mama?" asked Gianni. "Do we let her in on this?"

"No, idiot!" Paolo snapped. "She'd beat the hell out of us. We keep the guy in one of our guest apartments and keep Mama away from the barn. That means we do all the work around here. We do everything. Show Mama we're changing our ways. Let her know we want her to take it easy like she's always talking about. We keep Mama in front of the television or in town. Better yet, we send her off to spend time with Angela. That won't be a problem.

She's always anxious to get out of here and see the grandchildren."
He paused to think about what he would tell his sister.

"Anyway," Paolo continued, "I'll make him give us the name
of his big television boss, and I'll phone him. We'll demand pay-
ment in cash and give them two days to deliver. They will receive
some of his hair so they'll know we're serious about the kidnapping and we are holding him."

"I get to cut his hair," said Carlo. "It was my idea."

"What do I do?" asked Gianni.

"You get yourself and Carlo some ski masks. No one must
ever see our faces or be able to identify us. I'll disguise myself for
the meeting at the airport. I will blend into the crowds, be unno-
ticeable. Gianni, you prepare the room: chairs, table, rope, tape,
and something we can use to keep him gagged. Have everything
we'll need to keep him bound and silent."

"What if they don't pay?" Carlo asked.

"Of course they'll pay. Angelo said he's their television news
star. He makes fortunes for them. They have no show without
him. They'll pay, don't worry. I've thought of everything. It will
work. It will be an offer they can't refuse."

"An offer they can't refuse," repeated Carlo and Gianni in
unison, remembering that wonderful movie scene they had memorized and played out so often. It was their favorite line, and they
looked forward to the day they could use it. "That's beautiful. An
offer they can't refuse."

Two weeks later, at the Palermo airport, Larry Lincoln was
approaching the car rental desk when he felt someone grab
his arm. He turned around and was startled to be facing a
full-bearded man in a World War I uniform and leaning on
crutches. He wore glasses, had a large nose, a bushy mustache,

and was wearing what was obviously a woman's wig that reached down to his shoulders.

"Mr. Larry Lincoln, the newsman?" the stranger asked.

"Yes, I'm Larry Lincoln. You wish an autograph?"

"Yes. That's good. Sign this while I talk" He held up one of the crutches. "I have a message from Angelo Vocino. There has been a change. Your rental car has been cancelled. For your safety, you are to follow me. Try not to look conspicuous. There is a chance we are being watched. Follow behind me." With that said, he turned and headed toward the exit.

Lincoln stood there a moment in confusion, watching the stranger stumble along on the crutches. The man stopped, turned around, and motioned with his head for him to follow, causing the wig to shift across one eye. As he turned back to continue toward the door, he tripped over the crutches and fell to the floor.

Lincoln ran over to help him. "No, no," Paolo whispered as he shoved his fake nose back in place. "Just follow. But be discreet. No one must notice. You are in terrible danger!"

Getting back on his feet, Paolo continued hobbling across to the terminal doors, only to be knocked down when he attempted to leave through the automatic entrance door rather than the exit. Picking himself up again, he shoved the crutches under his arm and pushed forward, receiving several pushes from passengers as he made his way through the crowd.

Lincoln picked up his luggage and looked around to see if there might be any underworld characters among the crowd of people who were staring at him. Overcome by fear, he quickly swung around and ran out of the terminal to find Paolo, who was at the curb holding open the rear door of a dented Fiat van.

"What the hell is this? You don't expect me to get in this thing?" Lincoln asked, noticing for the first time the rubber surgical gloves the man was wearing.

"Quick, quick," Paolo hissed. "We are using the truck for a disguise. We have no time to lose." He pointed past Lincoln's shoulder. "They have spotted us and they're coming fast. We have little time. Get in."

As Lincoln turned around to see who was attacking, Paolo moved quickly behind him, grabbed him by the seat of his pants, and with a violent heave, sent him hurtling into the van. Instantly, Gianni stuffed a towel into his mouth while Carlo tied his arms and legs.

Lincoln attempted to shout, only to feel a clammy hand slam down over his stuffed mouth. "Silence!" Carlo shouted, as he clicked open a switchblade knife. "Or I cut off your ear."

Lincoln let loose a long, loud moan while shaking his head.

Paolo grabbed the luggage, threw it into the truck, and slammed the door. The luggage hit Gianni in the head, causing him to fall across Lincoln, who moaned again.

"You won't listen, eh?" Carlo shouted into the darkness of the truck. "This will teach you not to fool with the Black Hand Mob." He raised his fist and brought it down hard in Lincoln's direction, slamming it instead into the back of Gianni's head. Both men screamed with pain as the van lurched forward, throwing them back against the rear of the van and driving Carlo's knife into Gianni's buttocks.

In his urgency to get underway while at the same time remove his disguise, Paolo had only an instant to see the car pull out in front of him before crashing into its rear, pitching him forward into the windshield. The sudden stop also threw both Carlo and Gianni forward, landing them on top of Lincoln, who once again let out a loud moan.

An hour later the farm truck was speeding across the Sicilian highway in the direction of Monte Castella with Paolo at the wheel, alternately cursing his luck, the driver of the car he had run into, the police, and the violation he received from the policeman, which he was now using to dab his bloody head.

"The price just went up," he shouted to his brothers in the rear. "They'll pay for this blood. They'll pay big time. They'll find out. Yes, they will soon learn that they're dealing with the Polucci Black Hand Mob."

In the back of the truck, Gianni removed his pants to inspect his wound while Larry Lincoln lay silent, his thoughts switching between what he would do if he ever saw his agent again, his five-room apartment in New York, and his financial portfolio.

New York

I t had taken Alex LaRue a week of working with Pearl Necklace to realize he was in a trap. Even though he had kept Tanner aware of the time and place of his training sessions, his boss never showed up. For the first few days, there were lame excuses for not joining in. After that, his telephone calls were unanswered, and at the office Tanner rebuffed any discussion of the matter. After a few training and rehearsal sessions, LaRue realized he had been set up to be the fall guy.

The bastard, LaRue thought. *He never intended to be a part of this. This is now my baby, and if it's a fiasco, I'll be the guy they hang. I won't be able to get a job doing weather reports after this. If it does work out, he'll take credit and be a winner.* The entire scheme came to him much too slowly, making him lose confidence in his own calculating mind. *I bet he had the tape running when we first discussed this project.*

He was right. Tanner understood LaRue too well to leave himself unprotected, knowing his scheming little manager would sabotage him given the chance. It wasn't that he wanted the blame to fall on LaRue. He simply wanted to guarantee his cooperation. After he left the room, Tanner turned off the recorder and locked his desk safe.

It will take the little snake a couple of days to realize where he stands and stop screwing around with the training program, Tanner thought *After that, he'll work overtime to turn her into a competent television news anchor.*

Everything worked out exactly as he had planned. During the first few days, LaRue tried every trick to weaken Pearl's confidence, while at the same time attempting to hit on her after each session. Much to his annoyance, he failed in both attempts. Rather than being discouraged, Pearl Necklace, a name she refused to change, learned quickly from her mistakes.

Realizing his inescapable career-ending predicament, LaRue used every available minute to teach one of the most beautiful and engaging women he had ever met everything he knew about television news anchoring: How to appear totally involved in every story, how to show concern over tragic news, how to switch instantly to a smile if the next item were lightweight, and how to use facial expressions and voice modulations to fit the tenor of the story.

After that, he taught her to emphasize certain words to show she knew what the story was about, how to give the impression that she had written the story herself, how to hold and shuffle papers in her hands, and most important of all, how to project a cheerfulness at the sign-off to leave her audience feeling pleasant as well as informed. Basically, he was teaching her the art of acting.

LaRue did not know that after she left him, she met Steve Tanner, his associate and director Tom Dauber, and the studio manager Walt Summers to plan and rehearse the content of the new YOURchannel evening news.

Pearl Necklace had never been a slow learner. It was in high school when she first realized she was not only smart but also had something about her that made men feel uneasy and perspire, and she enjoyed using that asset. Although she did not need this particular skill to gain the scholastic honors she achieved throughout her college years, it amused her, and she honed it to perfection whenever she had a conference with a professor.

After four years at UCLA, she moved to New York to enter the modeling field as a stepping stone, an activity in which she was successful but that left her bored within a year. She knew she didn't have the classic model's figure except for lingerie, but she also knew she did have the perfect centerfold numbers. In a short time she achieved that feat and moved on in pursuit of her bigger plan. There was no question in her mind that her future was in television, and every step she took was in that direction.

It was not long after her centerfold publication when, as a representative of the magazine, she met Steve Tanner at a fund-raising party and in the space of a half-hour explained to him the shortcomings of television news programs and how he could create the most exciting news show on television. She also let him know how she would be part of it.

That evening worked wonders on Tanner. He changed from a demoralized executive with a barren daily television news show to a man on a mission. It wasn't from the perspiration he felt that night while talking to her; it was from inside. Thirty years of experience came alive, and he had no doubts about what he would do. That feeling spread to every fiber of his body, and he knew instinctively it was the way to move and that he would do it.

It may be my swan song, he thought, *but I'll show what has happened to television journalism. If it's great hair and feel-good they want, I'll give it to them in spades. I'll swing that pendulum out so far it'll have to come back. Maybe not back to that time between the fifties and seventies, but at least in that direction. If that happens and television news can be separated from entertainment, it will be worth getting fired.*

Tanner was too well practiced in the field of corporate politics to leave anything to chance, and eliminating chance meant keeping LaRue from upsetting his plans. Taping their conversation provided proof that he was a coconspirator in the idea, and he could use it if necessary to assure LaRue's cooperation.

An hour before show time, Alex LaRue escorted Pearl Necklace into the new YOURchannel evening news television studio. The set was entirely white—the floor, the background—everything except for a bright yellow trapeze swing suspended from the ceiling that would be out of camera sight when the show started.

As she walked from the doorway to her position on the set, the chatter of the crew quickly died down. All movement stopped. The only noise came from her spiked heel footsteps. She removed the dressing robe she was wearing to reveal a tight-fitting, one-piece, red sequined outfit that stopped at and hugged her thighs and featured a severe plunging neckline. Except for the director Dauber and his studio manager Walt, no one in the crew on the floor or in the control room was aware of who was taking Lincoln's place, only that it would be a woman. Everyone involved in the production of the show had been carefully selected for their experience and competence.

"Oh, my God!" Walt whispered into his headset when he saw her walk onto the stage and take her position on the swing.

"Mine too," Dauber answered.

"Let's move it," LaRue demanded, playing his news manager's role to the fullest and shattering the silence. "Haven't you seen a woman before? We have one hour to prep this show. Move it." His strong commands were a cover-up for the queasy feeling in his stomach. Tanner had kept him busy and away from the show's preparation, and he had no idea what was going on. But he knew it wasn't good, and he felt he was going to be sick.

Ignoring LaRue as they always did, the crew moved slowly and quietly into the routine they all knew, at times bumping into each other, but never looking away from Pearl Necklace. Cameras, lights, and booms were rolled into positions. A ten-foot image of Pearl Necklace suddenly appeared on the backdrop screen.

Necklace sat on the swing, crossed her legs, and smoothed out her outfit. Looking around the room, she paused to make eye contact with every member of the production staff, giving each one her most engaging smile. In return she received a thumbs-up sign, and with that she knew she had them with her.

In the control room, the director, Tom Dauber, stared at his monitor, oblivious to the whistles and howls filling the room.

"Okay, take her up, Walt," Dauber spoke into the microphone that connected him to the floor crew. Slowly a hydraulic hoist lifted Pearl up and out of camera view.

"Camera one, give me a full view her backdrop photo. When she descends completely into your camera's view, move in slowly for a full-body shot, and hold it until she steps off the swing. The photo behind her will fade as she is lowered. Then move in for a close-up from her waist up. Okay, let's try it. Lower the swing gently. Like she's floating down. The screen should show ankles, legs, torso, and then a complete body shot.

There was complete silence in the control room as the monitors presented a very calm Pearl Necklace descending, staring directly into the camera and through it into the eyes of the technicians and cameramen. Ever so gently she touched down, and the camera zoomed in for the close-up.

"Stop there," Dauber ordered. He switched to the studio speaker. "Pearl, can you use your foot to give yourself a gentle push so that you're swinging into the camera? But very little. Just a hint of a swing. Now let's do it again. Give me fluid motion bringing that swing down, like honey from a bottle. Walt, I want to keep the background dark until she begins speaking, and I want portrait lighting on her up to that point. This is our opening. I want audience meltdown. Everyone got it?"

The stage crew sprang into action, and cameraman one willingly rehearsed his directions over and over until Dauber shouted, "Perfect! Do it just like that. No more tests, Billy. You have it down pat. With this opener, every channel surfer in America will stop here."

He hit the switch that allowed him to speak directly to Necklace through her earphone. "Pearl, we need to work on sound. Would you go through your opening and the first story introduction? Just look into the camera and hold the look until we have you full view and we cue you. Then go to the prompter. I'll give you the word. Alright, everyone, from the top. Let's go from black to lights."

The rehearsal continued, with Pearl Necklace going through her introductions of the several news segments that would make up the half-hour show. When they were finished, Dauber turned on the stage loudspeaker. "That looks good. No, that was great! I think we have it. There shouldn't be any problems. Fifteen minutes to relax and make ready. Great job, Pearl." He switched off the speaker. "How about that, she handled that last go-through without ever using the prompter. Lincoln would have had a coronary. Remember the time the prompter stuck and he read the same line three times before he realized it? How do you think she did, Steve?"

Steve Tanner had been standing in the back of the control room, watching the rehearsal. "She did good, Tom. As you said, great. I'll watch from my office." He walked out of the control room and down the hall, stopping everyone on the way to tell them to watch the show. He was in high spirits by the time he reached his secretary's desk and shoved the telephone in front of her.

"Margaret, drop everything you're doing. Pull out that list of reporters and reviewers I gave you this morning. You have just a few minutes to call everyone. Tell them to watch today's YOURchannel news show. Don't get into conversation. Just tell them they'll miss the biggest thing in television news if they don't watch."

He laughed, dashed into his office, and turned on his monitor.

"Dynamite, dynamite," he shouted as he lit up a cigar and eased himself into his chair, throwing his feet up on his desk. "I haven't felt this excited since the day I directed my first television show."

"Five, four, three, two, one. You're on, Pearl."

Pearl Necklace's descent into the world of news broadcasting went as smoothly as the rehearsals, including parts she added. Moving gently in the swing, she looked into the camera, smiled, and just before speaking ran her tongue over her lips. "Good evening. I'm Pearl Necklace, and I'll be with you for the next two weeks, substituting for Larry Lincoln, who is away on assignment."

"Did you see that?" Dauber asked, turning to his assistant.

"Am I alive?" answered his assistant.

"This week YOURchannel's news presentation will be totally different from anything you've seen before," she spoke softly. "We hope you'll find it exciting, entertaining, and informative. Join me now, if you would, for a whirl around today's world … and a totally new way to watch the news, presented as you have never seen before."

The blaring, hot rock music of Pearl Jam filled the studio as a huge blow-up photo of Pearl Necklace in a halter and shorts and the words "YOURchannel Presents the Pearl Necklace News Show" burst onto the screen. Necklace came back on the screen, and the set came alive with music and movement. Pearl stopped the swing, uncrossed her legs, stood up on her red spiked heel shoes, and walked across the set with the long strides she had learned in her modeling experience, switching her gaze into another camera.

"Billy, keep your camera on that walk," Dauber said. "Hold on camera two until she starts talking again. Now! Close-up!"

The music toned down but continued playing. "Let's start tonight as we will each night with our new Hip-Hop News Wrap-up, our opening segment to keep you current with what's going on in the world. It takes only six minutes—just six minutes—and you'll know all you need to know about what's new in the news. Let's start tonight in the Big Apple with our New York NewsStar Cindi."

"Go to tape one," Dauber directed, and on the screen a smiling, statuesque young woman with long blonde hair flowing down over her shoulders and dressed in a halter and mini-shorts appeared on the floor of the New York Stock Exchange. A crowd of applauding and cheering traders stood behind her. She removed her black horn-rimmed glasses and brushed her hair back.

"Hi, I'm NewsStar Cyndi reporting from Wall Street, and I'll be with you every night, right here in the power center of the financial world. We'll give you a get a quick recap of what's been driving these hot guys behind me. As you can tell from the sounds and smiles from this happy gang of financial movers and shakers, it's been a good day on the stock exchanges. That means everything's up, right guys?"

The men roared their agreement.

"Aren't they a fun bunch? The bulls are certainly running today." She blew them a kiss, put on her glasses again, and reached into her bra to pull out a slip of paper. "Let's see now. The Dow ended with a forty-point climb. That should put you investors out there on the sunny side of the street. I hope as sunny as these money movers." She made a half turn, lifted her arm, and pointed to the cheering behind her. "Hey, let's keep it going. The NASDAQ and Amex were up, too, so we really had a good day all the way around. Details later. No need to say more, Pearl, so I'll turn it over to you." She smiled at the camera and blew a kiss.

"Thanks for the good news, Cyndi. Let's go directly to NewsStar Jenni at our nation's capital. What's going on with the elected ones, Jenni?"

"Not a lot to report, Pearl, if you don't count the dinner offers I've received. The chamber was empty most of the day except for constant meaningless speeches. Real yawners! The morning started with enough prayer breakfasts to create a halo over the capital."

Jenni was seated on the Capitol steps with legs crossed and dressed in the identical outfit Cyndi was wearing. "There were more lobbyists in the halls today than congressmen. But then what's new about that? Those blue suits never pass a chance to score points, and I can tell you that from personal experience."

She pulled out the notepad tucked in her shorts. "Let's see. There's an epic battle still going on over the president's budget, and that certainly had the Brooks Brothers scurrying around here with cell phones glued to their heads. Of course, the entrée of the day was pork, and everyone was piling as much as possible on their plates. All in all, an ordinary day in the people's capital. I was going to show an interview I did with two congressmen with opposing views but I thought better. Hey, why lose our audience? We'll try later in the show. Back to you, Pearl." Jenni stood and began walking up the capitol steps as the camera followed closely behind.

"Thank you, Jenni. Step carefully and watch out for the stray congressional hands. Let's go back to New York, and this time we have NewsStar Luci with the international news. What's up around the world, Luci?"

"Go to tape three," Dauber ordered.

Dressed exactly as the previous NewsStars, Luci stood in front of the UN building. Six men in military uniforms from different countries stood behind her in a relaxed at-ease position.

"Thank you, Pearl. Love your outfit. The guys here really like mine." Walking back and forth in front of the soldiers and reading from the notes on her cell phone, Luci continued. "Lots of speeches today, Pearl. Every nation seems to be terribly upset over the growing refugee crises, the financial inequality that is spreading worldwide, the heightening level of terrorism, and finally the oncoming of global warming. I mean, a really depressing day. Then everyone broke for dinner to get over it. Back to you,

Pearl. Don't you just love these hunks behind me?" She pressed her back against one of them and took a selfie.

"You've got a great assignment, Luci. Let's keep it rolling and get the news flashes out of the way. And speaking of flashing, here's NewsStar Britni in Tinseltown, getting ready for the Grammys. Go, girl."

Dressed in her NewsStar outfit, Britni appeared on the screen standing on a red carpet and surrounded by six models dressed in designer evening dresses.

"Hi! NewsStar Britni here at the Grammy gala rehearsal with these beautiful models, who are showing the clothes the divas will be wearing at the awards show next week. Wow, have you ever seen so much material covering so little flesh? And I thought I was exhibiting. Turns out, I'm overdressed. Pearl, these models are all smiling, and well they should. When posing, they all know what to do with their arms. The designer gowns they're wearing are worth thousands of dollars, and designers love the exposure. Turn around, girls. You have so much more to show, and we will show it all later in the program. Back to you, Pearl."

"Up on camera one," Dauber snapped.

"Thank you, Britni. It's time now to take you to the president at his latest news conference. No, don't surf. Our coverage of the event will be different than anything you've seen before. We call this segment The Prez and The Press. Let's skip his announcements—they've already been leaked—and go right to the questions. We'll keep the music playing, but low. But first, a commercial. We'll be right back, and I hope you will be, too."

Necklace blew a kiss to the camera as the image faded, then moved quickly for a clothes change. When she reappeared on the screen, she was in the swing again wearing a bikini.

"Hi there, and welcome back." With a gentle leap, she landed on the floor and did a complete turnaround. "Do you like my outfit? Not too daring, I hope. Now for the promised Prez and the Press that took place this afternoon. I think you'll learn from this segment. And love it at the same time."

"Go to tape," Dauber ordered.

The screen showed a close-up of the president behind the podium, and it appeared he was scanning a paper he was holding. He put the paper aside and spoke to the group. "Okay, let's go to Rose for the first question."

"Mr. President, is it true you do not intend to meet with …"

"Go to split screen," Dauber ordered, and immediately, while the reporter was finishing her question, the monitor in the control room showed the press conference on one half of the screen, and on the other half a fashion show appeared with models parading up and down the runway displaying the latest line of lingerie from the design house Your Bedroom Secrets.

The President gave a prolonged answer to the first question and called upon a reporter for the next one. Dauber gave the order for the second split screen. Immediately the lingerie scene changed to female mud wrestling, and the music switched to "Stomping' at the Savoy." The control room and camera crew broke out in cheers.

The questions and answers continued for a few more minutes during which the wrestling was replaced by a wet T-shirt contest while the president continued to answer questions from the press.

"Three … two … one, you're on, Pearl."

The screen faded out, and a smiling Pearl Necklace reappeared with both thumbs pointing up. Cannonball Adderley provided the background music, playing "Mercy, Mercy, Mercy."

"Hey, people, what do you think about that? How about that mud wrestling? Listen, you can tell us which segment you thought the best by going to our website, Facebook, or Twitter and voting for your favorite. We'll interview the winner tomorrow. Well, there's more where that came from, but first, let's take another commercial break. In two minutes and eight commercials I'll be back in a new outfit that I know you'll love with the latest news about congressional campaign contributions. It'll be fun, so stay with us." She gave the camera a wink and a kiss as her image faded to black.

"Two minutes commercial time," Dauber warned everyone. "Ready up on camera one. He switched to Necklace. "Good job, Pearl, very smooth."

Pearl Necklace looked at Dauber through the camera, gave him a wink, and ran off to change.

He switched off and looked around the control room, surveying the expressions of his crew. "You are witnessing the end of a career," he told them. "This should do it for Tanner. He's finally getting it off his chest, but he'll be out the door in an hour or less." He shook his head and turned back to review the schedule of the next segment.

Over the years, Dauber had spent many nights with his boss at their favorite bar, listening to him rage on about the condition of television news. "We have some really bad people in our government," Tanner would constantly harangue, "terrible people with enormous power and influence. Yet we don't say anything when they misuse it. Then add into the mix all that money floating around. The lobbies are in control of our elected pols, and money is controlling the lobbies. What do we do? We all sit back and telecast the latest fad in dieting or show cute kittens or the latest weather report. Instead of expanding international news, we're reducing news bureaus around the world, renting wire guys, and replacing vital information with YouTube feel-good stories."

His anger would push him on. "Do you think Congress would have slammed the door on McCarthy if Murrow had not spoken out? He was followed by some great ones, but where is that journalism today? What happened? Now we create TV news stars, celebrities. We're taking the big paychecks and running up to Martha's Vineyard to party, talk about ratings, and gossip about the latest scandal. We don't take sides because we don't want to offend anyone, or we're afraid to speak up. Today, except for public broadcasting, television news delivery is in serious trouble."

Dauber well understood what was going to happen as a result of the Pearl Necklace news show. "Okay, everyone, move! I want the cameras zipping around following Pearl. Try to get every angle of our new anchor possible. She may not be with us too long. This is her fifteen minutes. Let's make it good."

Watching the show in his office, Tanner flicked the ashes from his cigar onto the floor. "You're good, Pearl. You're a winner. You may be fired today, but you'll be on television somewhere."

He walked across the room to lock the door. Looking through the glass panels of his office, he could see activity picking up in the office as people crowded around the various television monitors. "Yes, Pearl Necklace, you're getting their attention. I think we have something here. Can't wait to see the ratings."

While he had never attended the training sessions with Alex LaRue, Tanner did spend the evenings with Pearl Necklace and Tom Dauber, going over every detail of what he wanted the show to be and how to do it. He had arranged all the videos, photographs, sets, scripts, and recordings.

Necklace was well prepared when the time came before the telecast to review the script and think about how she wanted to handle her presentation. She would have to ad-lib considerably, but Tanner had coached her, and she had worked hard every minute of every day to be ready. Saving television journalism was not on her agenda, but having her own TV show was, and she knew this was her big opportunity.

The only one in the dark was Alex LaRue. After Pearl had left him to walk onto the set, LaRue stepped back into the shadows of the studio. He had felt good all day, almost giddy with the confidence that his dream of promotion was soon to be a reality. Three weeks with her was not only a delightful experience that he looked forward to each day but also a surprising one. She never made the same mistake twice, and her performance to his suggestions was usually better than what he had in mind. He never relayed his exuberance to Tanner. He wanted him to sweat it out. Now, however, what he was seeing started a terrible churning sensation in his stomach. "No, no," he continued muttering. "No, no!" He could not find another word to express his horror, and his knees buckled as he sank down to a sitting position on the floor.

"Three, two, one," Dauber counted down. "You're on, Pearl."

Pearl Necklace was back on screen in a full body shot, now wearing a different plunging neckline blouse and miniskirt. She was standing behind a large executive chair with her arms resting on the back of it and leaning well forward for her close-up. In the background the wailing saxophone of Earl Bostic could be heard playing a blaring rendition of the song "Flamingo." Behind her, a new image flashed up on the screen. It was her magazine center spread, resulting in various responses from everyone in the studio and control room. To the music's jazz beat, she walked up to the camera for a head and shoulders shot.

"It's time for Strip and Consequences. It's a little like that old radio game. I'm sure some of you remember. Only in this case, I tell the truth and they pay the consequences. You should have fun with this."

Pearl Necklace smiled. "Have I got your attention? Hint number one: He loves to attend morning prayer meetings. Hint two: He has recently been voted the annual Fast Hands Award by congressional pages and interns. Hint three: Last month he spent two weeks in Jamaica with a female lobbyist studying the education system there. Hint four: While he constantly lectures against the misuse of campaign money, he has been working hard behind the scenes to kill campaign financing reforms. Hint five: Congressional lobbyists joke that he always shakes hands with his palm up. There, we've stripped him bare. Now you name the name." She paused. "Okay, one more hint. He's the chairman of the House Ethics Committee."

Pearl Necklace winked at the camera again as the song "I'm in the Money" started playing. With that she danced her way back to the chair, leaped into it, and slowly crossed her legs.

"Oh, my God," Dauber murmured. "We'll be X-rated."

Pearl then swung both legs over the side arm of the chair, rested her back against the opposite arm and tilted her head back, allowing her long hair to flow downward. She swung one leg up, flipped her shoe into the air, and struck the centerfold pose. She waited for the camera to zoom in for a close-up.

"I'm sure you're watching now. Well, hold on while we cut to YOURchannel reporter Michael Oakland in Washington for his daily take on what's happening on Capitol Hill. Entertain us, Mike!"

A stunned Michael Oakland appeared on the screen, staring at Necklace on the monitor next to the camera. Dauber waited a few seconds and then hit the switch connecting him with the reporter's headset. "Say something, Mike. You're on! Read what's there in front of you. Just read!"

"Thank you, Pearl," Oakland responded weakly.

"That's a good start," Dauber said. "Now underneath that, where it says 'I'm Michael Oakland reporting from the capitol steps.' Read that!"

"I'm Michael Oakland reporting from the capitol thighs."

Steve Tanner looked up at the door to see his secretary pounding against the glass, frantically waving a phone receiver in her hand and mouthing the name of the YOURchannel news president. Behind her were three other secretaries at their desks also waving phones. He smiled, waved back, and turned to the television set to watch the remaining minutes of the show.

What he didn't see was a white-faced Alex LaRue running down the hall while retching into a wastepaper basket he was holding. Upon reaching his office, he dropped into his chair and reached for another waste basket.

"Alex?" his secretary shouted at him, looking down at the back of his head. "Alex?" she repeated to the writhing body. Finally she screamed. "Alex! There's a phone call for you!"

"Is it Ingersoll?" he murmured without lifting his head, knowing it would be minutes before he got a call from the CEO and his life would be over.

"No. It's some guy calling from Italy. He claims it's a matter of life and death. Something about Larry getting a haircut for millions of dollars. I can't quite understand what he's trying to say, but you better take this. It sounds serious."

"You don't know serious." He looked up, took the phone from her, placed it gently to his ear, and stuck his head back into the basket. "Who is this?"

"Ten million dollars!"

"Who?"

"Ten million dollars if you want to see Larry Lincoln alive again," Paolo shouted. "Ten million in one-hundred-dollar bills."

"What?"

"I talk and you listen. Listen with care. We have kidnapped Larry Lincoln, and if you ever want to see him again, you will deliver ten million dollars in one-hundred-dollar bills to us here. The day after tomorrow. Otherwise, Larry Lincoln will be with the fishes."

"Larry's going fishing?"

"Tomorrow you will receive his hair. That will show I do not joke. Ten million by Wednesday or we whack him. I'll call later with details." Paolo hung up.

LaRue dropped the phone into the basket, leaned back into the chair, and stared at the television set. He listened to Pearl Necklace, now wearing a designer evening dress composed primarily of netting tell her listeners that every night she would conduct a five-minute interview with one of the twenty greatest celebrities in the world. The segment is be called Celebrities Countdown to Number One. The winner will be selected from among the top ten at an hour-long television show. All of this would be a part of the daily evening news.

She also invited the audience to vote immediately on which of the outfits she wore during the news show they liked best by going to the YOURchannel website using Facebook or Twitter. Photos of her outfits would be posted and numbered. She then blew a kiss to the audience as the music "Show Business" came up and the screen faded to a commercial.

Monte Castella

Burt Baywatch's nervous condition was beginning to show. He tried desperately to cover his anxiety over Lincoln's failure to appear in Monte Castella, but he could not conceal his perspiration. He was also very tired. In addition to experiencing the impact of jet-lag fatigue, he was affected by the four hours he spent accompanying Angelo Vocino on a driving tour in and around Monte Castella and two other villages. At the insistence of his host, he had filmed the entire countryside and practically every establishment in Monte Castella. At each stop, Vocino provided a well-rehearsed emotional description of what they were viewing and upon finishing, handed the agent a typewritten copy of his travelogue in triplicate. What Baywatch found most irritating, however, was the musical trio consisting of a violin, viola, and accordion that followed them everywhere, offering continuous background music to the tour. On several occasions, he applauded as a means of ending their accompaniment, but this only brought about many bows and handshakes followed by numerous encores.

Later, he was introduced to Mayor Vocino, who gave him a history lesson of Monte Castella from the Athenian invasion of Sicily in the fourth century BC to the American Third Army liberation at the height of World War II. More than once, the mayor interrupted his story to remind Baywatch of his televised interview by Lincoln.

"Not only will the members and friends of the Luciano, Gambino, and Gotti families be interested in seeing a show about the beloved town of Monte Castella," Mayor Vocino explained, "but it will also bring back wonderful memories for those American soldiers still living who marched through here on their way to Palermo. Some left children here. Like my cousin Francisca. That was the army of the famous General Patton, you understand. This town has a history that will touch a great many people in America. I shall cover all of that when Mr. Lincoln interviews me. I'm sure Don Marcasi will insist on it. He is a man people listen to, if you know what I mean."

Baywatch assured the mayor that he understood and promised that his interview would be an important part of the story with Don Marcasi. After the mayor finished his town's history, he forced Baywatch to film a religious ceremony moving through the streets, led by Father Autobelli and followed by two accordion players and two dozen farmers and townspeople who constantly smiled and waved frantically whenever he turned the camera on them. After the procession moved on, he was escorted around the town again, this time with the mayor offering the local color. The tour included the Grand Hotel Vocino, the Vocino sidewalk cafe, the Vocino bakery, the city hall, a freshly painted World War II Jeep, and the mayor's lovely granddaughter, Nina, who appeared in a different dress every half hour.

Then there was the food, more food than he had ever eaten in a week. They lunched at different restaurants, and in each one an excited chef insisted that he eat everything from a variety of plates placed in front of him. And always there was the music by the trio. It did not help his nervousness and digestion that in each restaurant, three short men dressed in black pinstripe suits showed up and glared at him from their table while smoking furiously and periodically slipping their hands in and out of their jackets. One of them would occasionally take out a push-button knife and clean his nails.

Finally the tours came to an end, and Baywatch and Angelo sat down at a table in front of a restaurant to have what seemed to Baywatch like the eighth cup of espresso. Angelo Vocino was beginning to show some impatience. "This is dangerous business, Mr. Baywatch. Your newsman Mr. Lincoln should have been here hours ago. It has not been an easy matter to make all the arrangements, and it cost us a great deal of money. Besides, the don does not like to be kept waiting."

"I understand," Baywatch answered while once again tipping the musicians playing behind him. It was the fourth time that day he had tried tips as a means of stopping them. Each time he made a mental note of the amount, which he was determined to pass on to Lincoln. And all the time he silently cursed his client every time Angelo mentioned the don.

"He is not a man to fool with," Angelo Vocino continued. "The last man who was late for an appointment was punished in the piazza as an example. Are you sure Mr. Lincoln was on the plane?"

"I'm positive of that, Angelo. No question about that part. He is on this island. He called me the minute he stepped off the plane. The airlines have confirmed that. Larry Lincoln is a famous man. He was seen getting on and off the plane. The only thing I can figure is he's lost somewhere between Palermo and here. He has always had a terrible time with maps. For some reason his phone is turned off or it needs a charge."

"The mayor is getting anxious, too. He does not want another nasty public display in this town. You must understand his position. Especially since his interview was part of the deal we made with Don Marcasi. We are cousins and very close. It was only with the mayor's help that we were able to make the arrangements. I hope you understand his position."

"Angelo, baby, I know where you're coming from. But you

must know that Larry Lincoln is a man who can be trusted. You can see it in his face. It's a face that millions of Americans trust. Every night they wait for him to read the news. He is so well-known that everywhere he goes, people say, 'That's Larry Lincoln. I watch him on television.' You should have seen him the day he did a live show of a man about to be executed. He was spectacular. He threw up, but that was due to his compassion. But I must tell you, it got us great press."

"From the signed photographs you sent us, it would appear he is losing his hair," Angelo answered. "Is that why he combs his hair that way?"

"It's a hereditary thing, Angelo. No problem. He still has two or three years to go."

"He could lose more than that if he doesn't show soon. The don demands respect at all times."

Baywatch crossed his legs and tried to find a way to get away from the brothers for a few minutes. "Look, Angelo, let me go back to my room. All that coffee, you understand. Also, I need to check in with my office. I have so much going on with other clients. But don't worry. Obviously something has happened to him on the way here. He wouldn't miss this interview for anything in the world. It's the newsman's code. Never miss an interview. Larry lives by it."

"He may have to," Vocino said.

As Baywatch stood, he heard three other chairs slide back.

"Who are those guys, Angelo?" he whispered, motioning to the Polucci brothers without turning around.

Angelo Vocino looked across the room at the Poluccis as they stood and prepared to leave. "Don't worry, Mr. Baywatch. They are only here to look after you. They are the don's bodyguard. One is the don's godson."

Baywatch turned and nodded at the three men, and each responded by sliding his hand inside his jacket. Instantly, he spun around and headed for the hotel. "I'll be right back. Believe me,

Angelo. No more than twenty minutes. We will spend an extra day for the mayor's interview. We have plenty of time."

He had not walked more than three blocks from the restaurant, when a Fiat van with a smashed front grille pulled up alongside, and a man with a paper bag over his head and wearing a trench coat stepped out and dug his hand into his trench coat pocket.

"You're coming with us," Carlo said.

"You have the wrong guy," Baywatch answered, looking at the bulge in the pocket pointing at him. "I'm Burt Baywatch. Like the television show. I'm sure you've seen it. It's on every day here. I'm Burt Baywatch. Here … let me show you my passport. It's not a great picture, but you can see it's me." He started to put his hand in his jacket pocket.

"Freeze!" Carlo shouted. He shoved his pocket forward, causing a button to rip from his coat and drop to the pavement. "Oh, shit!" He exclaimed. Without taking his hand from his pocket, he reached down with his free hand to pick up the button, forcing his finger to press against the trigger. The gun fired, and a bullet ripped through his jacket and glanced off the pavement inches from Baywatch's foot.

"Right, right," Baywatch responded. "You're absolutely right. No passport. I'm with you." He quickly climbed into the truck cab and slid next to Paolo, who was also wearing a trench coat and a paper bag over his head.

"Hi, my name's Baywatch. Let me show you my card. Agent to the stars. I'm sure this is simply a case of mistaken identity. I'm here to interview your boss, Don Marcasi. We are American television news."

Carlo jumped in and shoved Baywatch up against his brother. Paolo reached across Baywatch and slapped Carlo across the head and at the same time slammed down hard on the accelerator. The truck lurched forward into the back of a parked car, sending all three men into the windshield. Loud curses came from the back of the van. Paolo threw the truck into reverse almost hitting the three musicians who had been following Baywatch. They leaped to the safety of the sidewalk and let loose with a barrage of abuses.

"Fuck you, too!" Paolo shouted back as he shoved the gearshift into first, screeching the tires and racing directly toward Father Autobelli's religious ceremony in the middle of the street. The priest was reading from his prayer book and facing his parishioners, unaware of the oncoming van. Everyone else in the procession saw the disaster rushing toward them and scattered. Finally, confused by the panic in from of him, the priest turned around to see the truck heading his way and had only a few seconds to close his eyes and drop to his knees in prayer.

Paolo spun the steering wheel sharply and swerved to the right and up on the walkway, scraping the side of his truck along a number of storefronts before cutting back onto the road, narrowly missing the policeman who had squeezed himself into a doorway. Never taking his hand off the horn, he sped off through the street, occasionally looking into his rearview mirror to see Angelo Vocino running down the street after him, shouting and frantically waving his fists.

Two blocks away from the scene, Paolo turned a sharp corner and shoved down hard on the brake pedal, again hurling Baywatch and Carlo into the windshield. Once again, Gianni's curses came from the rear of the truck.

"Get out! Out, out, out!" Paolo shouted at Baywatch.

"Who, me?" Carlo asked.

"No, you idiot! Him! Let him out. Quick! Get him out of the truck."

Carlo leaped from the truck, and Baywatch followed quickly but tripped and lurched forward. In a desperate attempt to break his fall, he grabbed Carlo with both arms, and the two men fell to the pavement. As they struggled to free themselves, Baywatch felt as if he were once again in his television drowning scene.

"My trench coat!" Carlo shouted. "You're ruining my trench

coat." He looked up to see the van begin to move away, and unable to break loose from the bear hug Baywatch had around him, he drove his knee into his groin. Baywatch screamed and rolled away in pain, allowing Carlo to leap to his feet and chase after Paolo.

Baywatch grabbed his crotch with both hands, and felt the urine soaking through his pants. He looked down the street at the truck speeding away with Carlo on the running board. "I should have stayed in acting," he moaned.

The Polucci brothers knew they were in for another beating as they walked up the stairs to the mayor's office in front of the policeman who had arrested them.

At the top of the stairs, Angelo and Tomaso Vocino waited in silence, their arms folded across their chests and their eyes glaring down at their tormentors with the fury of volcanoes about to erupt. Nothing was said as the Poluccis walked one by one between the Vocinos. Gianni had the misfortune to be the last to pass, and he received two simultaneously applied kicks, sending him and his brothers tumbling into the office.

"Thank you, officer," Mayor Vocino calmly addressed the policeman. "We will handle it from here. There will be no charges at this time."

As the door closed, Angelo exploded verbally and physically. "You imbeciles. You chicken-brained fools," he screamed, issuing the first of many blows to come. "Did each of you drop from your mother's womb to the floor headfirst?"

"What the hell did you think you were doing?" the mayor joined in, taking his turn at slapping heads. "You could have killed him. Then what would we do? The whole plan—everything we have worked for—up in smoke. The town would have lynched all three of you without a trial. Right in front of the church! And Father Autobelli would have been the one to kick away the stools."

"Only if he had won the lottery," Angelo added.

"We were only trying to add a touch of realism," Paolo answered meekly as he rubbed his head. "How was I to know Carlo's gun was loaded?"

"It was an accident," Carlo said, trying to cover his head with both arms. "Look, it's only a target pistol. It wouldn't have hurt him badly." He started to reach in his pocket but was stopped by a blow to his head.

"The only accident was your mother giving birth to three sons without brains," Angelo shouted. "God have mercy on that poor woman." He kicked the chair from under Carlo. "Have any of you any idea how much money this town has spent on this and how much everyone is depending on its success?"

Not waiting for an answer, he grabbed Paolo by both ears and pulled him out of the chair and screamed into his face. "You were told to do nothing but sit around and look like gangsters. Nothing more. No grabbing people off the street, no guns, no shooting. Not even talking. It was only due to Carlo's natural clumsiness that he missed Baywatch. Now the man is dead drunk in his room, and we can't even talk to him." With that said, he shoved Paolo back into the chair with such force that the leader of the Black Hand Mob was sent flying backward, tumbling over the chair and across the floor.

"*Mama mia*," he groaned.

"Be careful of the furniture, Angelo," Mayor Vocino said quickly, grabbing his brother to restrain him from further violence. "We must think about what we do now."

"If it were not for the fact that these three idiots are the only ones in all Sicily stupid enough to own gangster clothes, I would replace them in this plan and throw them in jail right now."

He turned to Paolo, who had remained on the floor to avoid further blows. "Get up! Get out of my sight. Go put on new pinstripes. And if you dare make one more stupid move, with God as my witness, I will personally tie the ropes around your necks."

Paolo responded immediately, quickly scrambling to his feet and rushing to the door.

"Wait!" Angelo Vocino shouted. "Something I don't understand. Tell me, what in the hell were you going to do with him?"

Paolo turned around but continued backing away to avoid further blows. "We were only going to drive him to the edge of town and drop him off. We wanted to let him know that he would be in serious trouble if the newsman failed to show up. That's all we were going to do. We were only trying to help," he lied and quickly darted out the door.

"That's all," Carlo said, backing up his brother's lie. "We were helping." Seeing that the mayor was making a move toward them, the brothers scrambled out of the room. In their rush to escape, they tripped over each other and fell headlong down the stairs.

The truth of their motive in taking Baywatch captive was far from what Paolo had told the mayor. Flush with the success of kidnapping Larry Lincoln and taking him to the farm, Paolo immediately developed a new plan to kidnap Baywatch and squeeze money out of him to add to their loot.

After preparing lunch for Lincoln, who appeared to take great pleasure in their cooking, they tied him to the chair again and drove into town to play their role of providing a criminal ambiance. On the way he revealed his new idea to Carlo and Gianni.

"That's what I said. We kidnap this other guy. It will be so easy. We simply follow him everywhere like we are supposed to and the moment he is alone, we nab him."

"What if someone sees us?" Carlo questioned, thinking about the possibility of a beating they might receive from the Vocinos.

"That's the key to our success. We must not be seen. We must be good at this. Make it appear he has simply disappeared. We have had practice now, and that will help a great deal."

"Things did not go too smoothly the first time," Banco murmured.

"One must expect the first time to be a little rough. That can happen. Remember how they failed to kill Don Corleone in *The Godfather*. They had plenty of experience, and still they failed. Besides, if that driver had not pulled out in front of me at the airport, we would not have had problems. That reminds me, we must pay a little call on that man to make sure he knows better than to be a witness against the Black Hand Mob."

"We'll cut off his ear," Carlo responded quickly. "That should clam him up."

Paolo ignored his brother. "This time will be different. But we need a new disguise. That is why I brought our trench coats. We will wear them with the collars up like Bogart. But we need something new to hide our faces. I am tired of the ski masks. They're too hot."

"I have trouble with the mouth opening," Carlo said.

"When we arrive in town, Carlo, we will drop you off at Filipelli's, and you can pick up something new."

"Leave it to me. No problem."

"After we have this guy, we will return to the farm and tie him up with Lincoln."

"How much do we get for him?" Banco asked, pulling out his cell phone that showed exchange rates.

"Half a million dollars. I don't think he is as important as Lincoln. He's not on television. But he may be a celebrity, and those people always have money."

"You're a genius, Paolo," Carlo said.

"You are to call me Don Paolo from now on," he answered, straightening his shoulders, squinting his eyes and waving his right hand.

"Don Paolo Polucci," Carlo and Gianni responded in unison, each in turn kissing his hand.

A few hours after discussing their plan to kidnap Baywatch,

they were sitting at their table across the restaurant from where Baywatch and Vocino were having coffee. Paolo talked in hushed tones about their future.

"Kidnapping is the way for us from now on," he whispered. "I can see that clearly. This is only the beginning. The Black Hand Mob will become famous throughout all of Italy. There will be no stopping us. I promise you there will be no more beatings. No more insults. No more kicks. From now on the people of this town will bow their heads to Don Paolo Polucci when they meet me on the streets."

He paused a moment to enjoy his thoughts. "They will come to me for favors. Then I will nod my head and wave my hand, but I will say nothing. They will understand. In return, they will kiss my hand and thank me and ask how they can be of service to me in the future. I will shake my head and shrug them off but I will remember. That's the way it will go. Next time someone needs a movie role, he will come to Don Paolo Polucci."

"I will be your consigliore," Gianni said.

"And I will be your bodyguard," Carlo added, pulling his gun out of his pocket.

"Put that thing away," Paolo said quickly while looking around to make sure that Angelo had not seen the gun. "Just keep your eyes on that man. The minute he leaves, we follow. The truck is in the back and ready. You have the masks?"

"Certainly," Carlo answered and held up the paper bags he had purchased before joining them at the restaurant.

"Paper bags? Why the hell did you buy paper bags? Where are the holes?" Paolo hissed, desperately suppressing the urge to slap his brother.

"You don't need holes. They're transparent, you can see through them easily. It's fantastic. No one can see through the bag but we can see out. I saw it done in an American movie about robbing a payroll. What was that movie, Gianni?"

"I remember the movie, but I forget the name. Who was in it?"

"I think it was Al Pacino."

"No, no, no. That's *Scarface* you're thinking about. He never wore a bag in that. Maybe it was …"

"Stop it!" Paolo hissed. "I don't want to know. We'll make do with the damn bags. But God help you if we can't see."

"Paolo, he's getting ready to leave."

"Quick! To the truck!"

New York

Ahalf-hour after the Pearl Necklace news broadcast ended on Monday, Steve Tanner, Tom Dauber, and Alex LaRue were fired. The following morning, after the overnight ratings came in, they were rehired and ordered to report to a two o'clock meeting. To George Ingersoll, CEO of YOURchannel, the importance of the quality level of television newscasting never came close to the importance of high ratings. In fact, the concept of quality never made it to his list of values.

At the afternoon meeting, Ingersoll was seated at an enormous conference table in the center of his office. William Saxton, president of YOURchannel News, sat to his right. Henry Handleman, the president of YOURchannel Entertainment, and Carl Macon, president of YOURchannel Public Relations, sat on his left. Philip Sanford, president of YOURchannel Legal Affairs, sat next to Macon. Tanner and LaRue sat at the other side of the table.

"Alright now, first things first," Ingersoll snapped, a favorite phrase he used to open every meeting. He paused to glance over a report he held, the third time he had read it. After a few moments, he dropped it on the table, removed his designer glasses, and looked across the table at Tanner.

"I must tell you, Steve, at first I was somewhat taken back by your news program yesterday. Wait, that's not quite strong enough. Actually, I was shocked down to my toes, and the first thing that entered my mind was not to fire you but to have you killed. I can do that, you understand. It must be in our contracts. I really thought you had lost your mind. Don't get me wrong. Your mental collapse would not prevent me from killing you. Especially after witnessing the leg crossing bit."

Tanner flinched. Even he did not know she was going to pull that trick.

"However, when I read the ratings this morning, the brilliance of your idea hit me full force." He held up the report. "My God, by the time the show reached the last five minutes, the number of viewers had taken off like a rocket. We were at figures we had never reached with our evening news. Definitely brilliant thinking, Steve. Maybe the legs crossing was a little too much. But maybe not. You have to listen to the ratings, and from the ratings I see, it didn't bother the audience. And it certainly ignited the news world. Why did it take you so long to develop the concept?"

"I agree, George," Saxton cut in immediately. "A brilliant idea, Steve, but you should have cleared the concept with me first. After all, I am president of the news division. I would have bought into it immediately. I would have been right at your back one hundred and ten percent. We're a team here, and we must play like a team. Just read what it says on the wall."

Everyone swung around to face one of the walls, where in six-inch, gold script lettering were the words

YOURchannel Is a Team Effort,
And a Team Effort Gets Good Ratings!
　　　　—George Elliot Ingersoll, Florida State BS, Harvard
　　　　　　　　　　　　　MBA, CEO

"No question about that, Bill. I agree wholeheartedly," Macon jumped in. "If my public relations division had been alerted, we could have been out front with a great PR campaign. Now it's catch-up time. How long do you think it will take the networks and the other cable news departments to match us? A great idea is like adrenaline to the people in this industry, especially if it's not their own. Like George said, this was a brilliant idea. I saw it right away. George, you put your finger right on it. A brilliant idea."

"Do we have her under contract, Steve?" legal affairs president Sanford asked, glaring at Tanner and LaRue.

This was not at all the reaction Tanner had expected, and he was not feeling good about it. He thought of Alec Guinness at the river Kwai, mumbling, "Good Lord, what have I done?"

"We certainly do," LaRue answered quickly before Tanner could break from his thoughts. Seeing the reaction to the news program, he wanted to make sure everyone was aware of his participation in what was now being considered a masterstroke. "We have her locked up for six months and with an open option. We're all set."

"You call that a contract, you idiot?" Sanford shot back. "If the ratings continue going up, she could hang us by our balls."

"Just a moment, Phil, first things first," CEO Ingersoll interrupted as LaRue sank down in his chair, regretting having answered the question. "The first thing is to dump Lincoln from the show to make room for that beauty. Lightly, you understand. Don't want to make it look brutal. Do we have any problem there, Phil?"

"I doubt it," Sanford answered. "We have the hair clause, and his hair is falling out by the hour. We can work a deal with him. Maybe a half dozen assignments somewhere plus a gradual but substantial salary cut and then farm him out to one of the locals with a small bonus."

"Good. Done and done. Have it all worked out by the time he returns from vacation."

"Sir, there is something I should bring up," LaRue said, almost inaudibly.

"Carl," Ingersoll continued, "put out some good spin on Lincoln. Paint him into a corner before he can whine publicly."

"No problem. We'll plant some stories on the wire services, the locals, and the Internet. Something about his desire to get back to hard reporting or writing the great American novel. Everyone will pick it up. Then we'll place some of our people on the cable talk shows to back up the story line. To round it out we'll drop some inside stuff to the gossip columnists and entertainment TV shows about his mental difficulties. No problem. There will be so much out there, Larry will believe it himself."

"Good. Done and done," said CEO Ingersoll. "Now, I want to hear some ideas on how we are ..."

"Sir, about Lincoln," LaRue said, speaking a bit louder, "there ... there is something that's come up."

The room went silent as everyone turned toward LaRue.

"What is it, LaRue?" snapped Ingersoll, tapping the table with his gold-rimmed glasses.

"Well. I did not bring this up before, but ..."

Ingersoll cut him off. "I don't like sentences that begin that way, LaRue."

"Well ..."

"I don't like sentences that begin that way either. I'm asking a simple, direct question, and I want a simple, direct answer. Is that understood? Now, what is it you have to say? And say it in as few words as possible."

LaRue started to perspire profusely as he began talking rapidly. "It's about Larry, sir. I've received some really strange phone calls from Italy ... about him ... about him being kidnapped and held for ransom." He paused and braced himself for the outburst. Instead, his report was answered only with silence. Everyone in the room sat still and continued to stare at him while waiting for a reaction from Ingersoll, but the CEO remained silent.

LaRue continued hurriedly to break the chill that had filled the room, "At first I thought it was some kind of joke, sir. But then I was fired and escorted out of the building, and it slipped my mind in the confusion as I packed, and then I was hired again, and around noon I received his hair in a FedEx package …"

"His hair?" Ingersoll questioned.

"Yes, sir, I mean a swatch of hair. There was a photo of him with a terrified, wide-eyed look and something stuffed in his mouth and a chunk of hair missing from the side of his head, and I knew then that it could be serious. But all of this just happened, and I didn't have a chance to bring it up sooner as I intended to—really. But, I mean, you know, with the firing and the packing and the hiring again, sir, and then I … I …"

Ingersoll continued staring at LaRue as he searched for words and then turned to Sanford from legal affairs. "Will this affect the hair clause, Phil?"

"It's possible, George. I'll have to read the contract again. One way or another, I'm sure we can still dump him."

"Good. First things first. Let's get that put to bed." Ingersoll turned to Saxton, president of the news division. "I may be wrong but I think we have the makings of a pretty damn good news story here, Bill. What do you think?"

"Not only good but exclusive if we can keep it under wraps until we're ready to pump it." Saxton answered excitedly. "One helluva story, George!"

"Hey, can't Entertainment get part of this?" broke in Handleman, jumping to his feet. "It sounds perfect for my *Celebrities Galore* show." He instantly regretted bringing up the subject of his show. *Celebrities Galore* had been his brainchild, and based upon its initial success, he had been promoted to the position of entertainment president. Recently, however, viewership had been falling off precipitously, in part because of its reliance on rock stars who showed up either high or deaf.

"Absolutely not," shouted Saxton, who was constantly on his guard against presidents of other divisions gaining influence. "At least not at all during the first week. The news division should have first bite on this. He's one of our guys. He's our Larry Lincoln.

Maybe after a week of milking, yeah, put it on *Celebrities Galore* if your show is still on.

"A week!" Handleman screamed. "He could be dead in a week!"

"Hold on," CEO Ingersoll interrupted. "We're getting ahead of ourselves. Let's take care of this Pearl Necklace thing first before we jump on the Lincoln thing. Let's back-burner that for a while. Steve, she's your brainchild. What was your plan?"

Steve Tanner felt as if he had been shaken from a bad dream. He never thought there would be a need for a long-term plan. "Well, the original plan was to use Pearl Necklace only as a replacement for Larry and then give her a segment of the show when he returned, depending on the ratings."

"That might have been a good plan then, Steve," Ingersoll answered, "but not now in the face of the reaction to that little honey. As far as I'm concerned … if everyone agrees … this is her show. At least as long as the ratings hold up. But first things first. Get her contract problem straightened out. Work closely with Legal on this." He paused and smiled at Tanner. "By the way, Steve, have you got something going with her?"

The last remark generated a round of laughter. "You should be so lucky, eh, Steve?" Saxton said before turning to Ingersoll. "I think you're absolutely right about Pearl Necklace, George. The news show is hers. My thought from the get-go. What do you say to this? Starting tonight we'll call it *The Pearl Necklace First Things First News Show*. If that's okay with you."

"Well, I'll let you guys work that one out later," a beaming Ingersoll responded, pleased with the idea of using one of his pet phrases. "Now about Lincoln." He paused to take a cigar out of the inlaid pearl and walnut humidor on the table, light it, and blow a huge cloud of smoke toward the ceiling. "What's the agenda on that, LaRue?"

"They said they will kill him if we do not comply quickly."

"I'm talking about money, you dick! M-O-N-E-Y! Don't

waste our time here with their goddamn threats. How much are they asking?"

"The last amount for the ransom was ten million dollars. When we agree, he will be calling me with details for turning him loose. We are to talk to no one, absolutely no one if we ever wish to see Lincoln alive. He kept repeating that over and over. I think they are serious about not releasing any information about the kidnapping."

CEO Ingersoll looked around the table. "Well, team, I'm open to suggestions on how we get this story underway. Saxton?"

"Without question, we break the story on Pearl's *First Things First News Show* this evening, but we start immediately after this meeting to build viewership with promos every fifteen minutes plus all the horns and whistles: press releases, leaks, Facebook, Twitter, Instagram, etcetera, etcetera. We'll make it Pearl's opening story, a full-seven minute intro. Lay the groundwork but without too many details. Leave the audience hanging. Turn it into a tune-in-tomorrow thing. Create suspense. We'll go full steam on the social media side. Then each evening …"

"Sir," LaRue interrupted, "this guy did repeat several times the part about killing Lincoln. He seemed to enjoy talking about the variety of ways it would be done. He was very graphic."

"Then each evening," Saxton continued, "we start doing interviews. You know, Lincoln's father and mother, his high school teachers, classmates, priest, etcetera, etcetera. You know, sob it up a bit. Throw in some quickies with his landlord and doorman for the personal side. Then we'll get the official view with the State Department, FBI guys, United Nations. Really make it international. Give it a serious spin, like it's a really big deal. I know we can find some senator who wants publicity to say something outrageous like threatening to break off relations with Italy. Senator Jamison would jump at the chance. If he resists, I could call in a few chits I'm holding to change his mind."

"Great ideas, Bill!" Ingersoll broke in. "Pump it up. Make it an international impasse. You're getting me a bit excited on this thing. Take it up a few more notches."

"What we need immediately," Saxton continued, knowing he was on a roll, "is a great new title for the story and a balls-grabbing logo. Logos are everything. There's no great news story without a great logo and great graphics. I'm thinking something like … Hero Held Hostage! The letters will be in the form of a gun or knife and colored in Italian green, white and red stripes."

Ingersoll interrupted. "I think I'm going to leap across the table and hug you, Saxton," he exclaimed. "You've got your thinking cap on today. Okay, what about you, Henry? Follow that act if you can. Give us the Entertainment angle. Step up to the fire."

"I'm thinking about the *Celebrities Galore* program again," Handleman answered nervously, knowing Saxton had scored and he had to perform to at least create a tie. "I'm thinking we open the show with a close-up on Lincoln's hair swatch, which would be placed inside of an antique iron neck-collar, both of which would be resting on an Italian flag with a barber's scissors stuck in the center of the collar … right in the middle of the swatch of hair. Of course, we'll have to add some hair."

Seeing he had Ingersoll smiling, Handleman rose from his chair and continued. "Then we have cast members from *The Sopranos* TV show appear for interviews interspersed with some top flight models parading in outstanding fashions by Italian designers. Top name guys."

"You're making me feel warm all over, Henry," Ingersoll laughed. "I'm getting close to tap dancing."

A new feeling of confidence flooded over Handleman. "For the showstopper we do an interview with Gotti's son talking about kidnappings past and present. Get him to throw in some things about extortion, murders, wise guys, and all the standard mob stuff. During the interview, we do cutaways to some excellent turn-your-stomach photos that we can pick up from our police files library.

"You're rounding third, big guy. Go all the way."

"Finally, to end on an inspiring note, we close in tight on the photo of Lincoln with tape across his mouth while some Italian tenor is singing the *Ave Maria*. We'll fix up a Lincoln publicity photo from our files. We don't want to use the one they sent. Might not be good enough. Maybe a towel in his mouth with the name of an exclusive Rome hotel on the towel."

"Oh, my God! You scored! Oh, my God!" Ingersoll shouted. "But make sure you work Pearl Necklace into the show. Let's start showcasing her. Give her some exposure, if you will excuse the pun. You agree?"

"Of course I agree, George! Great idea! We'll have her handle the fashion show."

"Oh, I almost forgot." Ingersoll said. "This is ratings sweeps month. What a fantastic break. We'll cream the competition." He suddenly jumped to his feet, followed in like manner by everyone at the table. "Okay, team, this is a wrap. Let's get this steak on the grill. I want to smell the meat burning within minutes."

"What do I tell the kidnappers?" LaRue asked quickly when it appeared the meeting was over.

"Negotiate," Ingersoll snapped. "Try to get the price down. Tell them how rotten his ratings are. Talk about how difficult it is to transfer ransom money out of the country. Tell them anything but stretch this thing out. Tell them we're checking out the hair to make sure it belongs to Lincoln and our scientists need more samples. Ask for some from the back of his head. Just get us some time to milk this thing dry. Keep him alive for a week at least. Then we'll give them some money. Remember, I said *some*. Don't even think about ten million. Maybe a hundred thousand."

He walked quickly toward his desk, then stopped and turned to face Tanner. "Steve, send me a video of Pearl's television appearance yesterday. I want to see that again."

TV

"Up on camera one," program director Dauber ordered, starting the YOURchannel evening news show.

To the music of "Arrivederci Roma" the *Pearl Necklace First Things First News Show* opened that evening with a smiling Pearl Necklace in her swing and behind her a huge photo of herself wearing only an Italian flag wrapped tightly around her body.

As the camera closed in on Necklace, her smile melted away, and she took on a look of intense concern. Suddenly, the music changed to theme from *The Godfather*.

"Well, people, Pearl Necklace here again, and we are going to skip the NewsStar girls tonight and go right to a fantastic breaking news report." Suddenly, on the screen, NewsStar Lindi appeared walking along a beach and wearing a bikini. She waved as the camera closed in on her, then struck a seductive pose and held up a sign that stated in immense letters: BREAKING NEWS!

Pearl Necklace appeared once again. "I have terrible news for you tonight, people. I want you to fasten your seat belts and get ready for a real shocker. This is a breaking news special, and it might cause you to drop your remote so put in down. Tonight we are opening with a YOURchannel exclusive story. Are you ready for this, Mr. and Ms. America? You may find what I am about to tell you too difficult to believe but here it is. Straight out. Nothing held back."

She paused, stepped out of the swing and turned to another camera. "Larry Lincoln, our own Larry Lincoln, star anchor of the YOURchannel daily evening news show ..." She paused again and brought her hands to her moderately exposed breasts, "Larry Lincoln has been kidnapped! You heard me correctly. Larry Lincoln has been kidnapped—in Italy! Stay with us. We'll have more on Larry Lincoln, who is now our Hero Held Hostage— after these commercials."

Monte Castella

"**W**hat the hell are you talking about?" Paolo screamed into the phone, at the same time tugging at the wool ski mask covering his head. "We sent you plenty of hair. The poor guy doesn't have too much to spare."

Paolo Polucci and Alex LaRue were in the middle of a telephone discussion about ransom and it was not going the way Paolo expected.

"I'm having a problem understanding you, Paolo," LaRue said. "Do you have something in your mouth?"

Paolo straightened his mask so that the mouth opening would be in the correct position. "Is this better?"

"That's much better. Look, my friend," LaRue continued. "We're talking a lot of money here. I can't even figure how much that would be in Euros. My boss insists that we must be sure you actually have Larry before we fork over what you're asking. You're demanding serious money, Paolo. Besides, asking for ten million in one-hundred-dollar bills really slows down the transaction."

"How would you like it if I send you his hand? Then you could check his fingerprints." Paolo had his phone speaker on but did not let LaRue know. He turned to look at Lincoln, sitting close by, tied and gagged, his head shaking violently and his eyes wide open, expressing terror he had never felt before.

"Well, that's an idea," LaRue answered. " I'll certainly check that one out with my superiors. Could you call me back tomorrow? In the meantime, you might reconsider the amount you're demanding. Try thinking in the neighborhood of maybe one million. Or less."

"One million!" Paolo screamed again.

"We're not sure he's worth more. We must consider value in these matters. I told you how we've been having a terrible time with his ratings. It's the least watched evening news on television, and you're asking ten million dollars. Think about it for a while. Think about one million instead of ten. One million dollars is still a lot of money. I'm not even sure about that but I'll try."

"The only thing we'll think about is how to cut off his hand."

"I don't think that's really necessary. Oh, another thing before I forget, I must bring up the time difference. I don't mind you calling me at home, but it's four in the morning here. Could you make your next call a little later? About five hours later. I would really appreciate it."

"Go to hell," Paolo shouted and threw his phone across the room.

He turned to Larry Lincoln. "Can you believe that, mister big-time newsman anchor? They don't want to pay. I thought you told me you were the number one TV news guy. Your ratings are in the toilet. Now they're talking one million dollars. Two hours ago, it was five and now it's one. Even after you talked to him he doesn't believe we have you. What kind of people do you work for? Now they want more hair."

Lincoln shook his head while making loud garbled sounds through the sock.

Gianni had his face buried in his hands, once again thinking about the exchange rate, changing dollars into lire and lire into euros. "Does that come to nine million lire or three million, nine hundred thousand lira?" He raised his head. "Whichever is correct, it comes to a lot of money, Paolo." He approached his brother and whispered in his ear. "Maybe we should take it. We can't keep him here forever. God help us if Mama should come back and find him."

"After all this trouble, you want us to let him go for only one million? Maybe less? Never!" Paolo screamed.

This time Lincoln began nodding with equal vigor, making loud sounds and blinking his eyes frantically.

"I think he's trying to say something, Paolo. Should I remove the sock?" Gianni was sweating under his own ski mask and his resolve was weakening.

"Okay, but if he starts to scream, shove it back in."

Carlo pulled out the wet sock and wiped the saliva from his hands on Lincoln's jacket.

"If you don't mind, sir, this is cashmere," Lincoln snapped while spitting out remnants of the sock. The recent events had not been pleasant, especially for a man whose previous major problem in life outside of his hair was finding a cab on a rainy New York night. Though he could not really say he had been mistreated, his emotional level was at an all-time low. The truck ride was terrifying, and the materials that were continually being stuffed in his mouth were distasteful. Also, the bindings around his wrists and ankles were painful, and the absence of companionship produced a loneliness he had never known. Some of his depression was offset by the delicious meals he had enjoyed. If they did nothing else right, his captors knew how to cook.

More harmful than the physical hardships was listening to the phone conversations between Paolo Polucci and Alex LaRue, the one person at the network he considered to be his friend and whom he thought he could rely on to help him. It was LaRue he directed Paolo to call. He simply could not believe the nightmarish conversations. The endless bickering about money was bad enough, but the threats of dismemberment, not to mention another session with the hair clippers, was sending him into periods of depression comparable only to those Monday mornings when the weekly ratings were published. In moments of despair after the phone arguments over money, he would start to ponder the possibility of a career change, a line of thought he never pursued too far because he could think of no other profession that paid so well while providing such a satisfying life style.

There were moments when left alone by his captors, Lincoln's mind would drift back to the good life he was leading. Often he would think about those occasions when he would enter a restaurant, causing conversations to stop, heads to turn, and stares to follow him to his favorite table. Waiters would leave other customers to serve him, bantering gleefully with him and indulging his every desire. It didn't matter or wasn't known to these people that his ratings were terrible. He was on television five days a week.

Almost equal to that immensely satisfying experience was the use of the limousines the network provided for him on special occasions, a perk he thoroughly enjoyed and rushed to like a kid to a toy store. He always found it exhilarating to step out of one of those long, sleek machines to attend a charity function, a Broadway opening, a Madison Square game, or a political gathering and see the awe in the eyes of the people who had stopped to wait for the door to open in anticipation of encountering a movie or television idol, famous musician, sports star, or political luminary and experience the thrill of close contact with someone who had reached the high level of star, diva, or celebrity. It never failed to make him feel giddy, almost delirious with self-importance. This was a reality he could never relinquish.

Not to be overlooked, of course, were the requests for autographs. Those were uplifting experiences he looked forward to and thoroughly participated in whenever he appeared in public. Pretending indifference, he would sign with a practiced nonchalance but he loved doing it and bathed in the excitement he caused. Weekly viewership ratings never entered his mind during those delightful signing moments.

In addition, he would remember those wonderful evenings

when, dining alone in a restaurant, he might receive among the materials to be autographed an invitation to a rendezvous from some beautiful woman seated somewhere in the room. On occasion it would be just a key and hotel or apartment address. At times he took advantage of the situation, satisfying both his desire for a sexual adventure for himself and accommodate his lover's desire to sleep with a man with television fame.

No, he could not, would not turn his back to this life. It was a marvelous existence, and he would endure the current nightmare with its depressing phone calls if it meant a return to the life he loved. Simply thinking about it strengthened his resolve. He was determined to get back there somehow if for no other reason than to get his hands on his agent and Alex LaRue. The image of their battered faces lifted his spirits. Whenever depression started to set in, he would think about punching them severely and repeatedly or choking them, listening to and enjoying their screams for mercy.

"Would two million dollars do it?" he asked Paolo. "If so, you've got it. I'll pay it. I'll pay it myself. Two million in cash and I go free. Let me use your phone and I'll call my accountant right now. A quick wire and you'll have the money in your bank account today."

The offer stopped the conversation between the brothers immediately. "You want to pay your own ransom?" Paolo asked.

"Of course! I see now it's the only way. Don't you realize they're playing with you? Believe me, I know them. I've negotiated with them. They'll eventually work you down to much less, a great deal less. You're dealing with sharks, and they'll take you down. I guarantee you they're thinking about two hundred thousand, if that. My offer is a flat two million. Just give me your bank account number and you've got it. Think of the money you'll save on telephone calls. How about it?"

Paolo was puzzled. He had never seen anything in the movies quite like this to provide him with some guidance. He paused for a few moments to think about the offer and then motioned to his brothers to join him in a corner of the room. After an intense argument that included occasional slaps to both Carlo and Gianni, he turned to Lincoln. "Three million dollars. Nothing less."

"Two million," Lincoln answered sharply, sensing a weakness in Gianni to settle.

"Three million dollars," Paolo responded, "and no more bickering, or I will not be responsible for what Gianni and Carlo will do to you. They're animals."

"One million and not a dime more," Lincoln countered, seeing a compromise possibility and their desire to achieve some gain for all the trouble they had gone through.

"One million!" Paolo shouted. "You just said two million. Son of bitch, I don't believe this. You're just like your bosses. This is your life, and you're getting cheap about it."

"One million dollars is not being cheap," Lincoln answered. The stock market has not been good to me this year even with my contacts and access to inside market information. To help you out, I'll even throw in the services of my investment adviser, and I'll pay the fees. How about that?"

"You just told me he's no good."

"Okay, here is my absolute last offer. One million dollars, season tickets for your friends in New York to the Knicks, Yankees, and Rangers, and the use of my Visa card for one week. I have a fifty-thousand-dollar credit limit."

The Polucci brothers huddled in a heated discussion once again. Finally, Paolo turned to face Lincoln. "One million, the Visa card for three weeks, first class tickets to Hollywood, and you can keep the sports tickets."

"You have a deal."

"One more thing," Paolo said, returning to stand in front of Lincoln. "Listen to me very carefully. You forget this thing ever happened. No police, no television story, and especially—are you listening carefully to this?—not a single word to Mayor Vocino or his brother Angelo. They are the people you are to meet for the interview. Otherwise, we cut off your balls. Like I told you, we have family in New York. They have a specialty."

"As far as I'm concerned, this never happened. What's for supper?"

Angelo Vocino tried again. "Mr. Baywatch, I told you this was a very dangerous business." He was shouting in order to be heard through the closed door of the hotel bedroom in which Baywatch had barricaded himself. Angelo was there with Nina, the three musicians, and Father Autobelli.

"Something like this can occur when you deal with the mafia. These people can be ruthless. The don will deal with those men. They will not see the sun rise tomorrow. You have to understand, Mr. Baywatch. You must expect to encounter danger under these circumstances. You are operating in a world of crime. I explained all of this at the beginning. Remember? Can you hear me? Are you alright?"

Following the attempted abduction by the Polucci brothers, Burt Baywatch, wet pants and all, ran back to the hotel and locked himself in his room, stopping only once on his way to purchase three bottles of wine. He wanted whiskey, but it was not available. He was followed closely every foot of the way by Angelo Vocino and the group now at his door. Not once throughout the entire episode did he respond or even pay attention to their apologies. Upon entering the safety of his room, he slammed the door in their faces and dropped to the floor.

"You must calm yourself, Mr. Baywatch. We will straighten everything out, I promise. Can you hear me?" Angelo repeated, standing outside the hotel room Baywatch had locked himself in.

"Yes, I can hear you," Baywatch screamed. "Can you hear me? Can you hear me say I never want to see you again? I never want to eat again. I never want to be blessed again. I never want to hear another violin as long as I live. Go away."

He shoved as much furniture as he could find against the door, discontinued answering their pleas, and quickly began drinking the wine. After a half hour and consuming a bottle and a half of the wine, he fell across the bed and passed out.

The following afternoon the pounding on the door began again, and Angelo Vocino's shouts revived him from the best sleep he'd had in months. As he slowly regained consciousness, he became aware of a terrible headache and that he was not in New York.

"Everything is just fine, Mr. Baywatch," Vocino called out in a gentle, soothing tone. "You can come out now. It's entirely safe. No more problems. We have talked to Don Marcasi and he absolutely guarantees your good health. More importantly, here is the best news of all … I hope you can hear me … Larry Lincoln has arrived. He is in his room now catching up on his sleep. He is fine except for a problem with his hair. He said he would talk about what happened later. Believe me, everything is back on schedule."

Baywatch heard every word, but at the moment he was concentrating on bringing the room into focus and getting out of bed.

"Our famous chef—you remember him—is right now preparing a meal that you will remember for the rest of your life. Cozze al pomodoro, followed by ziti con finocchi, followed by osso buco ala Milanese, for which he is famous. And for desert, torta Giadula al cioccolato. For the wine we have selected three varieties."

The mention of wine revived Baywatch instantly, and he did not hear anything further as he rushed into the bathroom to relieve himself of the excessive food and wine he had consumed the previous day.

"We will meet at the Ristorante Vocino at eight and plan tomorrow's activities," Vocino continued. "Bring your camera for the interview with the mayor. Mr. Lincoln is in his suite, number

204. I must tell you he is very anxious to see you. He wanted to get together with you so badly he was threatening to tear down your door. It took quite an effort to stop him. Would you pick him up around seven thirty? Can you answer, please?"

"I hear you! I hear you!" Baywatch screamed. "Eight o'clock! Now go away and let me be sick."

"*Arrivederci,*" Vocino called back. He turned to the musicians. "Play for him a little while. Consider his condition and change the music from what you've been playing. Try some gentle classics. Maybe he'll slip you something under the door."

Angelo turned to face the door again. "I'm leaving now, Mr. Baywatch. See you and Mr. Lincoln tonight for dinner. He will explain everything. The mayor and Nina will be joining us. We will plan the interviews. Tomorrow will be a big day. The don is looking forward to meeting you and Mr. Lincoln. Everything is fine now. Ciao."

New York

Pearl Necklace removed her new contract from her briefcase and tossed it into her desk drawer. *Not bad for a few days work*, she thought.

They had been very busy days. In addition to her regular evening news show and guest appearances on *Celebrities Galore*, Pearl had conducted interviews with major magazines, newspapers, and radio shows. She was also invited to be guest host on one of the late-night television shows. There was not a talk show that did not devote a portion of its time to her performance and her impact on television news.

The *Pearl Necklace First Things First News Show* had run smoothly with Pearl's screen time extending beyond the normal five minutes usually assigned to anchors. Then when the Lincoln kidnapping story broke and the new program name changed to *Hero Held Hostage*, her viewership ratings moved higher each day, reaching record levels for YOURchannel. Her appearances on *Celebrities Galore* were also primarily responsible for that show's increased viewership, saving it from cancellation. Almost overnight, advertising revenues for the entire lineup of YOURchannel programs increased dramatically, resulting in her office being filled with flowers from the men and women of the company's advertising sales force.

Then there was her relationship with CEO George Ingersoll,

who would stop by her office to visit, always spending at least fifteen minutes, shaking her hand, praising her performance, encouraging her, and never leaving without an extended warm hug.

The television news competition on the other channels was not happy, and many members of the news media were outraged at what they considered the irresponsible intrusion of blatant sex and entertainment into the serious business of news reporting. Both YOURchannel and Pearl Necklace in particular were savaged on every television talk show and the op-ed pages of every newspaper. The only support she received was from viewer call-ins, letters to the editor, and the social media. Her Twitter following soared immediately. The decimal level on the cable news talk shows increased with sanctimonious bombast from pundits over the debasement of the profession to which they had all dedicated their lives and fortunes. The exposure she received from this combined clatter was a public relations man's dream.

The nightly *Hy Volume Show* television talk program was typical. Proclaiming he was speaking on behalf of all newscasters and journalists was Hy Volume, a television news commentator who created his name on the advice of his agent who saw the trend of memorable names led by hip-hop, rap, and pop music performers. He was determined to let his viewers know he was offended by the Pearl Necklace performance. However, what really enraged him were the viewer ratings her show achieved. They were at a point he had never attained no matter how outrageous the political positions he and his guest reporters acted out on his television show. He cut short a book tour of radio and television interviews to rush back to New York, where he gathered his usual vocal guests to attack the *Pearl Necklace First Things First News Show*.

He began shouting the moment the director cued him while simultaneously pounding the table with his fist so his viewers would understand that this night he was going to erupt as never before.

"She's a knee-jerk liberal flat out," he screamed into the camera.

It was his standard procedure to open with a strong salvo to grab the channel surfers and then increase the volume to hold them. "I can smell 'em a mile away. For my money—which I might tell you is considerable due to my many easy-to-read biographies—she is nothing but a tax-hiking, deficit-building, government-loving, welfare-sucking, gun-hating, abortion-pushing, gay-supporting, regulations promoting, foreign aid-advocating, moral relativist. And I'll bet my next five lecture fees that those goose-stepping feminists are behind her. You can just tell by the ..."

"Gee, that's original," interrupted Lily Saint Sear, who was a show regular as a voice from the left. She was once known as Marilyn Cummings, but she also saw the future blending of television news and entertainment and the importance of a memorable name. "You couldn't get two minutes of air time anywhere if you were ever to run out of smug, sneering, slanted, snide, shady opinions that you repeat incessantly and are as empty as a dry well. I speak truthfully and use facts while you and your look-alikes at this channel get marching orders in the morning and spend the entire day repeating the company line word for word. You spend most of your time either throwing incendiary bombs to excite your thin base or promoting books you have someone write for you. You have no more idea what honest journalism is about than ..."

"Pearl Necklace is not a real journalist, that's for sure," interrupted another show participant, Simon Wise. "Not what she's doing. That's simply sexual exploitation. What we do here is journalism, honest journalism. We turn loose a flow of thought-provoking ideas that are explored and expounded upon by people like us who have the dedication—I repeat—*dedication* to honestly separate the truth from the trauma, the bark from the trees, and the snow from the sidewalk. What she does ..."

"I'd like to know what they're paying that ball-cruncher to parade her sweet ass in front of the camera," screamed Sledge Hammer, another guest, this one from talk radio. He was a former disc jockey who changed his career and name when he discovered the enormous income to be made in ultraconservative talk radio and lectures. "She better never appear on one of my programs. I'd show her what truthful news commentary is about. I'd tear her a new …"

"Pearl Necklace slants the news," Hy Volume screamed, spitting to the side to emphasize his disgust. "That really revolts me. That's a no-no in this business, an unforgivable violation of the journalist's honesty compact with the public. Honesty and balance are what people deserve when they tune us in. They want the facts that a paltry pundit …"

"The only facts you uncover," Saint Sear bellowed, "are slanted views placed in your head by your bosses who pay you and your toady pals to play them like a record, spinning around and around all day long. You should be a poster boy for …"

"Dedication," Simon Wise screamed as he leaped up. "She lacks our dedication. And proper clothing."

Saint Sear snapped back. "The only dedication you practice is running for president every four years so you can land a host job on television talk shows and spew…"

Sledge Hammer jumped up. "Are you a socialist–communist?" he asked Saint Sear as he climbed onto the table and started doing push-ups. She answered by slamming her coffee cup into his head.

"Now, folks, that's what I call making a statement," shouted Hi Volume. "What a great show! We'll race Pearl Necklace to the ratings finish line any day. Let's break for a commercial. But first, I want to tell you the *Hy Volume Show* will be on its national Four Horsemen tour next month with stops in Chicago, Atlanta, Dallas, and Los Angeles. Check your local listings. By the way, on this tour I will rap my monologues."

For Pearl Necklace the excitement of the past few days was capped off by what she felt was a successful contract negotiation meeting with Sanford of Legal Affairs. He was full of confidence as he waited for her in the conference room, expecting to be facing a beautiful but empty-headed arm candy similar to his second wife.

"Not to worry, Steve," he told Tanner who was already there and waiting. "This will be a cakewalk. I know just how to handle this centerfold. I only hope she knows how to read." Tanner smiled but did not respond.

Sanford stood and greeted Necklace when she entered. She was wearing a finely tailored suit jacket and short skirt. They sat down facing each other across a glass coffee table. Watching her cross her legs, he somehow did not feel quite at ease as he usually was in these circumstances. It was the first time he had met her, and her beauty distracted him, creating a different balance of power to which he was not accustomed. He did not quite have that certain in-charge attitude that he had nurtured in law school and which was his essential mental state whenever he negotiated contracts. Necklace never took her eyes from his while she unbuttoned and removed her suit jacket both to make herself comfortable and to give Sanford the time to look at her and her legs.

"This contract isn't bad for a starting position," she said, never ceasing to smile. She took the contract from her briefcase, leaned forward, and pushed it across the table, providing Sanford an ample view. "You're in the ball park alright, Phil, but unfortunately, you're seated in the nosebleed section. Let's talk about the box seats, shall we? I have a show in an hour."

She paused to brush off an imaginary speck from her skirt, allowing a little time for the shock of her opening statement to throw him. The few minutes Ingersoll had spent in her office each morning and, in particular his hugs, gave her the leverage she needed in the negotiation with Sanford.

"Excuse me?" Sanford managed to answer.

"Let's talk about the money first," she continued before he could say more. "I want thirty percent more than the amount you are offering. Beyond that, a five percent raise for every rating point increase from the level the news show was at on my first day. Also, let's make it a three-year contract, which includes an hour weekly show of my own in the future at my option. In addition, it should cover the use of my image and my name only upon my approval. That should do it."

Sanford jumped to his feet. "What the hell are talking about? You're out of your damn mind. Just who the hell do you think you are? Who the hell do you think you're talking to?"

"I'm talking to a man with sweating palms." Without a moment's hesitation, she picked up her briefcase and turned to Tanner. "It's been good working with you, Steve. I have the show to prepare for and then some appointments."

"Wait just a minute, honey," Sanford snapped. "We have you under contract right now. We own you lock, stock, and barrel for the next six months. After that, you could be on the street."

"You have a point there," she answered, reaching into her briefcase to pull out a large envelope stuffed with an old contract she had with her former magazine employer plus some blank papers. "However, I have here an offer to join your competition after six months. Would you like to read it?"

Pearl stood, straightened her skirt, and waved the envelope. "The way I see it, you have three options. One, you can sue me. Two, you can force me to work for six months, which would certainly make me a bigger and more valuable celebrity, at which time my demands will be greater. Or option number three, you can give me what I ask and have the most lucrative news show on cable television. Not to mention a bigger audience for that idiot's delight, *Celebrities Galore*. Seems like a no-brainer to me. That's something I'm sure you're capable of handling." Her demands stunned Sanford into silence.

Slowly tucking the envelope back into her briefcase, she put on her jacket and walked across the room to the door, stopping only to make one last demand. "Sanford, don't ever call me *honey* again."

After she left the room, Sanford, his face flush red with embarrassment and rage, turned back to Tanner. "I told you something like this would happen. You should be fired for messing this thing up. It's entirely your fault. I'm not forgetting this."

"That makes a lot of sense," Tanner answered quickly. "I should be fired for turning a dead-end news show into a hot money-maker! Take a look at the ratings, Phil. Take a look at what those higher ratings will bring YOURchannel in advertising dollars. Just do the numbers, and if they work, give her what she wants. Money is what we're here for. She's right, it's a no-brainer. Like you said, it's a cakewalk."

That evening the show opened with a backdrop photo of Pearl Necklace tied to a gigantic oak tree by a yellow ribbon bound across her breast. The Hero Held Hostage logo was painted above her navel. The background music was "She Wore A Yellow Ribbon."

Pearl Necklace stepped onto the set wearing a short, tight-fitting yellow T-shirt bearing the logo Hero Held Hostage and yellow mini-shorts. As the camera closed in, she dropped her smile and assumed a serious look.

"Another day," she began softly, "means another day for our Hero Held Hostage." She paused and the music changed to Samuel Barber's *Adagio for Strings*.

"I am sorry, but I am here to tell you there is no word yet on the whereabouts of news anchor Larry Lincoln. But negotiations are underway. We at YOURchannel are working every minute of the day and night and through every worldwide source at our disposal to free Larry Lincoln. I know that's what you want and what you are hoping for. I can't disclose those negotiations now nor with whom we are negotiating. That information must remain confidential at the present time for fear of breaking down our communications with the kidnappers who call themselves the Black Hand Mob. Yes, that much we can tell you. It is a mob operation. It is the dark, dangerous, sinister underworld that has committed this monstrous act. The question is ... why? Why Larry Lincoln? What is going on, and how are we going to bring this appalling episode to a successful and happy conclusion? Those are the questions we are facing today. One thing I can say is Larry Lincoln knows you are with him, worrying about him, and hoping for his safe and soon return."

She turned to another camera and continued with a smile. "Let's move on to the cheerful side of this story. I do not use the word *love* lightly, but right now yellow ribbons are being tied to trees, telephone poles, traffic lights, billboards, and porches of homes across the country. The American people are behind Larry Lincoln and showing their feelings. Now that's love."

She turned and walked toward another camera. "As a demonstration of those feelings, let me take you right now to the street outside our studio, where hundreds of Larry Lincoln's fans are standing and waiting and hoping to be seen on television. They are with our weather forecaster, WeatherStar Maggi. It's all yours, girl."

"Thank you, Pearl, loved that yellow ribbon shot. Wow!"

"Thank you, Maggi. You're looking pretty hot yourself."

"Up on camera three," director Dauber ordered as the song "I'm Just Wild about Larry" came blaring out of the loudspeaker set up on the street. "That's good. Keep panning across. Get all those people in view a couple of times. Zoom in on some of the signs."

When the handheld camera's red light flashed on, the crowd of people standing behind barricades turned into a screaming mob, with everyone jostling for front positions, all the while frantically waving their ribbons and signs.

"Maggi, start the interviews," Dauber said. "Camera one, zoom in."

"Well, who do we have here?" Maggi asked a group of three teenage girls holding a sign with the words Framingham High Cheerleaders, Cleveland, Ohio.

"And where are you girls from?" she asked.

"Cleveland, Ohio!" they yelled, laughing, jumping, squeezing each other, and waving at the camera. Suddenly they threw their arms up high and called out in unison and on cue, "One … two … three … four, who the heck are we for? Larry Lincoln, Larry Lincoln, rah! rah! rah!"

"That's fantastic, girls," WeatherStar Maggi shouted over the noise, "but tell us, what do you think about the situation with Lincoln that you've been watching on television news?"

"We never watch television news," one of the girls responded quickly, "but now we follow YOURchannel on Twitter. It's awesome!"

"Thank you. Let's move over here," Maggi said quickly, smiling at the camera and walking along the line of waving arms. She stopped in front of a man shouting the Hero Held Hostage logo words. "What about you, sir? What's your reaction to the kidnapping of news anchor Larry Lincoln?"

"I think it's terrible, simply terrible. Why did they have to cut his hair? I watch television news every evening and I tell you I just don't know what is happening to the world today. You know, there was a time when just showing an American passport was enough to be treated royally. Now you can't even get a good table. Can I say hello to my grandchildren?"

"Go right ahead," Maggi answered as she turned to face the camera. "Now let's go to the WeatherStar map for the latest highs and lows, shifting currents, sunny and rainy patterns." The screen cut to a national map and Maggie continued talking, reading from a script. As she finished, the screen cut back to Pearl Necklace. "Thank you, Maggi. That was wonderful."

"You're welcome, Pearl."

"Well, you can see the kind of effect this kidnapping is having on our fans on the street and the affection it is bringing out of them. But what about Larry Lincoln's family? How are they coping with this tragedy? For that we take you now to Los Angeles where YOURchannel reporter Bruce is standing by to bring you an exclusive interview with Larry's mother, Lillian Pendal. They're on the front lawn of the Pendal home. Take it from here, Bruce."

"Thank you, Pearl. Don't drop that yellow ribbon. Folks, as you can see, I'm here with a woman in distress. Look at those tears flowing from her blue eyes and cascading down her cheeks. I see those tears as a stream of love, adoration, and worry, tears every mother can understand. But who can blame her? She's the mother of Larry Lincoln, YOURchannel's Hero Held Hostage." Bruce took out his handkerchief and handed it to her.

"No thank you. It's the sun. I need my sunglasses."

"I know you're trying to cover up, Mrs. Pendal, but let me ask you this tough question for a mother who might lose her son," Bruce continued as he put his arm around her shoulders. "Tell the American people exactly how you felt the moment you heard he was kidnapped and undergoing terrible torture."

"I never heard they were torturing him."

"Oh, yes, Mrs. Pendal, mother of Larry Lincoln, we have heard from a very reliable source—though I cannot confirm this—that they were considering the use of procedures that cause unthinkable pain."

"I never heard that before either. Italians would never use torture."

"Well, I think it's certainly possible, Mrs. Pendal. This is tough on you at this moment, I know, going through what you are going through, but I must ask these questions, as painful as they are, because that's my job as we in the news say."

"I wish I had put on my sunglasses. That sun is so bright."

"Are you crying again, Mrs. Pendal? Yes, I see you are and I can't blame you. No need to cover your sorrow with excuses. This has to be a heartbreaking experience. I can feel your pain."

Bruce looked toward the camera and took his arm away from her shoulders. "Pearl, this poor woman is a basket case right now. I could go on with more penetrating questions, but I don't have the heart. This is a trying time for all of us in the newsy business, and I think we should go back to you and let Mrs. Pendal have this awesome moment in private. This is a very troubled YOURchannel News reporter Bruce coming to you from Larry Lincoln's home on an otherwise bright and sunny day in the City of Angels."

Before the screen went black, Brace took Lillian Pendal's hand away from her face and pressed it to his chest.

"Thank you, Bruce," Pearl Necklace responded as she looked up at the monitor that showed a close-up of the clasped hands of Bruce and Larry Lincoln's mother.

"You're welcome, Pearl," Bruce responded in a voice-over. "In a situation like this, Bruce can't help himself."

Pearl Necklace turned toward the camera and quickly broke into a smile. "You can get more of the Bruce interview with Mrs. Pendal on the YOURchannel website. Well, it's time for our new segment, "The Sunny Side." For that we'll take a quick whirl around the world's top cheerful news stories of the week, featuring our beautiful NewsStars.

The song "Sunny Side of the Street" provided the background as an enormous revolving world globe descended slowly down from the ceiling. Necklace approached the globe and placed her hand on it to stop the spinning. Behind her, the background photo changed to Necklace in a bikini, posing atop the globe.

"Let's start with NewsStar Sherri," she said, pointing to a spot on the globe. "She's in England at Wimbledon, where the major tournament of the tennis season is underway. When you talk about that great country, you must talk about the royal family. Give us the latest on Queen Liz and her fun kids, Sherri. Any new scandals?" "Yellow Submarine" began playing.

"Thank you, Pearl," Sherri answered. She was wearing an abbreviated tennis outfit created from the British flag. "Too bad about Lincoln, but I'm here to talk the sunny side of the news. A few of England's first family spent the day watching the action at center court. We'll skip the tennis action for now and go directly to film and present an exclusive YOURchannel fashion show featuring former Princess Diana's famous one-of-a-kind evening gowns, and more than that, we'll split the screen and compare Diana's gorgeous garbs with those of the newest and hottest royal, Kate, Duchess of Churchill. You can vote your favorite via Twitter or go to YOURchannel/royal/voteyourchoice.com! We'll announce the winning gown tomorrow."

As the split screen exhibited a continuing slide show of Diana and Kate in a variety of designer gowns, Sherri described each one, naming the designer and the event at which it was worn. At the end, she announced that YOURchannel would soon be publishing a new book containing every tabloid photograph ever taken of the Princesses Diana and Kate.

"Back to you, Pearl."

"Thank you for that news report, Sherri."

"You're welcome, Pearl. Love your backdrop photo. Talk about a ratings boost!"

"Now, let's go with another Sunny Side news report." Necklace gave the globe another spin, stopping it after a few turns and pointing to Libya. The background music switched to the song "Caravan."

"Since we are not fortunate enough to have our own YOURchannel reporter on the scene due to political problems there, we are calling upon a local correspondent, Labib of Libya, who will be taking us back in time for a reminiscing look at the great clothing fashions of the former dictator, Colonel Muammar Qaddafi. That man had an eye for fashion. Tell us about it, Labib."

"Thank you, Pearl, and may your beauty be preserved forever."

Monte Castella

The moment Burt Baywatch walked into Lincoln's hotel room, the anchor leaped on him from behind the door, grabbed him by the throat, and pinned him to the wall.

"You cost me a million dollars, you rotten bastard," Lincoln screamed, "and the worst days of my life. And my hair, look at my goddamn hair. How do you think I'll look on television with this savage scalping?"

"What scalping? I don't see anything," Baywatch responded, gasping for air.

"Don't start your goddamn bullshit with me. Total control, you told me. Nothing can go wrong. You were on top of everything. The only thing you were on top of was me, and it was the worst screwing I've ever had! I should have known not to listen to you."

Lincoln swung the gagging, struggling Baywatch in a circle several times before throwing him across the room onto the bed. "Let me show you what total control is," he shouted, looking around the room for a weapon.

Baywatch had only a few moments to react when he saw a crazed Lincoln standing before him with a chair raised over his head. With his agent's instinct for survival, he drove both feet into his client's stomach, sending him back against the wall, groaning and crumbling to the floor.

"I have no idea what you're talking about, Larry, but I'm the one who should be doing the choking. Whatever your problem, you're taking it poorly." Baywatch rolled to the floor on the other side of the bed. "So you got lost. What's the big deal about that? You've here and that's all that matters."

He raised his head slowly above the level of the bed to make sure Lincoln was not continuing his attack. "I don't know anything about your million dollars. But would you like to hear something really serious that happened while you were driving around enjoying the Sicilian countryside? I'll describe serious to you. First, I was dragged around this damn town three times and then shown more farmland than I ever want to see again. I filmed everything that moved or didn't move, listened to enough trio music to last a lifetime, and stuffed myself with enough food to withstand a week of fasting. Not to mention getting blessed every time I turned around. Let me tell you something else, Larry. Everything I've related up to this point has been the good news."

Lincoln continued to groan.

"Now I'll give you the bad news. I was attacked by some crazed mafioso, nearly had my damn foot shot off, was thrown into the front seat of a van that would have been tight with just two people, had my head smashed into the windshield, and I was dumped into the street and kicked in the balls. All to the tune of 'Volare' played by three off-key musicians. I don't know which was worse: the kick, the bullet, or the music."

Lincoln stopped moaning and raised his head high enough to face Baywatch on the other side of the bed. "That's a lot like what happened to me."

"Which part? The kick or the music? What in the hell did you do to your hair?"

"Is it that bad?"

"If it was a haircut, it was a bad one."

"It wasn't a haircut, you ass." Lincoln snapped back, gently raising his hand to feel the gap in his hair. "It was brutally chopped off by some maniac who kept telling me he really wanted to remove my ear. I was kidnapped, Mr. Total Control. *Kidnapped*, as in abducted. Thrown into a god-awful smelly fertilizer van, slugged repeatedly, gagged, tied, tossed, and threatened with a knife. And that, to quote you, is the good news. Oh, did I mention what they used to gag me? A sock!"

"No kidding?"

"No kidding, Mr. Ex-Agent. They grabbed me at the airport and threw me in a van they use to spread manure! Then I was driven somewhere, tied to a chair, and forced to listen to the most devastating, demoralizing, degrading, and humiliating telephone conversations you can imagine. All the time I am surrounded by three masked men who loved nothing more than anything else to talk about dismembering me. Is that something I would kid about? The only thing that kept me going was the thought of strangling you."

"That's fantastic," Baywatch responded. The scent of a great publicity story was quickly exciting him. "Now tell me the bad news. Skip the hair bit. Tell me about the phone calls."

"It was all about ransom money. They were arguing about the damn ransom price. They were refusing to pay it."

"Your parents wouldn't pay to free you?"

"No! Not my parents. My own employers! The great YOURchannel! Can you believe that? Those rotten bastards actually dickered with these butchers. So much for all that crap about how we were a team. Through it all they actually refused to pay these guys to free me. A few lousy million dollars. Ingersoll spends that much on his mistresses. Just wait till I get back. I'll kill LaRue. After I kill you."

"How much did you say they wanted?"

"They started at ten million dollars."

"Wow! That's a lot of money, Larry."

"Great! Now my own agent. Thank God they weren't negotiating with you. I'd be bald and earless by now." He slumped back to the floor. "Nobody gives a damn. I should have stayed in modeling. I was doing fine. A couple of radio commercials a week, some print, some TV. I could have been a top model by now. I was making great money, too. Of course, I had a good agent then!"

"That's not kind, Larry."

"I was doing well and really creaming it. Today I could be modeling Calvin Klein … Polo … Versace … Abercombie …"

"Not Abercombie, Larry. You're not Abercombie."

"Can you believe at one time I did shampoo commercials? Man, I had great hair back then. Just like my dad. Did I ever tell you my dad still has a full head of hair, no broken ends, no gray, and he's going on sixty?"

"Not more than a dozen times. So how did you get free?"

"I paid my own way out. One million dollars."

"Ouch! That much?"

"That much!" Lincoln sunk his face into the bed. "This is a bad dream. My own agent thinks I overpaid for my life. What did you want me to do, wait until they started cutting something besides my hair? There's something wrong here. This can't be a normal client-agent relationship. At least, I don't think it is. How about showing some concern?"

"Listen, Larry. I'm going to get that money back for you. That and more, pal, much more."

"Don't call me pal."

"More than you ever dreamed. We're going to turn this thing into a fortune. My mind is bursting with ideas, big-time money-making ideas. This will be fantastic. There are so many ways to go with your story I can't keep up with them. Just give me a moment to sort it out."

Baywatch jumped up and began walking around the room. "I'm talking top rung now, buddy boy. Listen to me. I'm talking more than a great television bonanza. I'm also talking about a book, Larry. I'm talking easily five million dollars advance at the least. And that's just for openers."

"I can't write."

Baywatch quickened his pace as he continued, "I'm talking lectures, too. Inspirational speaking engagements at big corporate sales meetings. Sixty, seventy thousand a crack. Stockholders meetings, political and religious groups, self-help seminars. The list is endless. I could get you booked a hundred days a year for starters."

"They told me never to talk about this or they would have me castrated."

Baywatch began pounding his fist against his open palm as he raced around the room, his mind rushing up and down all the avenues that were open to celebrities to cash in on their notoriety.

"You're in the news media business, Larry. For crying out loud, you know magazines and television shows will do anything to interview personalities in the news. Once you do something, anything that gets enough publicity to turn you into a celebrity, you have the media rushing to your doorstep. Then it snowballs. It just keeps getting bigger and bigger as it rolls along. The bigger you get, the more everyone in the business wants you. And the more they use you, the bigger you become. And the bigger you become, the more they need you. It doesn't stop. Can't you just picture Perkie Perky going crazy when we tell her we may not be able to fit her morning TV show into our schedule? I love it!"

"Maybe I can't do Abercrombie, but definitely Brooks Brothers."

"Larry, Larry, Larry, listen to me. You should know better than anyone that people in this business go mad when they see someone become a celebrity and they don't have them on their television shows, or in their magazines or newspapers. They go bonkers. They need celebrities to make themselves current, to make themselves worth seeing or reading. They have to fill all that time and space. They have twenty-four hours, seven days a week to fill."

He stopped pacing and bent down over Lincoln. "But this is the important point, pal. You have to take advantage of it when you're hot 'cause there's nothing colder than a cold celebrity. When you reach that level, you're an untouchable, a dead fish, a leper. This is the right moment for us, buddy. This kidnapping will put you in the hot category, the gotta-have-him stage."

"Didn't you hear what I just said about the New York family? I can't talk about the kidnapping."

Baywatch didn't stop."Think about it. Network anchor held for ransom! Pow! News anchor Larry Lincoln has to buy his way out! Pow! He lives to expose the mafia. Pow! This is without question the best thing that could have happened to us."

"To us?"

"We're in this together, Larry. Think about it. Did you have someone practically shoot your foot off? Well, I did, pal. It scared the piss out of me, but I'm back."

"I think having some maniac come at me with foot-long shears and practically take off the side of my head is much worse. I just wish I had those shears now."

"There's something else we'll get out of this," Baywatch continued. "Think about this one. Think about one big juicy lawsuit against YOURchannel. I would love to be in on that meeting. Ingersoll would rip out someone's heart. They'll settle out of court for any demand we make to keep their handling of this thing quiet. Think about that. You say you paid one million dollars? That's chicken feed. Think about the look on Ingersoll's face when that legal guy of his walks in to tell him that you're going public with their treatment of your kidnapping."

"That would be fun to see," Lincoln said. "I might even get a larger office."

Baywatch stopped pacing and stared at Lincoln with exasperation. "A larger office! Good God! I'm here talking about a suite and a full staff of secretaries and accountants just to handle all the stuff you'll be getting into and you're talking about a larger office. Come on, pal, stay up with me. This is the mother lode of public relations."

"I told you not to call me pal. That's how I ended up getting scalped."

"This is different, Larry. I can see it all now, and what I see is a lot of money. Books, speeches, endless interviews, your photograph—from the right side, of course—on every magazine and newspaper in the country. Think about it: the law suit, the *Larry Lincoln Variety Hour*, the *Larry Lincoln Reality Show*. All that and the icing on the cake will be this mafia story that we can now wrap up in a couple of days or whatever it takes."

"Are you crazy? You actually want me to go ahead with that after everything I've been through? You're not real. What about my life? Does that ever enter into your plans? These guys promised to do terrible things to me if I ever talked about this. They have family on Mulberry street. And I believe them. I did a story there once."

"Larry, I promise you I will never leave your side again. Once we're back in the States and we break with this story, they wouldn't dare touch you. I will be your guardian angel. I'll be right there to protect you. You're no good to us dead."

"Thanks."

"You're welcome. By the way, I have an even bigger plan for you, but I'll hold that till later. I'll just give you a hint: politics. Come on, Larry, perk up. The bad part is behind us. Nothing can go wrong. Trust me."

"Don't ever say that again."

"Get dressed. We're meeting Vocino at nine. You should hear what we're having for dinner."

New York

It had not been a good day or night for Alex LaRue. He spent a sleepless five hours tossing about on his bed, waiting for Paolo's usual middle-of-the-night telephone call. Giving up on the hope of restful sleep, he dressed in the darkness of early morning and taxied through the empty streets of Manhattan. At the office the morning dragged on as he consumed cup after cup of coffee while chewing pencils and thinking about every possible disaster that could end his career. A good deal of time had passed since his last conversation with Paola and that worried him. To pass the time, he pulled up his résumé on his computer to update it.

He could have placed a phone call himself, but he was afraid of hearing bad news or irritating the kidnappers. He was also concerned about how long he could stretch out the negotiations and how to handle an ultimatum if he were faced with one. It was not until noon that he finally heard from Paolo wishing him a good afternoon. Instantly, he detected a strange tone, a confident cheerfulness, and it frightened him.

"You don't sound your usual angry, threatening self, Paolo, or am I wrong? Is everything alright? You haven't done any more cutting, have you? Nothing nasty like you've been threatening? Maybe you've finally decided to accept our latest offer of five hundred thousand? I tried to get you more, but as I told you, Lincoln is not pulling in good ratings. I'm on your side, and I love the guy, and I want him back here as quickly as possible, and I will continue to plead your case. You're the man, Paolo. You're the man."

LaRue paused to listen to an angry response but when none came, he continued. "You have to understand the situation, Paolo. The guy who makes the big decisions around here is in the hospital this very moment having a kidney transplant. I really can't discuss this situation with him now. You understand that. He's not well. Give me the weekend to work things out. Maybe two more days. I'm sure we can increase the price up to maybe seven hundred thousand. How does that hit you?"

Paolo broke out in a laughter which sounded vaguely familiar to LaRue. Somehow Sidney Greenstreet and the *Maltese Falcon* came to mind. His stomach began to tighten again.

"That's more than a million lire, Paolo, my friend. Tell Gianni that will exchange into a bundle of euros. Should be enough to put a couple of Ferraris in your garage," he joked weakly.

"I already have a new Lamborghini," Paolo answered dryly, again breaking out in a laugh. This one, however, had a different sound, and LaRue recognized it instantly. It was Richard Widmark pushing an old woman in a wheelchair down a flight of stairs.

"Your time has run out, LaRossi."

"It's LaRue."

"Never mind. You tried to play games with the Black Hand Mob, and nobody plays games with the Black Hand Mob. Mr. Newsman Lincoln is no longer with us."

LaRue dropped the phone. "Oh, God. Oh, God, they've killed him. They've gone ahead and killed the poor bastard. This'll mean my job. No question about it. I'm through here."

He picked up the phone, turned to his computer, and started printing his résumé. "Why, Paolo, why? We were so close to a settlement. I would have given you eight hundred thousand, you know that. Plus tickets to see the Rockettes, the *Tonight Show* and meet …"

"You cheapskate!" Paolo yelled backed. "Lincoln gave us two million."

"And you killed him? Larry gave you two million dollars and you killed him? I don't understand. What were you doing to him, for God's sake? Where is his body?"

"Kill him? We didn't kill him. He paid us and we let him go. He's flown the coop. He knew better than to fool around with the Black Hand Mob. A smart man, that Lincoln, a very smart man. Great appetite, too. He loves to eat!"

LaRue's mind was spinning. *How the hell am I going to explain this to Ingersoll? He would have been angry enough with Lincoln getting killed, but this is much worse. And just when the publicity was building and the news show gaining momentum and the advertising was increasing and everyone around here was happy.*

Paolo broke the silence. "I will not be calling again. Our work is finished. But something I want you to remember and the reason I called. Don't ever try to find us or talk about what happened. We have family in New York. They would enjoy hearing from us. I told you about their specialty."

"What the hell do you mean, they're no longer holding him?" Saxton screamed with the volume of an army drill sergeant.

It had taken only fifteen minutes for LaRue to print twenty copies of his résumé, pack personal belonging from his desk, and walk swiftly through the aisles to Saxton's office. Now, standing before the president of the news division, he felt the full force of his high verbal volume and raging anger. LaRue's frozen face was not more than four inches away, receiving Saxton's words, his hot breath, and his spit. In all his life, he had never wished with greater intensity to be able to make himself disappear.

"No!" Saxton continued to shout, raising his voice another decimal level. "Don't you dare tell me he's no longer a Hero Held Hostage! I don't hear it. I won't hear it." He raised his hands to his ears. "Get out of this office and come back in and we can begin this conversation all over."

LaRue turned quickly to leave.

"Where the hell are you going?" Saxton bellowed.

"You said I should go out and ..."

"Of course I said that. I know what I said. You don't have to tell me what I said. Don't you ever tell me what I said. You're the idiot here. Now tell me what happened, and don't tell me Lincoln is free. You know what I said about that insane dribble."

LaRue stood motionless. He could not think of any reasonable response to the impossible demand. To his relief, Saxton broke the silence. "Wait! Don't say another word. Let me get Handleman in here. Handleman must be here to hear this."

Saxton had been around too long not to recognize an iceberg on the horizon. Experience had taught him how and when to make a dash for the lifeboat, especially if there were only one on the ship. Making sure Handleman, the president of the entertainment division, would be deeply involved when the ship crashed was an instinctive first move. The next steps involved clear thinking, artful maneuvering, and a plan. He had developed special skills when it came to survival, something in which he took great pride and which had served him so well in rising to the top level of the company. Year after year, his fellow employees had secretly voted him the annual Executive's Pointing Finger award.

"After Handleman gets here you can start your story all over again. Make sure you do it right from the beginning. At that point you can tell us both that everything is just fine and Lincoln still has his mouth full of towel."

"They're using socks," he commented softly.

"What the hell do I care what he's chewing?" Saxton shouted. "Sally, get Handleman in here."

"You let him escape?" Handleman screamed at the shaking LaRue. "You idiot. I simply cannot believe what you've done. You incompetent fool! You … you … you …"

"Try fuck-up," Saxton suggested.

"Fuck-up!" Handleman repeated. "Yes, that's the word. That's the perfect word. That describes you. Okay, fuck-up, how in the world did you let him escape? And how did that fool Lincoln come up with two million dollars on his salary?"

"I didn't let him escape," LaRue answered, summoning up what little courage he had in him. "I did everything you instructed me to do. You guys told me …"

"Our instructions? Are you trying to blame us?" Saxton answered, preparing LaRue's burial. "As I recall, and I have a damn good memory, the negotiations were placed entirely in your hands. Right, Henry? You were there."

"Absolutely, Bill," Handleman answered, seeing the game plan unfold and falling into line. "LaRue was given the entire responsibility, and I remember distinctly hearing him tell Ingersoll he could handle it. He was even cocky about it. Okay, fuck-up, what are you going to do now?"

Before LaRue could respond, Handleman continued, "Don't answer that. I'll tell you what you're going to do. You're going to leave here right now and walk directly to the chief's office and tell him how you screwed up the best news story and the best ratings YOURchannel has ever had. That's what you're going to do. Don't even think about suicide, you sniveling coward. At least, not before you go see Ingersoll."

"No sir. I won't, sir. I mean suicide, sir. Ingersoll first, yes." LaRue turned and quickly made a move to the door to escape the hell he was in and find an empty wastepaper basket as soon as possible.

"Wait a minute. Come back here." Saxton commanded as

LaRue was about to close the door. "I have a thought that just might save both your ass and our ratings."

Saxton turned to Handleman. "Let me run this idea past you, Henry. It's just an idea at this point but tell me what you think. Suppose we have our negotiator here get back in touch with the kidnappers. Like I said, this is just a thought, and I want your input here."

Handleman immediately felt the net falling on him. He knew that awareness of Saxton's plan guaranteed shared responsibility. "I'd love to hear you out, Bill, but I have a staff meeting in my office and I'm ten behind already. I'm really interested but can we discuss this later? I should be free this afternoon sometime or tomorrow morning."

"We'll discuss this right now, damn it. Time is essential. Listen, what good is Lincoln to us and our ratings if he is free? What kind of news is that? Once it's announced, the show is over. No more pizzazz, no more anticipation, no more excitement. Then it's back to Miss T-and-A for the news, and that broad is already gaining too much ground around here. I wouldn't be surprised if Ingersoll is nailing her already."

He paused for a few moments to think out a new plan while walking behind his desk and reaching to shut off his recorder. "Suppose LaRue offers them a deal, some more money, maybe two million dollars to kidnap Lincoln again before he has a chance to leave the country. No beatings, or at least they hold that stuff to a minimum, and they keep him under wraps for another five days. Five days will be enough to milk this thing dry. By that time we will have built up enough ratings to carry us through the entire ratings sweeps month. It means a huge increase in revenues and that means bigger bonuses. Five days will do it. We can hide the two million on our books easily."

"Your idea has a lot of sound and bite to it," Handleman responded. "We can always count on you and you alone to come up with the right way to solve problems." He was pleased for having had the foresight to wire himself before joining the meeting.

"I'm glad you approve, Bart," answered Saxton. "Let's move on it." He turned back to LaRue. "Now do you think you can handle our plan, LaRue? They kidnap Lincoln again, and we pay them. Can we depend on you not to fuck up again? This is going to be up to you to pull it off. Two million dollars, no more. Yes or no."

"I'm sure I can. You can count on me," LaRue answered, his confidence renewed by being included in a top-level plan and happy to hear his correct name being used again. "Yes, sir, I can certainly do it. And I appreciate your confidence in me. I'll get on it right away." He wheeled around and rushed out the door.

Saxton turned to Handleman. "Bart, this conversation never took place."

"What conversation?" Handleman answered.

"And, Bart, erase your recording."

"Come in, Pearl," George Ingersoll said to Pearl Necklace, who was standing in the doorway of his enormous office and pausing to take in the full scope of its grandeur. On one side of the room, an unbroken row of floor-to-ceiling windows extending almost the full length of the fifty-foot room offered a panoramic view of midtown Manhattan. On the opposite wall hung a series of original twentieth-century paintings and beneath them a twelve-foot overstuffed sofa and chairs. His desk, an early American replica, was highly polished and held only a telephone, pen holder, leather folder, and a calendar in a gold-plated holder.

George Elliot Ingersoll had been in the field of business man-agement his entire career from the day he graduated from the Harvard Business School. He was CEO at YOURchannel for two years following four years as CEO of High Summit Studios in Hollywood, a company he managed to drive into Chapter 11 bankruptcy through his incompetency. Upon his departure from that position, the board of directors gave him a seven-million-dollar contract buyout, which he promptly increased through a lawsuit. Based upon his experience as a CEO, his Harvard Business School degree, and business world contacts, he was hired to his current position at YOURchannel within three months after leaving High Summit Studios in shambles.

Seeing Pearl Necklace at the doorway, Ingersoll quickly jumped up from his chair and crossed the room to greet her, shaking her hand, then held it while walking her across the office and to the sofa.

"I've been looking forward to getting together and having this little social chat, Pearl." He continued to hold her hand as they sat down. "I can't tell you how pleased we all are with your performance on YOURchannel. You have added a spark of life to the evening news program and, I might add, to our company. Just look at the increase in viewers. From the ratings we've been receiving, I guess I speak for all of us in the company when I say: glad to have you aboard."

"Thank you, Mr. Ingersoll," she answered, gently sliding her hand away from his grasp. As she crossed her legs, she noticed CEO Ingersoll's fleeting glance at the considerable amount of bare thighs beyond her short skirt. "This is a fantastic opportunity for me, and I hope I can continue to justify your confidence in me. You took quite a chance to allow me take over the news show. I've heard it was your idea. I mean, here I am, a raw beginner. It's like a dream, and I owe all to you." She locked on to his eyes and smiled.

"No need to call me Mr. Ingersoll," he responded as he inched closer to her. "Make it George from now on. You're an essential part of the team now, Pearl." He pointed to the company slogan on the wall. "We're family here, and I want you to think of me as George." He reached across to place his hand on hers. "Is that alright with you? I mean calling me George."

"It will be George from now on. Whatever you desire."

"Good girl." He paused and smiled, giving her hand a slight squeeze. "But first things first. I heard we have the contract business out of the way. Are you happy with it? Everything go smoothly?"

"Yes, it was quite easy, really. Mr. Sanford was very generous. It's a dream contract."

"Glad to hear that. He can be tough at times, really hard-nosed, but a good man. For a lawyer he shows a lot of common sense. He knows when to sign and when to walk away."

"He certainly does, George. I can definitely vouch for that." She knew immediately that Sanford had relayed the entire conversation of their meeting.

"Well, now we have that behind us, let's move on. First things first, I always say." He slid closer to her, closing his hand tightly around hers. "Pearl, this may sound a bit sudden but I'm sure you felt the electricity during our morning chats and warm hugs. I felt it and I won't deny it or hold back what I feel right now and what I feel I need to express. I'm a believer in free expression. I hope you won't think me forward, Pearl, but I want you ..."

"You have me, George, for three years at least, plus an option. That's in the contract. I couldn't ask for more than that. As I said, it was very generous."

"I don't mean just as an employee of YOURchannel. I'm not talking contract, Pearl. I don't want to hold you in a contract; I want to hold you in my arms. I mean, I want you. I want you now. I want you as I've never wanted another woman. I want you here on this sofa, on the desk, on the spacious conference table, on the floor. That's the want that I mean, Pearl."

"George, George, George. I've seen your wife. She's a beautiful woman, and she's around here all the time. Why don't you just call her in here and, following your descriptive tour, hump her all around the room? You could have a great time."

CEO Ingersoll stiffened. "Pearl, you're talking about the

stepmother of my college-age children. I can't just hump my own wife right here in my office as you so brutally put it. Out of the question; we're married."

"George … can I still call you George?" She continued to smile and look into his eyes.

"Yes, yes. Call me George. Call me George when we're going at it. Oh, yes, that sounds so sensuous. Scream George if you want. Yes, that's it. Scream! That would be delicious! Don't hold back. This room is soundproof."

"That's not what I meant. There's something I must tell you, and I hope this doesn't come as too much of a shock, but you see, George, I don't care for men."

"That's wonderful to hear, Pearl. Just me. Right here." He patted the cushions. "On this overstuffed Italian sofa, on the Thomas Jefferson desk, on the custom-made, solid walnut conference table, on this soft, deep wool antique Turkish prayer rug. Forgive me if I'm repeating myself."

Still clasping her hands, Ingersoll slid off the sofa and onto the floor. He planted himself on his knees in front of her. "Just feel this rug, Pearl." He pulled gently on her hand. "How did you put it? Hump! I'm beginning to love the sound of that word. It's so graphic, so organic. We can hump a couple of times a week. Is that too much to ask?"

Pearl leaned forward so that her face was close to his, and she spoke slowly and distinctly, "You don't understand what I just said, George. I don't make it with men," she lied and then shouted, "I'm *gay*, for crying out loud!"

"That's fine. I don't care what you do outside the office. I'm liberal sometimes. Oh, Pearl, this is getting better. Now I really want you more than ever. More than when I thought you were straight." He laid the side of his head in her lap.

"Can't we just be friends, George?"

"Yes, yes. We'll be best friends. BBF as they say." He laughed and lifted his head to look at her. "Twice a week we'll be the best friends the world has ever seen."

"I'm sorry, George. It wouldn't work," she pleaded, trying another approach. "I might fall in love with you."

"I'm not exactly talking love here, Pearl. I'm talking about humping. Oh, what a great word. Your word, my lovely."

"But it might turn to love. You know something like that can happen. Soon twice a week wouldn't be enough. There would have to be more. It would have to be every night. Then every day and every night."

Ingersoll's eyes widen with excitement. "Oh, yes! Yes! Every day and every night. You're right, Pearl, darling. We'll hump away. Every day and every night and every night and day, Pearl. It's just like the song: 'Night and day, you are the one. Only you beneath the moon and under the sun.' Oh, I do love Gershwin."

"Cole Porter," she corrected.

"I love him, too." He started to hum the melody.

"Word would get out, George," she said, deciding to try yet another way to turn him off. "You know how people gossip. In no time at all everyone in YOURchannel would know about us. Think about what they would say. More importantly—are you listening, George?—think about what Sanford, the president of Legal Affairs would say."

The word *Legal* struck Ingersoll like a lightning bolt, and he dropped her hand and backed away quickly. It was a word he understood, and he also understood the message. He saw Pearl in a totally different light. "Right, you're absolutely right. That bastard with his picky little lawyer's mind. Probably would raise hell. Well, as I say, first things first. We must keep him out of this. Must stay away from Legal. Just our little secret. Between you and me."

"Our little secret," she answered, pretending to draw a zipper across her lips. "Yours and mine, and not Legal's."

He paused a moment. "Not even once ... on the prayer rug? A little quickie?"

"It wouldn't work, George. Not even a quickie. Once always leads to twice."

"An excellent idea!"

"Remember Legal, George." She looked over his head at the enormous windows. "George, you have a great view of New York from here. It's fantastic. I wish I had an office with a view."

That evening, sitting at the bar next to his director and friend Tom Dauber, Steve Tanner took another sip from his second Manhattan. He felt like the week had been on fast-forward and he was confused.

"I can't believe what has happened, Tom. I initiated what I thought would be a wake-up call to the news media, and now I'm being hailed as a communications genius. It's incredible! Did you read that article in the paper today? 'With the brushstroke of a master artist, YOURchannel vice president Steve Tanner has changed the direction of television's evening news.' Can you top that one? I thought I was destroying my career, and I end up getting a raise. I thought I would be turning back the television news pendulum, and instead I pushed it on in the same terrible direction. I failed at what I was trying to accomplish, and I was rewarded because I failed."

"Not bad for what I thought was a terrible mistake to begin with. Take it and run," Dauber answered.

"You warned me, but you never saw this result. And now you think it's okay?"

The two men had worked together for several years. Tanner had hired Dauber away from one of the locals when he was just beginning as a junior director handling early morning newscasts. Their friendship and loyalty to each other was established quickly, forged by the pressures and frustrations of doing live daily news and specials.

"Come on, you should have known better," Dauber answered. "I'm sorry, but I don't buy the good old days and golden years stuff. Maybe those were great times, but times change. They'll change again. Maybe even for the better, but we're not going back. And that's where you always want to go. Technology has changed everything. You have to admit, the show has been a helluva lot of fun. Look at the crew. They can't wait to get started each day. It's exciting. I know you hate to hear me say this, but look at the ratings."

"But that's my point."

"What is your point, Steve?" someone behind them asked. They both swung around to face Pearl Necklace.

"Hi, Pearl," Dauber said. "Steve is doing his soapbox thing. Join us, but please don't ask him what his point is. We'll be here all night."

"I promise," she answered as the three moved to a table and Necklace ordered a beer.

"How did your meeting go with Ingersoll today?" Tanner asked. "Did he hit on you? I know that's a silly question."

"Of course he did, but everything worked out well. You should see my new office. Fantastic view of the city."

Tanner threw back his head and laughed. "Will this never end? See what I mean, Tom? The three of us should have been thrown out on our asses, and instead she's the hit of YOURchannel. Hell, the hit of television news! Where do we go from here?"

"I'm glad you asked that, Steve," she responded with a smile. "Where we go from here is my new show. Would you like to talk about it?"

Both men put down their drinks and almost in unison said, "Your new show!"

Tanner added quickly, "Yes, certainly, we should talk about it!"

"And how you got it." Dauber joined in, then wished he hadn't.

"I'll pretend you didn't say that."

"I'm sorry,' he answered meekly.

"Forgiven. We move on," Necklace shot back, then smiled. "Anyway, it's just an idea at this point, but one I've been thinking about for a long time. That's what I want to go over with you guys."

"Am I forgiven enough to do the directing?" Dauber asked.

"Of course, and Steve Tanner, the man who has changed television news programming forever with just one brushstroke, is going to produce. That is, if he hasn't forgotten how and can stop playing Don Quixote long enough to have some fun. As it says on Ingersoll's wall, we're a team."

"Why do I have a feeling," Tanner responded, "it's not just an idea you have but a firm concept of what your show is going to be?"

Necklace answered, "Sort of, basically. I think it could be exciting, and I wouldn't do it without you. Both of you."

"Pearl, It's been a different kind of a week, and I'm still reeling. But yeah, let's hear your plan."

"Before I begin, I must ask: Whatever has happened to Alex LaRue? I stopped by his office, but his door was locked and he wouldn't come out. Later I saw him running down the hall, and he looked like the blood had been sucked out him."

"It probably had been," Tanner said. "He had a meeting with the big two. He wouldn't tell me anything except that he's in charge of some top level plan. That's enough to scare anyone. Forget LaRue for now. Go ahead with your show idea."

"I think you'll like this," Necklace said. "It will be a combination news show, interview program, and reality show rolled into one. However, it will be much more than that and it has to be different than anything done before. Totally different. We'll concentrate on members of Congress, the Washington press, and the people who overload the interview television shows. Everything that really goes on inside Washington."

"Death Valley," Dauber interrupted. "It won't last two months."

"You're wrong, Tom," Tanner answered, "It wouldn't go that far. Saxton wouldn't allow it. Bad idea, Pearl. Anyway, there's stuff like that around now. Try something else."

"I forgot to tell you, I don't report to Saxton. I report directly to Mr. CEO, to Ingersoll himself. Saxton will have nothing to say regarding this, and I can easily handle Ingersoll."

Necklace paused to take a sip of beer. "Anyway, I'm not thinking of the comedy routines you refer to or the standard interviews that you see on Sunday morning where the politicians are only too happy to appear and the interviewers too eager sucking up or too afraid to challenge. I'm thinking of stripping the clothes off these people. Show how they distort, deceive, or doubletalk, if you like alliteration. We go at both sides of the aisle and the lobby money changers. We go for the jugular, but we'll do it in a way that will grab the audience. Make them laugh, yes, but angry, never content. We'll do on it Sunday mornings. The setting for the show will be the Capitol."

"Excuse me," Tanner said. "You want to take cameras and crew into the Capitol and do a live show there ridiculing congressmen and the Washington press corps?"

"I would love to, but that's impossible. No, we will rent a studio and construct the setting. Most Americans are very familiar with the Capitol, so we must duplicate everything to make them think we are actually there. That's where all the action is."

"How do you expect to have anyone come on the show and take all that beating?"

"They can if they want, but we don't really need them. We have them on film, we have their voices. This will all be staged. We'll take advantage of the technology that's available to us now. It's the technology that will make this show different from anything in the past or the present. There's no limit to what we can create. We use material from campaigns, congressional speeches, television interviews, talk shows, and even their own campaign advertising. We can have them participate if they want, but on our terms."

"This could be fun," Tanner said, catching her excitement. "We could create press conferences, closed committee sessions, cloakroom conversations, meetings between congressmen and lobbyists, congressional hearings, secret arrangements … it could go on and on."

"Now you're getting it." Necklace laughed. "The key is the technology that we have today. We use every effect we can think up, off-the-wall stuff to keep the show jumping. We entertain but with an axe, a constant viciousness. That's what will draw viewers. Right now Congress has a fifteen percent public approval rating. The press is close to that. And lobbyists have no friends. We tap into that anger, vent it, let the volcano erupt. We want our audience to say: Go to it, hang those bastards. We won't take one side or the other. There's too much of that crap now."

"The set costs would be tremendous." Dauber said.

"Not with the technology available. Plus a couple hugs and a few free feels," Necklace laughed.

"I like the idea, Pearl," Tanner said. "I mean the show idea. At least, I think I do, but I see a big problem we'll be facing. There will be a lot of pressure against this sort of thing. You might be able to handle Ingersoll. But Schumbeck isn't a fool. He might see this as an attack against everything he's doing. He keeps an office and a large staff and a couple of hotel suites in Washington."

"Who is Schumbeck?"

"Arnold Schumbeck is one of the richest men in the world. He is the invisible, unpublicized head of the conglomerate that owns YOURchannel in addition to telecom and Internet firms, newspapers, magazines, tabloids, radio stations, movie studios, and distribution companies, theaters, movie houses, and everything else in the communications world. The list is endless."

"How do I get to meet him?"

Tanner laughed. "Don't worry about that. You will definitely meet him. He'll see to that. But that's for later. Let's get back to your show. We need to move. I'll draft a time frame immediately. By the way, have you thought of a name for the show?"

"*Washington Brothel.*"

Monte Castella

"**O**nce again, here's to your health, Mr. Lincoln and Mr. Baywatch," Mayor Vocino toasted, "to this evening of marvelous food and wine, and finally to the television interview tomorrow with Don Victorio Marcasi, the most respected man in the Italian mafia."

"To all that and more," his brother Angelo joined in.

"Thank you," Lincoln responded, "and to your health and also to the magnificent dinner you provided."

It was an evening in which a gourmet Italian feast was consumed along with a great many bottles of the finest wine to be found in Monte Castella. Mayor Vocino and his brother Angelo had gone to considerable effort and expense at the mayor's restaurant with Baywatch and Lincoln to convince them to look beyond the day's activities and renew their enthusiasm for the mafia story. It wasn't altogether necessary. Baywatch and Lincoln were already back on track after reviewing the monetary opportunities now available to them through the turn of events.

Prior to meeting for dinner, Lincoln brought up the threat from the Black Hand Mob against discussing the kidnapping with the Vocino brothers, going into detail what they would do if that warning went unheeded. Baywatch found that to be no problem and easily provided Lincoln with a story to cover his late appearance, avoiding any mention of his capture and ransom.

Angelo and the mayor were aided considerably in their efforts to calm their guests by Nina, who sat next to Lincoln, giving him her full attention the entire evening. Her youthful beauty and Italian exuberance alone would have been enough to charm Lincoln, but this, combined with the adulation she showed him constantly throughout the evening, made him forget his days as a hostage, if not his lost money. He was alive again and captivated by her, and he began to experience that glorious feeling of self-importance that was always there when he was in the company of people who knew him only as a television performer.

Her admiration for him was not a pretense. Nina had never met a celebrity before, much less sat next to one on a social occasion. Even his beret, which he wore strangely to the side of his head, did not diminish his attraction or the excitement of being in his company. He was from American television, a handsome newsman seen and heard by millions every day, and sitting next to him was emotionally and sexually thrilling. This was an evening she would never forget.

She also had the attention of Baywatch, who was sitting to her right, showering her at every opportunity with compliments while hinting at appropriate times and without subtlety his ability to possibly arrange a career for her in Hollywood, where he was a man of considerable influence. He did not know why Angelo Vocino insisted that he bring the video camera to dinner, but now he was thankful he did. He had her pose throughout the restaurant and kitchen while casually assuring her that the right people in Hollywood would view the filming.

His attempts to win her interest were in vain, however, for he could not compete with Lincoln talking about his career, his television show, his nationwide viewers, his fabled ratings, and the celebrities he knew on a personal basis, and whose names he was not shy to mention throughout their conversation. He fascinated her with stories about a world she had known only through magazines, television, and movies. Seeing the awe in her eyes, and affected by the wine the Vocino brothers continually poured into his glass, Lincoln began to unwind and enjoy the evening. *I'm myself again*, he thought. *I'm back in the real world.*

The dinner conversation at the beginning of the evening was forced and difficult, but the tension melted away with the serving of the ziti con finocchi and the fifth bottle of wine. By the time the chef presented the finale, the torta Giadula al cioccolato, and the waiter emptied the seventh bottle, an atmosphere of warmth and friendship had been created.

Lincoln had not felt this relaxed for months. His struggles at the offices of YOURchannel were forgotten, and with the wine-induced confidence surging through his body, he easily repeated the believable story Baywatch had made him learn to cover his delayed appearance in Monte Castella.

"There were problems at the airports on both sides of the Atlantic," he began with a slight slur in his speech. "I guess I created quite a traffic tie-up at the Kennedy boarding counter when people there recognized me. It was impossible to wade through the passengers crowding around me. Angelo my friend, my feeling has always been that it is unfair to refuse an autograph, to turn away from a fan. These are the people who watch me, the people who depend on me for world news every night. When they meet me in person, they want something to take away, something to help them remember the occasion. How can I deny them?"

"No, you cannot deny them. It would not be right."

"Of course, I apologized to the pilots for holding up their departure in New York, but they told me to think nothing of it. They even allowed me to use their on-board announcement equipment to apologize to the passengers. Let me tell you, their response was not something I expected, nor will I forget it. They actually cheered when I came out of the cockpit."

"I can believe that," said Mayor Vocino, prodding Lincoln on. He was now confident that everything that had been planned was fine once again. "Again, a toast. You are here, and that is what counts. I have explained everything to Don Marcasi and he understands. He can be brutal but also compassionate."

Lincoln drank to the toast and returned the kindness. "To you, Mr. Mayor, to Angelo, to the lovely Nina, and to this marvelous town—Monte Cassel."

Angelo let the mistake go without correction. "Thank you. Monte Castella is truly is a fine town. The weather is always good, the skies are cloudless, and the sun is warm year-round. Much like Hollywood, I am sure. A great place for making motion pictures, wouldn't you say, Mr. Baywatch?"

"I would say that, and I should know. I have spent most of my career in Los Angeles." Turning to Nina, he touched her glass with his. "You know, Nina, Larry is only one of my clients. In Hollywood I represent movie stars, writers, producers, directors, many of the makers and shakers in the film industry."

Lincoln interrupted. "Then when I arrived in Palermo, the same thing happened. The reaction of the crowd was amazing. I had no idea I was so well known in Italy. Once again I was forced to stop and sign autographs. In the middle of the mayhem I created, a gentleman approached and informed me that he was a local television producer, and he insisted that I appear on a popular celebrity show. How could I refuse?"

"Of course, you could not refuse," Angelo responded. "Did I hear you say something about Hollywood producers, Mr. Baywatch?"

"Yes, you did. Several are my clients. Of course, you've heard of Francis Coppola."

"Francis Coppola is your client?"

"Not at present, but my contract is on his desk right now just waiting for him to have a free moment to read and sign. It's only a matter of time. Do you know of Albert Einstein?"

"The great scientist?"

"No, the rock group. They're also a client. They play alternative music and stuff. They're going to be the biggest stars ever. No question about it. I just signed them with Holy Ghost Records. You can expect to see them collecting awards at Grammy time."

"What about Hollywood movie producers? We must talk further about them. I have an idea to discuss."

Lincoln continued, speaking directly to Nina, who was now the only one listening to him. "After I appeared on the celebrity shows, they held a press conference for me. They had a direct link-up with Rome television so reporters there could question me. They kept after me to tell them why I was traveling to Monte Castalo."

His last statement caught the attention of both the mayor and his brother. "You didn't tell them anything, did you?"

"Of course not. No reporter worth his salt would pre-empt an exclusive story or divulge his sources. Except for promos, of course. That's why we have the First Amendment. Here's to the First Amendment."

"Yes, to the First Amendment," Angelo toasted without drinking his wine. "Mr. Baywatch, let's talk about Hollywood producers. Do you think these people you know—or represent, as you say—might be interested in coming to Monte Castella to make a movie? Your interview with Don Marcasi will put this town on the map. It would be a perfect place to make a movie about the mafia. We can guarantee full cooperation and low costs."

"I toast again the town of Mount Castle," Lincoln said.

Angelo answered. "Yes, yes. To Monte Castella, the future site of a great mafia movie."

Baywatch thought about the possibility of Angelo's suggestion, and it rekindled his dream of being a player in the film industry. "Very possible, Angelo, but you must have a script first. In the movie business, everything starts with a script and after that, money. Lots of money and the right contacts. It's not easy."

"After your television show of Don Marcasi, you will be a famous man. People will be coming to you, Burt Baywatch, the man who set up the greatest crime story on television. You will be able to do all those things you mentioned. We will be able to help. It could work. A Sicilian crime movie made in Sicily. Right in the home town of the soon-to-be famous Don Victorio 'The Brain' Marcasi. Think about it."

"I will. Yes, I definitely will. It definitely has a ring to it. I'll get back to you."

Overwhelmed by the intimacy and warmth he felt in the embrace of Nina's arms, Lincoln could not refrain from disclosing to her the kidnapping ordeal he had experienced at the hands of the gangsters.

"You were kidnapped?" she asked with surprise. "Right here in Sicily? Larry, it sounds so exciting. But it must have been terrible. You must tell me everything about it." She snugged closer to him.

Still feeling the effect of the considerable amount of wine he had consumed earlier in the evening and the relaxation of having made love to Nina, he opened up and related everything to her that had occurred—plus a great deal that did not. He could not help himself. He wanted to impress her with something beyond his experiences in television and the celebrities he had known, something personal and character building. He knew those celebrity stories could only go so far before wearing out. However, he also told her emphatically that disclosing his story to the world would endanger not only himself but also the mayor and Angelo and others in town, and only after receiving a promise of confidence from her, he related his trial of courage in elaborate detail. He created a story involving threats of torture, the possibility of murder, the ruthlessness of the hardened criminals, and the spiritual strength that held him together in the face of such savagery.

Nina responded to each revelation with alternating sighs and squeals of sympathy and excitement.

"I will relate the entire saga, Nina, but you must promise not to tell anyone until I have left Monte Castella."

"You have my word, Larry. I will keep it a secret until you are safely out of Italy. I promise."

"It's one of those things you learn to live with as a celebrity," he began. "Being on television has made me so recognizable that I am an open target. The constant publicity given to my enormous salary also makes me susceptible to this sort of thing. I must be constantly on guard. That's why I take Tae Kwon Do lessons. My focused mind and trained hands are my defense, but in this case I had no chance. It was an ambush."

"Oh, Larry, an ambush." Nina ran her hand across his chest. "Go on. I want to hear every detail."

"Well, my darling, it all began when I turned off the autostrada and took the road to Monte Castella. I was about fifteen minutes out of Palermo when I spotted a man lying on the road beside his truck. Naturally, because of my reporter's instinct, I stopped to see what happened and if I could provide some aid. When I knelt beside him, someone came from behind me and delivered a powerful blow to the back of my head. When I regained consciousness, I found myself tied to a chair with tape across my mouth. I had no chance to use my defensive skills, which are considerable."

"Did you see who they were?"

"No, whenever they were with me, they wore ski masks. I never had a chance to see their faces. Although they were men of extreme cruelty, I was not afraid, and they knew it. Even when they cut my hair, I laughed." Unconsciously, he removed his hand from her breast and gently felt the bare spot on his scalp. "My hair—that was the worst of it."

"It will grow back, Larry. You have beautiful hair." She placed his hand back on her breast. "Thinning a bit, but beautiful. Please go on. Tell me more. It's so thrilling. Did they torture you?"

"Does it look like it's thinning?" Once again he removed his hand to touch his hair.

"It's lovely hair. Please … the story, the torture." She moved his hand back to her breast.

"The torture was much more psychological than physical. Unless you count the tape. They were at me constantly. One of them desperately wanted to cut off my ear. He was the one who assaulted me with the shears."

"Oh, Larry," Nina moaned as she slid her hand down across his stomach while pressing close to kiss his neck.

"Then the phone calls to my company began. Right in front of me, they described in the most horrifying detail what they were planning to cut off next if their demands of ten million dollars were not met. Of course, my network was willing to pay them immediately all the money they requested, but I said no. I took over the negotiations, and they soon realized that threats of violence meant nothing to me. Ouch!"

Nina had bitten hard into Lincoln's ear. She moved her leg across his.

"When they saw how willing I was to accept pain, they eventually gave up and accepted my first and only offer. After that, they released me, and I came here to Monte Castella … and you."

Throughout Larry's story of crime and agony, a volcano of sexual excitement was building up in Nina. Barely had he finished when she erupted, suddenly grabbing his hand again and pulling it around her back. "Again, Larry, again!"

"The whole story?"

"No, not the story!"

It was early in the morning when Burt Baywatch, Larry Lincoln, and Angelo Vocino stepped out of the car in front of the mayor's home. Angelo had told them it was the home of Don Victorio "The Brain" Marcasi, the boss of bosses in Sicily, a man most honored and respected throughout Italy and the United States.

Outside the front door they were met by the Polucci brothers, standing guard with their hands inside their suit jackets. They were dressed in what they considered their finest for the occasion. Gianni and Carlo wore double-breasted black suits with pink pinstripes, lavender silk shirts with pink ties, black and white shoes, and black fedoras with pink bands. To set himself above his brothers, Paolo used yellow as the offsetting color and had a rose in his label. All three were wearing sunglasses and sporting enormous black mustaches, which made Mayor Vocino close his eyes when he spotted them.

"Stop!" Paolo ordered and then motioned to his brothers. "Frisk them!"

"Frisk?" Baywatch whispered to Lincoln. "Humphrey Bogart was the last man to use that word, and the film was black and white."

Without removing his right hand from his jacket, Gianni quickly stepped forward and ran his free hand up and down their bodies. "They're clean."

"Wait!" Carlo ordered, attempting to take the video equipment away from Baywatch. "No pictures of the don. You must leave all that camera equipment here."

"We're here for the purpose of making a video, you idiot," an exasperated Angelo yelled at Paolo.

"Give it back," Paolo ordered, slapping Carlo across the head.

Lincoln gave the three men a puzzled look. "Slapping people seems to be a big thing with Sicilians," he said to Angelo, remembering the many blows to the head he had witnessed while in captivity.

"It helps to keep people in line," Angelo answered as they passed through the doorway. Turning around to look back at Paolo, he added, "Especially the dumb ones."

"Welcome to the home of the famous Don 'The Brain' Marcasi," Mayor Vocino said, leading the group through the house.

"You know your way around," Lincoln said to Mayor Vocino, who was walking swiftly to the room he used as an office.

"Don Marcasi and I are very close, and we have an arrangement. Something you news people might call a quiet relationship. He does not tell me how to run this town and I do not question or try to interfere with his business, if you understand me. I am very comfortable in this house. I have been here many, many times."

Lincoln winked at the mayor. "I understand perfectly, Your Honor."

Mayor Vocino opened the door and allowed Lincoln and Baywatch to enter the spacious office. "Gentlemen, it is my honor to introduce you to one of the most important men in all Sicily, Don Victorio Carmine 'The Brain' Marcasi. Don Marcasi, it is my pleasure to present the famous American television newsman, Mr. Larry Lincoln and his agent, the famous representative of Hollywood producers, Mr. Burt Baywatch."

The group stepped up to the desk where Don Victorio, better known to the citizens of Monte Castella as Guiseppe Palazzolo, the town's cobbler, was sitting, a heavyset man in his sixties with unusually puffy cheeks and wearing a crumpled suit, an old shirt with several buttons opened, and a worn, soiled fedora. A large gold cross hung from a necklace. He said nothing and did not rise from his chair but stared at Lincoln and Baywatch for a few moments and then with one hand motioned to the chairs. In front of him, lying on the large, ornately carved desk, were two hunting shotguns and a thick notebook.

Instead of sitting, Lincoln moved forward to shake hands. The don immediately put his hand on one of the guns. Lincoln backed away quickly, stumbling into Baywatch.

"Don Marcasi," Lincoln said after gaining his composure and finding a chair, "I find it difficult to express the pleasure, respect, and admiration I feel in meeting you at last and to have the opportunity to introduce you to the millions of Americans who watch my show every day. I have heard many great things about you from Angelo and Mayor Vocino."

Again, placing a hand upon one of the shotguns, Don Marcasi answered sharply, "What have they told you?"

"Nothing, nothing at all, sir, I swear. Can I call you Victorio or do you prefer Don Marcasi? Or The Brain. Whatever you say."

Without moving his hand from the weapon, Don Marcasi looked at Angelo Vocino. "Have they been searched?"

"Certainly, Don Victorio. We would not allow them in your presence without being searched."

"Then start with the camera. I have little time for this business. One never knows. The contract on my life, you understand."

Baywatch leaped into action and hurriedly arranged the lighting and prepared the camera while Lincoln opened a pad containing his introduction and questions. He cleared his throat and ran up and down the scales until he felt comfortable with the level and smoothness of his voice. "Okay, Burt, cue me whenever you are ready. Opening of the Sicilian Connection."

"Excuse me, Larry," said Mayor Vocino. "Shouldn't that be the Monte Castella Connection?"

"You're right, Mayor. That does have an original sound to it. Yes, I'll use that. I'm set if you are, Burt." He took a mirror out of his pocket, checked his appearance, straighten his beret and then practiced several facial expressions. He read his introduction five times and placed his script in front of him on the desk.

"Larry, I'll focus on you for the intro," Baywatch said, "and after that, I'll keep the camera on Don Marcasi. We can do the on-camera questions after the interview and edit them in proper sequence later." He looked around at the mayor and Angelo. "No noise, please. Whenever you're ready, Larry, four, three, two, one."

Lincoln looked into the camera with an expression as serious as he could manage. "Good evening, my fellow Americans. This is Larry Lincoln speaking to you from Italy, bringing you the first in a series of exclusive reports on the inner workings of organized crime that stretches from Europe to the United States. What you are about to hear has never been revealed before. It is the personal story of a man whose entire life is woven into the very fabric of crime in this century and beyond. We call it the Monte Castella Connection."

The Vocino brothers turned to each other and smiled. Lincoln stopped talking, turned the pages of his notepad and reviewed his lines again. "Okay, Bert, I'm ready to go again."

"I am reporting from the home of Don Victorio Carmine 'The Brain' Marcasi in the town of Monte Castella, Italy, with a YOURchannel television exclusive exposé of the Mafia here in Sicily and in America. Don Marcasi is a man you will get to know well over the next several days: his life, his family, and his crimes here in Italy and the United States. There is much to be told, so let us now begin. Don Marcasi, would you tell us ..."

Don Marcasi raised his hand and Baywatch swung his camera toward him. "I will talk. You will listen. My life may come to an end quickly. One never knows. There is a contract out on me. They want to silence me because I am about to betray them. But they have betrayed me. Me, a man of honor, and they showed me no respect. They have threatened me. That is why I now break the code of silence."

"Excuse me, Don Marcasi, but we are having a little difficulty in understanding you. Could you speak up and a little more clearly?"

The Don turned his chair around away from the camera and pulled the cotton padding from his mouth.

"A little medicine I must take for my heart," he said, swinging around again to face the camera. "No problem. Let me begin. Start the camera again.

"I was born here in the beautiful town of Monte Castella, a picturesque garden of Eden in the most beautiful part of Sicily, surrounded by rugged mountains, green valleys, and blue lakes, and where you will find the best wines in all Italy. The weather here, let me tell you, is ..."

"How did you become a don?" Lincoln interrupted.

"A blessing from God. Yes, I am the don of Monte Castella, the most powerful don in all Sicily. I was born into it. My father, Gaetano 'Nice Guy' Marcasi, was don before me, and his father, Michelangelo 'Fat Nose' Marcasi before him. My father's name, Nice Guy, was given to him by Don Luciano for his compassionate manner in conducting assassinations."

He paused to put his hand on one of the guns and turn the page of his notes.

"My father was the don here during the time of General Patton's army, which came to Monte Castella during the war. Many American soldiers will remember that time. Some even came back to visit after the war. My father met with the famous general and gave him permission to enter our lovely town. General Patton returned the favor, which was the honorable thing to do, by making him don of all Sicily. It was a time of great celebration."

"Can you tell us about the Sicilian ties to the American mafia families? How did that come about?"

Don Marcasi once again flipped over some pages. "You must understand that because of my age and the difficult life I have led, my memory for details sometimes needs to be aided. For that I need to look at my memoirs, which I am planning to print soon. Yes, we have ties to all of the families in the United States. But I tell you for the last time. Do not interrupt me. My life may be short. I have little time."

Don Marcasi paused to reach for his glass of wine while glancing at this notes. "I took over from my father when he was assassinated, may his religious soul rest in heaven. It was an ambush, and he was hit while buying oranges from a street vendor. Like my grandfather, Fat Nose Marcasi, he lived his entire life in Monte Castella because he loved it here. He traveled to many places, doing his thing in Rome, Naples, Florence, and Venice, but he always came back to Monte Castella because of its beauty. He also spent much time in the United States, setting up operations in New York, Chicago, Miami, Las Vegas ..."

"Las Vegas?"

"Oh, yes. He helped Bugsy set up the first hotel there. But he knew the man would not last. He even voted for eliminating him at the meeting of the families in New York. He told Salvatore the man was crazy and could not be trusted. That's why they called him Bugsy, a name my father gave to him."

"Who is Salvatore?"

"Salvatore Luciano, who else?"

"You mean Lucky Luciano?"

"We men of respect never used the name Lucky. In Sicily that would be disrespectful. My father and Salvatore were very close. He helped him develop the New York operation, and Salvatore wanted him to remain in New York and be his underboss, but my father could not stay away from Monte Castella. He told me that Meyer would have given him control of Miami and all of Cuba, but that place, with all its casino riches, could not pull my father away from Monte Castella with its magnificent landscapes and food and history and ..."

The sound of the song "Volare" came from the back of the room and stopped the don in midsentence. Everyone turned around to see the Polucci brothers, who had silently tiptoed into the room to watch the show. The sound of the cell phone in Paolo's jacket continued. The mayor made a move toward them, but they rushed quickly out of the room before his upraised arm came within reach.

"Don't come back, imbeciles!" Angelo shouted.

"I don't trust those men," Don Marcasi said. "They are here to guard me, but with the contract on me, one never knows. I cannot trust anyone."

"That's alright," said Lincoln. "No harm done. We can edit out the interruption."

Baywatch took advantage of the break to lean close to Lincoln and whisper in his ear. "This guy sounds more like a tour guide than a mafia don. Try to steer him away from talking about the town and toward the crimes and the people who carried them out. See if you can get him to talk about hits and how they carried them out."

"No, I'm not going to stop him," Lincoln answered. "You heard him get angry about interruptions. He's doing just fine. You don't understand. You're not a reporter. We need the local color to be part of the interview. It's great contrast. On the surface, a sweet, lovable old Italian discussing the good life he leads. Underneath, a killer. Believe me, I know honest television when I see it."

The don paused to glance at the notebook, turn the page, and after a moment of hurried reading, reach for the glass of wine again. He wiped his forehead with his sleeve, rearranged the weapons and then looked back toward Lincoln.

"I must tell you a story about my father. One day in June many years ago, he returned to beautiful Monte Castella after a business trip to Miami to discover that some of his own soldiers had been conspiring to take over his operation. They were led by Ice Pick Valachi. Naturally, he had them all rubbed out ... *whacked*, as we say in the society ... by his underbosses, Looney Louie Gottiano and Eleven Fingers Florenzo. Everyone got it except for one young boy who managed to escape and run off to New York. That turned out in the future to be my father's undoing. In his old age he became careless. But more of that later."

"Was that Valachi any relation to Joe Valachi," Lincoln asked, "the gangster who gave testimony about the Cosa Nostra to the Senate crime investigation committee?"

"His father. You can see how treachery is passed on. But you keep interrupting, and you are making me angry. I do not like being angry. I have my story to tell."

"I apologize, Don Marcasi, sir."

"For the next twenty-five years, everything in Monte Castella—this area of magnificent mountains, green valleys, clear water lakes, and truly the most productive and finest vineyards in Sicily—was peaceful as order was restored. Less than ten or thirty assassinations a year depending on how well my father's operations were doing. He returned to the States occasionally, but each time he stayed just a few days. One time was when Don Luciano asked him to come back and wipe out Joe 'The Boss' Masseria."

Lincoln interrupted. "So he was the one who killed Joe the Boss. That's amazing," he said with an air of authority on the subject even though he hadn't the slightest idea who the man was. Pretense of knowledge was one discipline he had mastered over the years, and he liked to employ it as often as possible when in a group.

"Of course. If you knew my father, you would recognize his touch. Even though he was young, he had a signature, so to speak. A bullet through the ear. Don Luciano was very proud of him for that hit, but that was nothing compared to the day of Maranzano. Now that was a work of art."

"He whacked Maranzano, too?"

"Certainly. A restaurant masterpiece. In between the zuppa di polpettine and the fusilli alla Rossi. A single bullet to the ear and Little Caesar Maranzano plopped headfirst into the fusilli alla Rossi. It was truly an Assassins Hall of Fame hit. People still talk about it."

Don Marcasi paused to take a cigar, light it, and glance at his notes. "My father remained in New York only thirty-six hours for the Maranzano thing because he had to return to Monte Castella for the wine festival that was being held about that time. It is a one-week annual celebration that continues to this day. People come from all over Italy to join in the festivities. This year it will be held the second week in September. But I tell you, reservations are a must."

"You say your father was an important man in the States as well as Sicily. How did he manage to arrange that?"

"He and Salvatore were boyhood friends right here in Sicily, and when the great man rose to the top in New York, he wanted to bring my father there to join him. They would have made a great team. Besides Salvatore, Lansky, and Siegel, there was Costello, Castiglia and Genovese. They controlled everything: bootlegging, thefts, hijackings, gambling, extortion, politicians."

"They controlled politicians, too?"

"No question. It is important to have politicians you can count on. It was necessary even though it cost a great deal of money. But I don't name names. The families were like today, you have … what is the word?"

"Lobbies?"

"I don't know that word. They were persuaders. If they wanted a favor, they would persuade. They always had an offer the politicians couldn't refuse. Like you say, lobbies. Most of the time the offer was money. But sometimes, there were other ways. Like using the head of a horse."

"I've heard about that," Lincoln said. "They showed that in a famous Hollywood movie. You're telling us that the horse head business started here in Sicily?"

"I don't go to movies. It doesn't surprise me that they stole the idea. Yes, that practice started right here in Sicily with my grandfather. Anyway, my father, like his father before him, could never leave this paradise of Monte Castella for any length of time because the weather …"

"Yes, yes. So your father was a friend to all these people?"

"What kind of talk is that, friend? They were not friends.

They were men of respect, I told you. They were all made men, they were like this." He raised his hands and interlocked his forefingers. "Like a chain. When there was anything important about to happen, they would call my father to New York. First class." He paused and picked up one of the shotguns and cradled it in his arms.

In another room, Paolo Polucci made a phone call to New York. "Why are you calling, Mr. LaRossi? Our business with you is finished. You are wasting my time. You can be in serious trouble for bothering me. I told you, we have family in New York."

"Wait, don't hang up. It's LaRue. L-A-R-U-E. But never mind that now. If you hang up you will miss out on a great opportunity, a chance to use your skills. How would you like to make another million dollars?" He paused, waiting for an answer. "Paolo? Are you still there? Speak to me."

"I'm listening. But I told you never fool with the Black Hand Mob. That is not healthy for you. And you must address me as Don Paolo Polucci."

"You've been promoted. That's great! Promotions are good. What I have for you could make you a super don or whatever the next grade up is. It will be easy because it's right up your alley, something you are so good at. We want you to kidnap Larry Lincoln *again*. That's all, just kidnap him. Just like you did before. No more hair business, though. We don't need that. Simply kidnap him nicely and hold him hostage for a few days or until we tell you to release him. You're good at that, I know."

"It is our thing."

"Yes, certainly. Listen, you kidnap him and then call me. In the afternoon your time, please. Allow me to talk to Larry. Once I hear his voice, we will wire the money to your bank. It's that simple and you get one million dollars. How does that sound?"

"That's not enough. The price has gone up. It is always more difficult the second time. Why do you want this? Are you setting a trap for us? If that is your plan, it would not be good for you."

"I remember clearly, Don Paolo. I promise you, this is not a trap. Think of it as a type of television show. I'll explain quickly. Do you understand television ratings?"

"Of course, and you told me Mr. Lincoln's ratings are in the dumpster and you wouldn't go over three hundred thousand."

"Let's not bring up the past. Now everything is different. I see you have a good understanding of ratings. You're with me. Ratings mean everything, and that's what this kidnapping is all about. Follow me now. We have replaced Larry on his television show with a girl with a great body. She's fantastic, and we have more viewers than ever before. Our viewer numbers are up—way up. She's packing them in, and we need a few more days without Lincoln to keep our ratings climbing. Understand?

"That means you make more money, right?"

"You're catching on to television news, Paolo."

"That's Don Paolo! The price is two million dollars, and I have no time to argue with you. Two million or I hang up. Then you have Mr. Lincoln and poor ratings."

"Okay, okay. Two million. We have a deal? You can do it?"

"I told you, it is our thing. What about the other guy?"

"What other guy?

"His friend from the TV show with the girls—Baywatch."

"I didn't know he was there, but it doesn't matter. Take him, too. Definitely, but not a dime more. He's for free."

"Alright, we throw him in. But you owe me."

"Great! This is really great. I won't forget I owe you, Don Paolo. Call me when you have him. One more thing. If you're ever in New York, let's do lunch. Ciao!"

Paolo put the phone away and turned to his brothers. "Didn't I tell you this is our future? I have good news. We kidnap Lincoln again. Two million dollars this time. Two million in the bank. We need a new plan. And better masks and disguises this time."

"Certainly," Carlo answered while Gianni reached into his pocket for the exchange rates.

Two hours later, Don Marcasi had covered in grim detail his father's involvement in the murders of Phil Mangano, Albert Anastasia, Frank Scalise, and the failed hit on Frank Costello, which he blamed on the flu. He also threw in a number of lesser known gangsters. In fact, many of the gangsters he mentioned were known to no one other than Guiseppe Palazzolo, who quite often would lose his place among his scribbled notes and would be forced to delve into his imagination to keep the interview flowing.

He soon found joy in creating fictitious characters because it gave him the opportunity to even the score for Italy by using other European nationalities, many of whom he felt were always over-looked when the subject of crime was exploited in the news media. His narrative included such notables as Buzzsaw Sorenborg from Sweden, Hatchet MacHenry of Scotland, Mad Dog Schlossman of Luxembourg, and Ivan Balavic the Great of Russia.

Throughout the interview he intermingled these crime ac-counts with constant forays into the tourist appeal of Monte Castella, covering every restaurant and their specialties, the charming antique and souvenir shops, the religious boutiques with articles blessed by the pope, the beautiful women, and the practice of nude bathing at the lakes.

During a break Baywatch pulled Lincoln outside the room. "Larry, my mind is exploding. I'm in overdrive. Something I didn't see before this old geezer started talking, but now I see it all. A whole new angle to this interview, and the don's father is the key to it. He's been at the center of the crime world from the beginning. Sicily, New York, Chicago, Boston, Las Vegas, Miami, Cuba. He not only knew everything that was going on, he was in on it. He took part in forming the most famous American and Italian mafia families and the really big-time murders in this country and the States. He knew all the rackets, the political payoffs, the murders, everything. His father, Nice Guy Marcasi, is a goldmine, Larry. We're getting more than a television program here. With him we're getting the makings of a great movie script or a TV reality show. He's the story. He's our score."

"I saw that."

"Good. Then keep him on his old man. We can go into his personal experiences later or tomorrow."

Lincoln had no idea what Baywatch was talking about, but he followed his orders the minute the taping began again. "How did your father die, Don Marcasi?"

"It was that little kid who got away when a few malcontents tried to take over the Monte Castella operation. He ran off to New York and grew up to be a big man in the crime there. Had his own mob and grew rich, but he never forgot. One day he returned here and tricked my father into thinking he was visiting as a friend. It was a terrible thing he did. He took advantage of the kindest, most generous man in this paradise we call Monte Castella, and he assassinated him."

"You mean he whacked him."

"You don't say *whack* when it involves family. My father was assassinated."

"That's amazing. The very same thing happened in the movie *The Godfather*."

Don Marcasi quickly looked past Lincoln to the Vocino brothers. Getting no reaction from them, he coughed a few times and continued with the interview. "As I said, I have no time for movies. If what you say is true, they were telling the story of my father. They should have made the movie here to be authentic. I did not tell you this before, but Don Luciano was in this very room with my father. It was during the time the great boss of bosses was in Italy right after he was forced out of the United States. In fact, he sat in the very chair you're sitting in now, and I sat on his lap. He and my father were like that." He pressed his thumb against his forefinger. "I went with my father to attend his funeral. That was when we talked Carlo Gambino into taking control of the New York operation."

"You knew Carlo Gambino?"

"Did we know him? Ha! He was my godfather. My father helped set him up as head of all the New York families." Don Marcasi paused to turn several pages of his notebook.

Mayor Vocino realized that Giuseppe had lost his place and interrupted the interview. "It is time we stopped for lunch. The don has been up since early this morning, when he had a meeting with his caporegime Big Belly Tognolliani. He needs to relax a bit, have something to eat, and take a little nap."

Baywatch turned off the camera. "I must tell you, Tomaso, this is great stuff. It has all kinds of possibilities. We must talk further."

"Yes, most certainly, we will talk. But right now, we will stop to have a light meal at my hotel restaurant, and Nina will join us. She insists on hearing more about Mr. Lincoln and all those famous people he knows. Everything is waiting for us. Don Marcasi, we have prepared especially for you insalata alla carnica, brodo de pesce, zucchini ripieni and a little granita de limone. For wine, we have a good selection from the local vineyards. How does that sound?"

"Thank you for your hospitality, Tomaso, but I must decline. I have much to study. My memoirs, you understand. There is so much to tell and so little time. Remember, the contract. It would be dangerous for you, too. But then, I must honor your generosity. Have the meal sent here. I am very hungry."

Three days later, Burt Baywatch stood in front of the mirror in his hotel room and was pleased with what he saw. He was in a state of happiness incomparable to anything he had experienced before. The interview sessions, though often interrupted with breaks for food, wine, coffee, or cigars, had been conducted without problems except for the occasions when Don Marcasi seemed to contradict himself or become confused in separating movie fiction from historical crime accounts that he had read about in his preparation. Baywatch allowed these mistakes to pass without question, attributing them to Don Marcasi's old age, which he also blamed for extending their stay longer than he had anticipated. He was too pleased with the prospects the future held to allow doubts to enter his mind. The books, lectures, tours, interviews, prime-time television show, lawsuit against YOURchannel, and now the possibility of a movie had elevated his spirits to new levels. His lifelong desire to be a major player as a celebrity agent now involved offices in New York and Beverly Hills; movie, television, and music deals; and multi-million-dollar contracts. Questioning anything in the interview was not to be considered. He was afloat in a new champagne world that blocked any suggestion that something could be wrong.

"You've come a long way from that drowning fiasco," he said to his image in the mirror. "Now that I think about it, that was my baptism, my passover to a new life of success. This means I immediately drop all those small-time losers I've been wasting my time on. I must make room for the great things to come, room to grow! Yeah!" He pumped his fist into the air.

First thing to do is change my name again, he thought. *This time in keeping with my career's divine path, it must have religious, spiritual connotations—but with pizzazz, yet cool. Like Solomon of Beverly Hills. No, no, no. No zing. I'll have to work on it.* He winked at himself in the mirror and walked out the door to join his guests for a parting breakfast.

Sitting across from his new friends and partners in the hotel's patio and sipping his morning espresso slowly, Baywatch relaxed in the warmth of the early morning sun. Across the table, the Vocino brothers chatted cheerfully, buoyed by the prospect that their dreams for Monte Castella's future would come true. Nina also shared in the group's contentment as she thought about the experience of having made love to a man, a celebrity, who was on television and watched by millions, a man who knew personally so many important people. In addition, he had shared the secret of his kidnapping with her alone.

Luggage, cameras, lights, and tapes had been packed in the car in preparation for their departure. They had come together one last time for breakfast and a quick review of the events that were to follow.

Mayor Vocino raised his coffee cup. "To the television interview and the future."

"And to the possible movie," his brother added.

"To all of that and more," Baywatch laughed. "Just keep that old man alive. We'll need him as a consultant."

"We'll take care of that. He is well guarded. You take care of the tapes. How soon do you expect the television show to be on, Mr. Lincoln?"

The question startled Lincoln out of his reverie. He had been staring at Nina and paying little attention to the conversation.

"Television show? Oh, yes, *The Monte Castella Connection*. That name has such a mysterious sound to it. I can't wait to see the logo our art department creates. How soon? I will show it to Saxton, the president of the news division, the moment we return. When he sees what we have, he'll want to start the preview segments on my evening news show immediately. The full one-hour broadcast will follow in a week. That's the schedule according to my agent and friend, Burt." He placed his arm around Baywatch's shoulders.

"That's just the beginning, Mr. Mayor," said Baywatch. "After that I begin two projects. First, I'll get a book underway based on the interview. What do you think of this title: *The Count of Monte Castella?*" There was no reaction. "No? Well, anyway I know just the writer who can turn it out in a week. Then I'm on a plane to Los Angeles to get a script going and contact the studios. The first will be Dreamworks. Spielberg will snatch it up in a minute."

He picked up his demitasse in order to give the Vocino brothers time to get the scent of the bait. "The one element I'm missing to grease the skids, as they say, is a little front money. Something for the book and script writers and to cover the expense of wining and dining the Hollywood crowd. Those people don't talk unless they have food in their mouths."

The Vocinos looked at each other and back at Baywatch. "We thought the television story would open the doors to a movie. How much money are you talking about?"

"Sure, the doors will be wide open after the show airs but I don't want to wait. Timing and contacts are everything. We sell the concept on expectations. Three or four of hundred thousand can really help build expectations."

The Vocino brothers stopped smiling. "That is a lot of expectations, Mr. Baywatch. The money you gave us for the interview all went to Don Marcasi. What he takes, he does not give back. Out of the question. I'm sure you wouldn't want us to ask."

Lincoln felt the chill sweeping across the table. It was not only interrupting the afterglow of his time with Nina and the amorous conversation he was having with her at the moment. It also reminded him that more than anything else, he wanted to leave Sicily before anything remotely resembling his kidnapping might occur. Unconsciously, he raised his hand to the spot where his hair had been cut by Gianni.

"Burt, we can get that much out of YOURchannel. Maybe even get the company to back the movie entirely. We certainly have the leverage now with the lawsuit against Ingersoll. Maybe Don Marcasi could have some of his men of respect pay a call on the great Mr. Ingersoll. An offer he can't refuse sort of thing."

Baywatch was dumbstruck. In all the time he had known Lincoln, he had never heard him present an original idea. Now it was not only somewhat original, but good. He felt there was only one thing that could account for the brainstorm. *This guy should get laid more often*, he thought.

"You're right, Larry. Absolutely right. I love the bit about using the don's influence. Does Ingersoll own a horse?"

Angelo brightened. "That definitely is a good idea, Mr. Lincoln. I will talk to Don Marcasi. But you must remember there is a contract out on him. He may not have the power to ask favors. But we will try."

Lincoln saw the opportunity to be underway, and he quickly rose from his chair, taking Nina's hand. "Let's walk ahead, Nina. There is much I have to say to you."

"Hold on a moment," said Baywatch. "I want to take some photographs. We'll need them for Larry's book."

After the photo session, Lincoln and Nina moved on ahead while Baywatch, the mayor, and Angelo followed a short distance behind with the agent reviewing the plans for the next few weeks and promising to be in touch with them daily. As they approached the car, Baywatch saw someone sitting in the driver's seat.

"Who is that?" he asked.

"He is your driver," the mayor answered. "He will take you to the airport. We thought it best you have a driver. We want to make sure you and the interview arrive safely at the airport. Remember the problem he had when he arrived. Palermo is a large city. Besides, the driver will be able to help you check in and return the cars. Everything is arranged. Another driver will follow with the second car you rented."

"That's very thoughtful of you, Tomaso, but it's really not necessary. I know the way."

"As mayor of Monte Castella, I insist. You are our guests. We want you and the tapes as safe as possible. Please accept this little show of hospitality."

After ten minutes of handshakes, hugs, kisses, and promises, Baywatch and Lincoln climbed into the rear seats and immediately opened the window to continue talking to their hosts. They continued waving out the rear window as Paolo, sporting a full beard, glasses and a wide-brimmed fedora, pressed his foot to the accelerator and drove the car away.

"Larry," Baywatch said looking at his client, "what do you think about my new name, Abraham Starmaker?"

New York

Alex LaRue leaned back in his chair, threw his feet up on the desk, and used his shoulder to press his phone against his ear. "Is that you, Larry? How do you like Italy?"

Paolo had turned on the speaker and was holding the phone close to Lincoln, who was once again tied to a chair. Baywatch was seated next to him in the same condition.

"LaRue, you son of a bitch!" Lincoln screamed into the phone. "What the hell is going on? Get me out of here. Now!"

"Calm down, Larry. Everything's under control. They're not going to hurt you or cut your hair, and it's just for a few days. We won't even count this as vacation time. I'll explain everything. In the meantime, relax and enjoy yourself. Paolo seems to be a nice guy. He told me you love his cooking."

Lincoln continued his frantic shouting. "I'll cook you in oil when I get back! I'll cut you into small pieces. Better than that, I'll sue you. I won't stop until I see you and that rotten team of lunatics on the streets. I'm warning you right now to have them put me on a plane within four hours or I'll sue YOURchannel all the way to bankruptcy."

"This is not like you, Larry. You've always been a team player. Just listen to me. You won't believe what your captivity has done for our ratings and for you. You're news, Larry, big news! This whole country is talking about you. You're in every newspaper and magazine and on television all day. You're a celebrity! More than that, you'll come home a hero. Public Relations has big plans for you. Like meeting the president. Better yet, maybe leading the Macy's Thanksgiving parade. Or a ticker tape parade. What do you think of that?"

"Down Broadway?"

"Just like Lindberg and every hero since. Larry, would I kid you? YOURchannel is behind you all the way. You're a major player on our team now. Just stay calm, cooperate, and enjoy yourself. I wish I could be there with you. I've never been to Italy, but I hear it's the place to visit. By the way, where exactly are you? I know it's Sicily, but where? I hear cows."

"In a barn, you ass. I can't tell you where. They threatened to cut off my fingers if I did. Can you imagine how that would look on television?"

"No problem. We'll work that out. See how we're thinking about you? You have nothing to worry about. This is top level action, Larry."

"What about my money? I had to pay a million dollars the last time I was kidnapped."

"I'll have to talk to the chiefs about that. I'll definitely work on it. You paid that much? I must say you didn't have to go that high. I had them down to three hundred thousand."

"I can't believe this conversation."

"Cheer up, Larry. Think about your fame. Think about people idolizing you, asking for autographs, taking selfies with you, touching you. Right now you have reached the top rung of the celebrity ladder. Just play along."

"How long?"

"A couple of days and then bingo! Larry Lincoln, Hero Held Hostage, is back in New York to the cheers of the nation."

"Hero Held Hostage! I want Hero Returns! And speaking of returning, who's been filling in for me?"

"Some dizzy broad. She's terrible. Doesn't know a thing about news. We can't wait for you to come back and begin reading again. Larry, I don't mean to be abrupt with you, but I have Saxton calling me on the other line. He's anxious to hear about you. See that? Saxton no less. We're all here for you, Mr. Celebrity. A parade down Broadway, people lining the streets, waving and cheering and shouting 'Welcome home, Larry.' And we'll have that new teleprompter you've been requesting for the last six months. Digital! I have a meeting to go to right now. Ingersoll has called for a big one. I'll call back later. Ciao!"

Saxton, Handleman, and LaRue huddled outside of Ingersoll's office waiting for the 10:00 a.m. meeting he had unexpectedly announced.

You're sure you didn't screw this thing up?" Saxton said to LaRue. "You're toast if I'm blindsided at this meeting just because you didn't carry out your plan."

LaRue was too full of renewed confidence to notice he was now the parent of the second Lincoln kidnapping idea. "Everything has been handled," he responded. "There was no problem. I talked to Lincoln on the phone a half hour ago and everything is under control. He screamed bloody murder at first but when I told him about the nationwide press he's been receiving and the welcome home celebration, he calmed down. I think he was actually a bit pleased by the end of our conversation."

"It's strange that he took it so well," Handleman said. "Maybe he's dumber than I thought."

"I promised we would get him out in a few days." LaRue continued. "He loved the Hero Held Hostage idea. He also wants reimbursement for the million he paid the kidnappers the first time around."

"Good job, LaRue. You finally did something right. That

million he paid was his decision, not ours." Handleman turned to Saxton. "Do you know what this meeting is about?"

"Not the slightest, and I don't like it. It can't be good. Janet said he had one meeting already, but she wouldn't tell me who it was with. This isn't like him. Ingersoll has never been in this early. I checked with his chauffeur, and he told me they arrived here at eight. Eight in the morning! He doesn't leave his house that early even on what he calls his busy days. Here comes Tanner and the bitch. Let's go in now and grab the good seats."

As they entered the office, both presidents reached in their pockets to make sure their recorders were operating. They were soon joined at the table by Macon, Sanford, Tanner, and Pearl Necklace. Ingersoll was still seated at his desk, and he did not respond to their greetings but continued to read through a thick report he was holding. His silence sent a message of impending unpleasantness to everyone in the group. There was no conversation while they waited for him to join them at the conference table.

Ingersoll finished reading the last page and dropped the report on the desk. "Dammit!" The word seemed to ricochet around the walls of his office. LaRue reached for his water glass. It was the only movement at the table. "Dammit all," he repeated and shoved the report in his leather folder bearing the ornately embossed initials GE–MBA–CEO. He paused to read the initials several times, run his fingers over them, then silently pick up the folder, walk to the table, and sit next to Pearl Necklace.

"You look smashing this morning, Pearl. Sorry about the language." He turned to face this staff and spoke solemnly, "Now, first things first. Gentlemen—and you, Pearl—we have a problem." He looked around the table, making eye contact with each person, intensifying their uneasiness.

Saxton was the first to gather himself together and react. "Whatever the problem, George, you can rest assured I for one will not leave this building until it's resolved."

"That goes for me twice over, George," said Handleman.

"All for one, George," Macon chimed in, angry with himself for not speaking up first. He attempted to make up for this negligence quickly. "We're a team here. Like you're always saying and like I've always said, I'll walk through fire to …"

"Shut up, Carl," Ingersoll snapped. "As I said, we have a problem, a poll problem. You all know what a poll problem is, I assume. I had an independent poll of viewers taken last night on the Lincoln hostage story on our evening news, and I received the results this morning. They are not good."

He opened the monogrammed leather folder and pulled out the top sheet of the report. "I won't bother with the details. The summary tells the whole story. Forty-two percent said they did not want to hear any more about Larry Lincoln until he was released or found dead. Seventy-one percent said we are repeating the same news every day. Sixty-three percent want more violence in the story. Seventy percent said they liked the music. Thirty-seven percent were against any kind of gun regulations. That subject wasn't even on the survey. Fifty percent wanted to see more of Pearl Necklace." He paused to look up. "If that's possible, I might add. No offense intended, Pearl. You and the music were the only positive responses we received. The survey company summed up the report in one word: *boredom*. We have a tired news story on our hands. We've peaked. In this business, it's time to bail out."

Ingersoll slowly placed the report back into the folder, closed it, and ran his fingers over the monogram again. "Like the astronaut famously stated: Miami, we have a problem."

Macon made sure this time he would be the first to speak up. "Polls always have a three to five percent margin of error, George."

Ingersoll glared at his Public Relations president. "Have you worked at being stupid, or did you inherit it? Does anyone have anything intelligent to say?"

There was a long period of silence before Saxton spoke. "I had a feeling we've been milking this thing a bit too much. Sagging teats, definitely. I have an email to that effect right now, directed to the entire staff. Susan was to send it out this morning. You'll all find it on your computers when you return to your offices."

That was true. Saxton wrote that memo and several others in his computer's drafts folder, ready for transmittal, each covering a different position for him to take depending upon circumstances. However, there were enough conditional phrases in each to allow an escape. He paused a moment and then looked across the table in order to shift the spotlight. "LaRue, where do you stand with your negotiations?"

LaRue's earlier exuberance was now gone. Instantly, he was aware of the significance of his previous conversations with Saxton. He felt the trap door drop, and the only thing he could grab was his glass of water.

Tanner spoke up to save him. "The first thing we do is get Lincoln back here. That will free us from repeating the day two, day three, day four bullshit. A big return celebration at the airport would at least add a news element to the story. We need news or at least a different angle like the ransom."

"You might have something there, Steve." Handleman said. He folded his arms across his chest and looked up toward the ceiling. "Let me think about that one. It definitely has possibilities. It might be a way to go if it works. Of course, it could be just a non-event. Let's pass it around the table. LaRue, you've been handling all the negotiations yourself. What's your take on this thing, and how fast can you get him back here?"

LaRue was still drinking water and he choked at the question.

"Not on the table, you slob," Ingersoll yelled, "and forget about how fast. First I want to know how much this is going to cost us."

LaRue quickly wiped the water from the table with his jacket sleeve. "I gave them two million dollars."

Ingersoll leaped up. "Two million dollars!"

Saxton slammed his hands on the table. "You gave them two million dollars! You mean you already gave them the money?"

"You said that …"

"I said? What the hell are you talking about? I said nothing. We all sat here and told you to stretch out the time of his captivity. Of course, that was before I had the feeling that the story was getting stale. Now we discover you have already paid the money."

"That's what I remember," Handleman snapped, joining the sacrifice. "You gave them two million dollars! Really, LaRue, I find that impossible to believe."

LaRue felt himself plummeting down a black hole, and he could think of nothing to say that might stop the fall. This time Pearl Necklace came to his aid. "Has he been released yet, Alex?"

"No. He is still being held hostage."

Handleman stepped in. "You mean we paid the money but they are still holding him? What have you done?"

"It's a little more complicated than that. You see …"

"Hold on a moment, Alex," said Necklace. "I have an idea."

"If you don't mind, Miss Necklace," interrupted Saxton, "We are at the presidential level with this problem LaRue has created. We don't need any more centerfold gimmicks."

Without answering, Necklace looked at Ingersoll, who turned to stare at Saxton, instantly silencing him.

"Okay, Alex," Necklace continued. "Forget your explanation. If he is still a captive, that's fine." She spoke to Tanner. "Think about this, Steve. Before we put him on a plane and welcome him home with a five-minute interview at Kennedy airport that would be the end of the story, let's add a new twist, an element of excitement. If Alex can arrange it, we go to where they're holding him and do an interview. I know it's been done before but never with a television news anchor. We do a live interview with Larry Lincoln and his captors, telling Americans what it's like for an anchorman to be held hostage. We might even hook up a telecom link between Larry and our viewers. They address their questions directly to Larry, and he answers looking right into the camera.

We could even bring his mother into the interview for the personal touch."

"I'm beginning to see light again, Pearl," Ingersoll said. He sat down. "This could be fantastic. I think I see a bonus in your future."

"Pearl in Peril!" shouted Macon. "That's what we'll call it. From *Hero Held Hostage* to *Pearl in Peril*. The logo could be a knockout. All the letters would be in the shape of Pearl's beautiful body. The letters 'P' could form her breast."

"Now you're coming alive, Macon," Ingersoll responded. "Must have been a blackout you were in before."

Macon beamed. "Thank you, George."

Tanner stood and held up his hands. "Wait a minute. We're talking about real kidnappers here. Real bad guys with real guns and real ugly motives, not some reality TV show."

"We're also talking real rating points, Steve," countered Handleman. "If we can pull this off quickly, it will be included in this month's sweeps. Think what that can mean to our advertising revenues. On my *Celebrities Galore* show we could have a few movie stars who have played hostage roles come in and talk to Lincoln. Get some politicians on, too. And I love the idea of his mother talking to him. Can't you just see her crying? It would be fantastic, as the chief said."

"Think about the risks," Tanner countered.

"It was her idea, Steve," said Saxton with a smile. "If she wants to do it, I say let her. I don't want to sound mercenary, but the ratings are well worth the risk. Don't be so melodramatic. I mean, look at Lincoln. He's still alive. Isn't that right, LaRue?"

"Oh, yes. He says the food is out of this world."

"Don't worry, Steve," Necklace answered, "I won't be alone. If LaRue can arrange this thing, I'll take a full crew with me. We'll devote the complete evening news half hour to the interview. In fact, if it goes well, we might even stretch this out for a couple of days. Then I come back with Larry and we do a live show at Kennedy airport. It should go like clockwork."

"Only if I go with you," Tanner demanded.

"I wouldn't go without you. We can work on my new show while we're there. That's coming up fast."

"What new show?" shouted Saxton and Handleman, simultaneously. "What's that about?"

"First things first," said Ingersoll. "I want Pearl and her crew on the plane today. Needless to say, Pearl, I'm going to miss our little morning chats. LaRue, do you think the kidnappers will go for the plan?"

"They seem to go for anything if there's enough money involved."

"Don't go over a half million. By all rights, with what we've already given them, he belongs to us now anyway."

"I just thought of something else," said Macon. "We float a story that Lincoln is really a CIA agent."

Following the meeting, Saxton spent the next few hours at his computer, composing a letter to Arnold Schumbeck, CEO of YOURchannel's parent company. In it he created a diabolical dissembling of Ingersoll, relating in extraordinary detail the CEO's incompetent management of YOURchannel, his inability to make decisions, and his wasteful spending on such items as a personal airplane, leasing hotel suites in three cities, cars for his two mistresses, rare paintings and antiques for his home and office, season tickets to every sport, art, and entertainment activity in New York, and credit cards for his two children in college. After that, he brought up the limited number of hours Ingersoll actually spends in the office, his constant attempts to seduce every woman in the building, his attendance at every major golf and tennis championship worldwide, and his total ignorance of television in general.

Once he finished making editing changes to improve the letter's flow and embellish the sexual encounters, he read the composition several times over. Pleased with the final result, he smiled, lit a cigar, and threw his feet up on the desk. "This is good … really good. No question about that. I feel so much better now. It's the best I've ever written." Ten minutes later, after thoroughly enjoying his Montecristo and dreaming of the reaction his letter would ignite, he stretched out his arm to reach the computer and hit the save key. "One of these days when the time is right, I'm going to send it."

Alex LaRue spoke into his speaker phone. "Paolo, have I got a deal for you. It's a deal that'll make you more money and you don't have to do anything. No more kidnapping."

"That is our thing," Paolo answered, speaking through his new President Nixon mask.

"I understand, and you do it well, but this is a little different. Are you ready? My company wants to conduct a television interview with Larry."

"Goodbye, Mr. LaRossi."

"Wait, Paola! Hear me out. And it's alright to call me LaRossi. We've already given you a lot of money for Larry, and that brings up an important point. Since we've already paid for him, he's really ours. Legally he's our property, not yours. We should be able to do whatever we want with him. We don't want to go to court over this because we would both end up with terrible legal fees. I don't know anything about Italian lawyers, but I do know ours. They would drag this thing on until you're broke. Believe me, you would lose everything you've gained. It's not worth the time and money. Do you understand? Do you really want to go to court?"

Paolo did not understand. He was confused, and another memory search of all the kidnapping movies he had ever seen produced nothing to resemble this situation. He wasn't sure how to answer. He turned to ask his brothers, but one look told him that would only result in an argument about movie stars and titles.

"Paolo, are you still there? You must help me on this. You owe me."

"I think I owe you a visit from my New York family."

"No, that won't help anything. Let's talk money. You let us do this interview—just a half hour. We will wire you a quarter of a million dollars. Now before you start raising the amount, I must tell you that's as high as I can go. Just a quick interview and we'll be out of there. To show you our good intentions, we'll wire you half the amount in advance. You'll get the rest when our people leave."

"It smells like a trap. I told you never to fool with the Black Hand Mob. You could end up with the fishes."

The mention of the mob's name gave LaRue an idea for resolving the deadlock. "How about this? If you let us do the interview, we'll give your gang a plug during the interview."

"It's Don Paolo, Mr. LaRossi. What's a plug?"

"A plug is a way to promote something. It's an announcement promoting something but made to sound like news. During the interview, Larry Lincoln will mention he is being held by the Black Hand Mob. In an instant your organization would be famous around the world. It could mean an increase in business for you. That's what a plug does. We do it all the time. How about it?"

Paolo was thoroughly confused by LaRue's fast talking, strange requests, and now this bewildering offer of more money. First, he would not pay to free Lincoln, and then he paid to have him kidnapped again. Now he is willing to pay for an interview and offering television fame. Things were getting out of hand, and he needed help. In desperation he turned to his brothers again, but a look at the Mickey Mouse masks they were wearing made him reject the idea. Then he looked across the table at his bound and gagged hostages, who were staring at him, trying to understand the phone conversation.

"Wait, Mr. LaRossi, I must discuss this." He pressed hold and addressed his brothers. "Remove the gags. We must talk." He waited until Lincoln and Baywatch stopped spitting and held up his hand before they could speak.

"I will talk, you will listen. Your boss wants to pay us a lot of money and he will plug us."

Baywatch looked at Lincoln and back again at Paolo. "They want to shoot you and also want to pay you a pile of money. I can understand that. That's YOURchannel all the way. I think you should definitely accept the offer."

Paolo held up his hand again. "You don't understand television, Mr. Big-Time Agent. A plug is a promotion. They want to promote us, make us famous."

The two hostages looked at each other again. "They've gone around the bend completely," said Lincoln, shaking his head. "I cannot believe this is happening. My own company has me kidnapped and now wants to turn the kidnappers into celebrities. To think the only thing I worried about was my hair." He turned to Baywatch. "You told me there would be no problems. You're fired."

"Enough," shouted Paolo. "Your boss is waiting for an answer. The other thing they want is an interview with you on television. I think they are trying to set a trap."

"No, it's not a trap," Baywatch shouted as he attempted to leap out of his chair. "It's a fantastic idea. Don't you see, Larry? They really want an interview. It's for ratings!" His mind was racing in high gear again as he recognized the interview plan for what it was.

"I know ratings." said Paolo. "It means more money."

"It's insane and I won't do it," said Lincoln.

"It's not insane and you must do it," Baywatch shouted again. "It's the best thing we could ask for. Think about it for a moment.

It will attract the biggest audience of your life on television. The greatest ratings ever for YOURchannel. This is an opportunity of a lifetime. Think about the effect it will have on your books, your lectures, your fees, your stardom, your celebrity level. It will make everything we've talked about bigger than ever. It guarantees you a prime-time show and the movie a slam dunk! We couldn't ask for anything better." He tried to stand up again in order to pace but Carlo slammed his hands down on his shoulders.

"You can lose an ear that way," he said through his mask.

"Sorry about that, Mickey," Baywatch answered, receiving a slap across the back of his head.

"Enough!" said Paolo. "I'm beginning to get the picture. If the ratings are going to be so big, we should get more money."

"Definitely!" Baywatch answered. "They're playing games with you. That's just part of negotiating. You can easily make them double whatever they promised. That's what they had in mind to begin with. I know these people. By the way, could you change that Nixon mask you're wearing? It might affect the ratings. Do you have a Kennedy? Or better yet, a Clooney?"

"Are you willing to do the interview, Mr. Newsman?" Paolo asked.

"Say yes, Larry." Baywatch pleaded. "Believe me, I know this is right. I can feel it. I'm right here with you this time. By the way, what do you think of the name Elijah Mogul?"

"It sucks." He turned to Paolo. "Okay, I'll go along. Tell that dick LaRue he can have his interview. But he has to guarantee this is the end of it. I come home with the film crew. What's for dinner?"

Immediately following Ingersoll's meeting, Steve Tanner met with Pearl Necklace, Tom Dauber, associate director Walt Graber, two cameramen, and the production engineers to discuss their trip and the programming and equipment necessary to conduct live television interviews from Sicily.

An hour later, LaRue burst into the room. "It's all set. They're going along with it. The kidnappers agreed and so did Larry. You can be on your way. By the way, Baywatch is with him."

"You did good, Alex," Tanner responded. "What is the plan?"

"You fly to Palermo using Ingersoll's private plane and pick up your transportation at the airport. I've made arrangements for that and with a Palermo TV company to aid us with transmittals, but you must take with you whatever equipment you will need for the interview. Your contact will be waiting at the airport's Hertz car rental lot. Look for a Fiat van with the outline of a hand painted in black on the rear door. Pull up behind it and sound the horn four times. Three short and one long. You are not to leave your vehicles or attempt to meet or talk to the driver but simply follow the van. You will be led to where they are keeping Larry and Baywatch."

Tanner picked up the phone. "Mary, have the limo meet us curbside in two hours." He turned to his crew. "We'll finish the interview details on the way over." He turned back to LaRue. "What the hell is Baywatch doing there?"

"I don't know. I guess he went on vacation with Larry."

"Dammit, he'll just be in the way. I know he'll want to negotiate something or try to direct the interview. No matter, we'll work that out when we get there. Let's break now and get the equipment packed. Mike, make arrangements to lease any extra remote equipment from one of the Palermo stations you think we might need. Have everything waiting for us at the airport. Tom, you stay and control the operation from here."

"I should be there," said Dauber, looking at Necklace. "Walt can handle things here."

"We'll need him, Steve," Necklace said to Tanner. "The action will be in Sicily."

"Okay, but remember, this isn't *The Love Boat*."

Monte Castella

"Why, Nina, Why? You should have come to us immediately," Mayor Vocino asked his granddaughter after she had finished relating the story of Lincoln's first kidnapping. "You should have come to us immediately."

Nina kept her promise to Larry to remain silent until he was gone and out of harm's way. She waited until long after Lincoln and Baywatch departed for Palermo and the airport before she met with mayor Vocino and his brother Angelo to tell them Lincoln's real story of why he was delayed in reaching Monte Castella.

"He asked me not to say anything to anyone until they were safe at the airport. He was afraid … no, not afraid, he was worried about what might happen to innocent people. They told him many would suffer terribly if he did not keep silent. He was concerned about your safety, too. His captors made terrible threats about what they would do even after he returned to New York."

"Did he say where they were keeping him hostage?" Angelo Vocino asked. "Were they close to Monte Castella?"

"He was unconscious until he found himself in a bedroom. That apartment was the only thing he could describe. He knew they were keeping him on a farm because he could hear cows."

Mayor Vocino looked at his brother, and then turned back to

Nina. "How many men did he say were involved in this, and did he describe them to you?"

"He saw only three but he knew there were more. They always wore masks so he never saw their faces. He did mention that the leader was always shouting at the other two and slapping them across their heads."

The two men jumped to their feet. "Those damn Poluccis," Angelo screamed. "It had to be them. They knew when he was coming. They were waiting for him at the airport."

"I'll kill them this time," said Mayor Vocino. "With my bare hands I'll choke the life out of them."

"Did Lincoln say how much it took to free him?"

"A million dollars."

Driving at great speed, Tomaso and Angelo arrived in less than ten minutes at the Polucci farm. They drove past the house slowly and as quietly as possible to avoid alerting anyone of their presence and came to a stop at the barn the Polucci brothers had turned into a bed and breakfast. Hearing Nina's story, neither doubted for a moment who had kidnapped Lincoln. During the trip, they took turns describing methods of inflicting excruciating pain and lifelong injuries to each of the three brothers.

"How could that newsman allow those three fools to kidnap him?" said the mayor. "Either he is dumber than I thought, or they are getting better with practice. Is that possible?"

"It can't be that," Angelo answered. "It was just a month ago they tried to kidnap Nina, and she beat the hell out of them. No, it must be him. It's hard to believe he's a television newsman. An 'anchorman' he called himself. Now I know the meaning of that word."

Angelo looked around for signs of the Polucci brothers. "I don't see their van. Maybe they're in town robbing the church."

"No, they tried that once, remember. Father Autobelli almost crushed Paolo's head with a cross. Let's go inside and wait until they return. A million dollars! That man is worth a million dollars? Television!"

They concealed the car far away from the barn, walked back, and approached the door, on which was painted a black outline of a hand. They gently slid it open a few feet and stepped inside.

"I don't believe this," said Angelo Vocino. "That's the car belonging to Baywatch. Do you think they stole it from Avis?"

"That would be the good news. No, I know the Polucci too well, and the sick feeling in my stomach tells me they have been doing something terrible. I'm thinking they're up to their kidnapping thing again."

Both men moved quietly to the car and opened the doors. "Thank God for his mercy," Angelo gasped. "All the equipment is here. At least we won't have to go through the interviews again. They must be ..."

"Paolo?" Carlo called from the upstairs room. "Is that you?"

Angelo put his finger to his lips and the two men climbed the stairs to the loft as quietly as their heavy bodies on the steps would allow. They were breathing heavily by the time they reached the top and tiptoed to the doorway. The door had been left ajar, enabling them to peer into the room where they saw Lincoln and Baywatch tied to chairs. Carlo saw the Vocinos and instantly threw up his arms. "It was only business," he pleaded, "nothing personal."

Both Vocinos burst into the room and simultaneously screamed out apologies to the captives as they ran to them and worked desperately to untie the bindings.

"Hold still. You're only tightening the knots," Angelo ordered. "Everything is alright now. You are safe again. This is a terrible mistake. We knew nothing of this. These people are traitors to the don, and they will suffer terrible deaths."

"The don will see to that," Mayor Vocino broke in. "He will

be shocked when he learns of this. These were his bodyguards. He will apologize to you a thousand times over. He owes you the favor of watching them die. Remember how he told you he could trust no one? This is proof. But you are in good hands again, and they will suffer great pain."

That was all Carlo needed to make his move. He darted for the doorway but not fast enough. Angelo stretched out his leg and caught him in midflight, sending him stumbling across the room. Angelo pulled the sock out of Lincoln's mouth and walked slowly toward the fallen Carlo with as much menace as he could create with each footstep. He leaned over him and lifted the Mickey Mouse mask enough to roughly shove the sock into his mouth and then snapped the mask back in place.

"If you move again, I will stand on your face. After that, I will throw you out the window and God will thank me for preventing another Polucci generation."

Freed from the ropes, Baywatch pulled the sock from his mouth and spit several times. "Thank you for providing us with a driver to the airport, Angelo, but please—no more favors."

"You must believe me, Mr. Baywatch. We did not know these people were part of the gang trying to destroy the don. He told you about the contract. As I said, they are traitors. But you are free now. No great harm done, the interviews are safe, and soon you can be on your way. I will drive you to the airport myself. You might even consider including this in your television story."

"I have enough story, thank you," Lincoln answered. "The only thing I want is a first-class seat and as much gin as they're allowed to carry on the plane. Let's get out of here."

"We can't leave, Larry," said Baywatch.

"What?"

"We have the television interview coming."

"What television interview?" the Vocinos asked in unison. "We have finished all the television interviews. The don will not permit more."

"No, we have one more to do. Our friends Mickey One, Mickey Two, and Nixon have arranged to have Larry's company come here to conduct a live interview with him. Nixon and Mickey Two are at the airport right now, picking up the television crew and bringing them back here."

Lincoln flung his hands in the air. "I've changed my mind. I want to go to the airport before anything else happens. I'm tired of all this. Tired of being tied up, tired of that awful sock in my mouth, tired of these lunatics. I want my life together again—in front of the cameras where it's safe and I have a prompter that tells me all I need to know."

"You'll get all that and more," Baywatch answered. "Larry, this interview is the key to everything. Like I told you before, it ties together the entire package. You remember … books, lectures, fees, lawsuit, your own show and more money then you ever dreamed of having. It all hinges on this interview."

"And the movie," added Angelo Vocino, who immediately understood what was occurring and recognized the overwhelming benefits it would provide Monte Castella. "A television interview would definitely make Larry Lincoln the most famous man in America and then a movie about you would follow. Your fans would demand it."

Baywatch was pacing the floor again. "That's right, the movie. A movie about you, Larry Lincoln. Hey, why didn't I think of this before? You play yourself in the movie! The whole thing starts off with you doing the interview with the don. Then we cut to flashbacks. The start of the Mafia right here in Sicily. That's how we bring the don's father into the story. This is beautiful!"

"In Monte Castella!" shouted the mayor.

"Yes, right here in Monte Castella. The camera opens on you. I can see it all. Up there on the big screen, YOURchannel anchorman Larry Lincoln, flashing his steely blue eyes, looks into the brown eyes of the infamous Don Victorio 'The Brain' Marcasi."

"What do I say?"

"We'll work that out later. Don't worry, I'll get the best script-writer in Hollywood. It's the start of a whole new career, buddy. It's a brilliant idea. Better than the one I had about you running for the Senate. We'll do that later. After three or four movies, the Senate will be a gimme!"

"Senator Lincoln," added Mayor Vocino. "Can I call you Senator right now? Your agent is a genius. We must go through with the television interview."

Baywatch swung around to face the mayor. "What do you mean by *we?*"

"*We*, of course. We meaning all four of us. We meaning my brother and me. Angelo and I will also be hostages. We'll be tied up here alongside of you. That will make it more realistic. Italian realism! We are world famous for it. Remember *La Dolce Vita* and Anita Ekberg. The interview will be with Mr. Lincoln, of course, but perhaps I could be on for a few minutes to back up your story and talk a little about the don and Monte Castella. It would add color. After all, we are the ones who know him personally. It would add to the interview. I'm sure the don would approve. He has always been disappointed about never receiving credit for his work, always living in the shadow of his father."

Baywatch began pacing again, stepping back and forth across Carlo's prostrate body. "Maybe you're right. We could make this a bigger deal than just Larry's kidnapping."

"Excuse me," said Lincoln, "but I think my kidnapping is a pretty big deal."

"No question about that, Mr. Lincoln," Angelo said quickly, not wanting Lincoln to think about leaving again. "You are the important person here. What Mr. Baywatch meant, I'm sure, is that with the mayor and myself involved, it is more than an isolated case but instead wholesale kidnapping by an underworld mob trying to prevent your interview with the don from being on television."

Carlo, still on the floor, pulled the sock from his mouth. "It is our thing! Are you going to mention us?"

Mayor Vocino walked across the room and placed his foot on Carlo's stomach. "One more word and I will squash your guts out through your eyeballs. Put the sock back in your mouth before I put my foot in it. The don will deal with you later."

He turned to Lincoln. "See, Mr. Lincoln, you really have nothing to fear from these people once you know how to deal with them. Believe me, Don Marcasi will deal with them."

"What about my hair?" said Lincoln, using his comb ever so gently and checking it for loose hairs. "What will my public say when they see the gap? It could affect my ratings in the future."

"You look great in the beret," said Baywatch. "You can explain that you don't want to expose the wound because children might be watching. We'll have them position the camera on your right side. I always thought it was your best side anyway."

"I agree with you there, Burt," said Lincoln. "I've always avoided the left side unless I'm doing a smile story. For some reason my left always looks best when I'm smiling. Mayor, you and Angelo should be on my direct left so when they talk to you, I can give them a three-quarter profile. I'll use the wrinkled-brow look I save for really serious matters."

"Now you're talking, pal. That's the old Larry Lincoln I know. Anchor man, *par excellente*. You like my Italian?" Baywatch turned to Angelo. "One other very important matter we must cover, my friend. What about Mickey Mouse there under your foot and his companions? How are they going to react? We can't have them screw up this television interview. This is critical."

"Do not worry about that," Angelo replied as he joined Baywatch, pacing back and forth and stepping over Carlo. "Before the other two return, this fool will tie all of us to the chairs and then he will do as we instruct him or he will spend the remainder of his life in jail. Do you hear and understand me, imbecile?"

Carlo started to take the sock from his mouth but thought

better of it and simply nodded vigorously while making a few positive sounds.

"Larry, I think I've got a winner this time," Baywatch said. "What do you think of my new name, Ezekiel of Hollywood? Don't you think that really says it all?"

Lincoln ignored the question as he gently replaced his beret and walked to the dresser mirror. "I hope they remember to bring makeup. That has me really concerned, along with one other very important item."

"What's that?" asked Baywatch.

"This will be the only time I'll be in front of a camera for a long period without a prompter."

Two hours later the Polucci truck drove up to the barn, followed by two vans carrying the YOURchannel television crew. Carlo finished tying the four men to their chairs and went down to meet his brothers. Still wearing his Mickey Mouse mask, he drew Paolo and Gianni aside to explain the new situation while the YOURchannel crew unloaded the equipment. Paolo received the news and the mayor's threats calmly.

"We must go through with the interview. I don't want to give back the money. After that, we will pay off the mayor. This is as good a time as any for us to start buying politicians. We must learn how to do this thing. Remember the Corliones. Another thing: don't mention to the Vocinos how much we have made on all of this."

"I'm still working on the exchange rate," added Gianni. Carlo looked over their shoulders at Pearl Necklace. "*Mama mia*, she's beautiful! Can I search her?"

Paolo tried to refrain from hitting Carlo for fear of alarming the guests, but his arm involuntarily swung out in his direction. The hesitation gave Carlo time to duck, and Gianni received the blow, which broke off one of the Mickey Mouse ears. Without apologizing, Paolo shouted to the group that had assembled by the van watching the strange conference of Richard Nixon and two Mickey Mice. "Come this way. Follow us and remember to follow the rules."

"What rules? What is he talking about?" Dauber whispered.

"I have no idea," Tanner answered. "I'm still trying to figure out why they're dressed like that. For some reason they remind me of gangster movies from the thirties. This is all really strange. I'm feeling a bit uneasy."

Tanner took the lead and followed Paolo into the barn and up the stairway. He stopped instantly at the open doorway, shocked at the sight of four men tied to their chairs and gagged. "What the hell is going on here?"

"This is our thing," Paolo answered. "No more questions. You are in the hands of the Black Hand Mob and we do not answer questions. Now you know the rules."

"No questions!" Gianni repeated.

"You could lose an ear," added Carlo.

Tanner quickly crossed the room to Lincoln, pulled the sock from his mouth, and began to untie him.

"Stop!" shouted Paolo. "Everyone remains tied. That was the agreement."

"Better listen to him, Steve," Lincoln said. "They're very big about cutting off ears."

"Thank God you're okay." Tanner said. "In fact, you look great, considering what you've been through. Actually, I think you've even put on some weight."

"They've been force-feeding me to keep me alive. Never mind that. Let's talk about how hard you guys worked to set me free. What friends you turned out to be! That really hurt me, Steve. I still can't believe it. Where's that bastard LaRue? Is he too ashamed to come and face me? The slime pot. Why are you looking at my head?"

"He isn't with us. I'm really sorry, Larry. I don't know too much about the negotiations, but I apologize for what they've put you through. Just hang in for a little while longer and it will all be over. Who are these other guys?"

"Never mind them. Who's the girl?"

"Her name is Pearl Necklace," Tanner answered. "She's been filling in while you've been away. What's with the beret?"

"It simply doesn't stop! LaRue told me she was a loser and we were dropping points. Look at her! She's beautiful. That lying bastard. He said she was obese, wore pants, had black curly hair and a lisp and doesn't read the news without stuttering."

"I'll explain later," Tanner answered. "There's no time now. You know about the interview. I have to go over the plan with you. We need to move fast. As soon as everything is set up, we're going to cut in on the regular programming."

Lincoln looked at the clock on the bed stand. "That's not what I would call prime time. Shouldn't I get prime time? Can't we wait?"

"Don't worry, it will be close enough. They've been running promos every fifteen minutes, and there is an all-out publicity campaign underway. Believe me, we'll have a great audience."

"I know about promos," Paolo interjected.

Ignoring Paolo, Tanner continued. "The show will also be repeated during prime time hours. Listen to me. This is the plan. Pearl will open with a very short introduction to set the scene, then she will turn to you with a few opening questions to enable you to explain the kidnapping, and after that we're going to switch to some questions from the audience. After her introduction, the camera will be on you all the time. It's all been set up in New York. They're actually running a contest to see who would have the chance to talk to you."

"Did you bring the prompter?"

"Of course not. This must be improvised."

"Improvised? What do mean, improvised? No rehearsal?"

"This is live television, Larry. We will screen the questions the audience will ask, and Pearl will review them with you. Listen to me. The network has been merchandising this interview from the moment these guys agreed. This is going to draw a colossal audience. Everyone is waiting to see you. We have it all worked out. Pearl will be handling the interview with you and the viewers' questions. Dauber will direct and transmit, and I'll control things from here. This will be easy."

"Can I have a copy of the answers in front of me?"

"No. Now tell me, who are these men and why are they being held?"

"First, I have my own questions," Lincoln said. "Number one, why didn't you bring a prompter? You know I never worked without a prompter. Number two, is she going to be on camera? Number three, I can't remember the third one. Number four, can you give the mayor here a couple of minutes air time? I made a promise to him. Last but definitely not least, how do I look in this beret?"

"Here are your answers, by the numbers. No prompter. I repeat, this is live. Pearl has all the questions she will be asking, and you can look them over before we start the show. Dauber will also have a copy of her questions, and he can prompt you through your headset. Pearl will be on camera only for a few minutes, but you will have it all after that. This is your show. I don't understand the part about the mayor, but the beret looks great. You should wear it all the time. He is mayor of what?"

"That's a terrific idea," Baywatch broke in. "It will be your new image, Larry. We'll have a logo drawn up the minute we get back. It'll be a totally new marketing concept. Like the Hathaway eye patch. Like the swish. Like the apple. Then we'll license the beret logo! Can't you just picture it? Lincoln beret shirts, ties, jackets, T-shirts, running shoes. There's no end to it. Lincoln beret games, posters, luggage, carpeting."

Tanner closed his eyes and again thought of Alec Guiness on

the River Kwai. "You still haven't answered my question about these other guys. Who are they, and why do you want them on the show? What have they got to do with your kidnapping."

"I can handle that one," Baywatch answered. "This is Mayor Victorio Vocino and his brother, Angelo. Say hello. Guys, this is Steve Tanner, an important man at YOURchannel television. Steve, they're from the town of Monte Castella. The two most important people there, as a matter of fact."

As Tanner nodded to the Vocino brothers, Baywatch continued with the full story of why Lincoln had come to Sicily, filling in the details of the interview with Don Marcasi, the tapes, the plan for using them on the evening news show, the hour-long finale, the mayor's part in setting it up, and ending with the story of this splinter group, the Black Hand Mob, that is trying to kill the don and take over his operation. Throughout the entire story, Tanner said nothing, stunned into silence by the story.

Baywatch continued. "The mayor and his brother were kidnapped because of their friendship with Don Marcasi. Of course, Larry will bring all of this out in your interview. We have to give the mayor a few minutes of television time. It's important. It will pull everything together. He will back up Larry's story. Your little arm candy there can just swing around and throw him a question at the appropriate time."

Hearing the last remark, Necklace walked up to Baywatch and swatted him across the face.

"Wow, you're a very fast learner. You've only been in Sicily a few hours and you already speak the language. May I ask if you have an agent? That's what I do. I can make you a celebrity. My name is Jeremiah Starmaker. You can call me Jerry. I'm a great talent agent."

"Is that how you got kidnapped?" she answered.

"Oh, that was mean, but I'll overlook it. We should talk."

Paolo walked up to Mayor Vocino and bent over to whisper in his ear. "You work with us and we'll work with you. There's plenty more where this came from." With that, he tucked two 500 euro banknotes into the mayor's jacket pocket.

Mayor Vocino's face turned red with anger. He rose, still tied to the chair, and butted his head against Paolo's chin.

"Damn!" exclaimed Baywatch. "That would have looked great on television. Can we stage that later in the show?"

Tanner looked over the group assembled in the room. He was beginning to question what was going on. Everything about the story he heard bothered him. He pulled Necklace and Dauber aside and whispered, "There's something about all of this that does not fit. I wish I could stop this whole damn thing. We're making a mistake rushing the interview. I can feel it."

"We can't stop now," Necklace answered.

Three hours later the equipment was in place, the cameramen positioned, and Dauber was directing from the adjoining apartment. He conducted a series of rehearsals, then made contact with New York and again tested the system.

In anticipation of being on television, the Polucci brothers had changed into their favorite outfits: white suits with white vests, purple silk shirts with yellow ties and large fake diamond tie pins, fuchsia handkerchiefs, and black and white shoes. Over their shoulders they draped long, black, double-breasted topcoats. Paolo had changed from a Nixon to a Reagan mask, but his brothers continued with Mickey Mouse.

"Everyone ready?" Tanner shouted. "We're going on. No noise, no talking." He spoke to Dauber through his headset. "Okay, Tom, tie into YOURchannel, let them know we're set, and take over."

After more conversation with the home technicians, Dauber counted down and cued Necklace. "You're on, Pearl."

"Good evening, America. This is Pearl Necklace talking to you from somewhere in Sicily ..."

"Monte Castella," Mayor Vocino interrupted, speaking off camera. Tanner frowned at him and held his finger to his lips.

Necklace continued without pausing: "And we are going to bring you a first in television news history. As we have been alerting you over the past several hours, I am with YOURchannel anchorman Larry Lincoln. As you know, he has been kidnapped and held in captivity for the past several days. He is our Hero Held Hostage and still in captivity, but we have managed to arrange a live interview with Larry to let him tell you himself what it has been like to live with his life held in balance by a gang of underworld gangsters. We're not sure what they have in store for our hero or why, but we shall soon find out through this live interview. Now you will learn all about this terrible saga from Larry himself. First, we'll take a commercial break, but don't go away. The excitement of this historical moment and dramatic story will soon unfold."

"When are you going to mention the name of our organization?" Paolo whispered to Tanner as the cameraman moved behind Necklace to get a full body view of Lincoln as the screen faded into the commercial.

"Look, people," Tanner said. "We can't have anyone talking during the interview. We must have total silence, or we'll have chaos on our hands. You must not interrupt."

"You must not interrupt," Carlo shouted to the group. He pulled out his switchblade and began cleaning his nails.

Lincoln was watching the cameraman. "Billy, would you move a little to your left? I want the camera angle to be on my right. Make sure you get some full right profile shots."

He turned to Necklace. "Let's get things straight right now. First, that was a long introduction. Second, you are to ask only the questions we went over. Don't stick in any stingers. Handle this properly and I may be able to find work for you when we return."

"Thank you. I'll stay with the script, Larry, just as we re-hearsed. Nothing new, I promise."

"Ten seconds," Dauber warned. We're opening on you, Larry. Everyone quiet. Three, two, one, take it, Pearl."

Lincoln turned his head slightly to the left as Necklace began speaking. "We're back again with Hero Held Hostage, Larry Lincoln. As you can see, his kidnappers have your favorite news anchor bound to a chair, but even in that condition he is anxious to speak to you. Larry, America is watching you right now. Waiting to hear from you. Tell your audience how you're managing this terrible ordeal."

Lincoln froze as a trickle of sweat rolled down the side of his face. Dauber spoke to him through the ear mike. "Say something, Larry, and please turn toward the camera. Tell them you're fine and then elaborate on that."

"I'm fine."

Necklace waited a few moments for Lincoln to continue. When he didn't, she quickly moved to the next question. "We're certainly happy to hear that, Larry. Everyone back home wants to know about your condition and how all of this happened? Why were you kidnapped? On your last newscast, didn't you tell your viewers that you were taking a vacation?"

"Yes, I came here on vacation to see don."

Necklace began to scramble. "Yes, the mafia don. So that's it. You told everyone you were coming here on vacation, but you were really here on an assignment—a very dangerous assignment involving the mafia. Is that right? I know you are in a life-threatening situation, but please tell us what you can … a lot more … about the real purpose of your trip here was."

Once again Dauber spoke into Lincoln's ear. "I was really here on assignment."

"Yes, I was really here on an assignment."

"And what was that assignment?" Pearl asked.

"I came to see Don Victorio 'The Brain' Marcasi, the most

powerful man in all Sicily. I had the opportunity for an exclusive interview with this man, who has ties to the underworld here and in the United States and that's what I was here for. In Sicily. With the don."

Steve Tanner stopped holding his breath as it appeared Lincoln had gained control of himself.

"You really put yourself in harm's way, Larry. What was the interview about? Can you tell us?"

"The don wanted to expose the mafia because they have put out a contract on his life. Both his father and grandfather had been dons before him, and he knows everything about the underworld, going back to the beginning of the twentieth century."

"And how did he happen to select you of all the American newsmen and news anchors?" Pearl asked.

"He chose to talk to me because of my accomplishments in the field of journalism and, of course, my television fame. You must understand that I am world famous throughout the world, especially in the United States. Word leaked out about my appearance here, and that made news in Italy. People here stopped me everywhere for autographs. That is what led to my first kidnapping."

Lincoln was on a roll now that he could repeat a story he had memorized. Words were tumbling from him with ease, but in the process of gaining self-control, he had moved completely away from the planned questions. Necklace looked at Tanner and shrugged her shoulders.

"Larry, You're telling us you were kidnapped more than once? That is something we and your viewers were not aware of."

"Alex LaRue certainly knew. When I get …"

Pearl interrupted quickly. "Tell us how you were taken."

"When I arrived at the Palermo airport, people instantly recognized me and practically mobbed me. I had to appear on television in Palermo. That's what led to the kidnapping before I met Don Marcasi and Mayor Vocino and Nina. Well, actually I met Nina later. I stopped for a dead man on the road who was not really dead and I was hit over the head from behind. When I woke, I was gagged by vicious gangsters."

"That's frightening, Larry," Necklace responded and tried to clarify Lincoln's answer. "Right here in Sicily in broad daylight. You stopped to help someone who was lying on the side of the road, and you were ambushed, tied up, and dragged to this barn."

"That's exactly what I just said, which you don't have to repeat. I can tell you have a lot to learn. Let's go on with the questions, please."

"Was that when they cut your hair?"

"Yes, that man over there did it. The one with the Mickey Mouse mask."

Tom Dauber spoke to the cameraman. "Billy, turn the camera around to show the kidnapper."

The camera and lights swung around to focus on Carlo, who turned toward the camera and raised his hand. Then he quickly grabbed the shears, opening and closing them a few times before Paolo slapped him on the back of his head.

"Camera back to Lincoln, quick!"

"See what I mean," Lincoln continued. "He's even proud of it. But it didn't frighten me. Not as much as the negotiations with my great company. I could not believe …"

Necklace broke in again. "How did you manage to escape? This is live television with no editing, Larry Lincoln, Hero Held Hostage, live from somewhere in Sicily. America is watching this show right now and waiting to hear about your escape."

"That was easy for me. I waited until they were gone and bounced the chair across the room and used the same shears to cut through the ropes. All I was thinking about was meeting with Don 'The Brain' Marcasi for the interview—an *exclusive* interview, I might add—and exposing the mafia. I managed to reach the town where I met Mayor Vocino and his beautiful granddaughter, Nina, who helped arrange the exclusive Brain interview. I mean the mayor did, not the beautiful Nina. The mayor was also taken hostage because he helped me." Lincoln paused, not knowing how to continue his story. "Can you show the mayor?"

"Hell, why not?" Dauber said from the adjoining room. "Go ahead, Billy, focus on the mayor."

The lights and camera swung around toward Mayor Vocino, and he smiled broadly. "Hello, America. I am Tomaso Vocino, the mayor of Monte Castella, garden spot of Sicily. But I will speak more of that later. This is my brother, Angelo, who owns the five-star Grand Ristorante Vocino. We were also kidnapped."

"That is our thing," shouted Paolo. "The Black Hand Mob."

Mayor Vocino glared at Paolo. "Yes, we also are Heroes Held Hostage," he continued, "but soon Don Marcasi will rescue us and make mincemeat out of Reagan here and his gang."

"That's enough, Billy, that's enough!" Dauber screamed. "Back to Lincoln. Larry, will you please face the damn camera. You look like you're talking to someone in the next room."

By this time Necklace had thrown her notes to the floor. "So now you have escaped and ..."

"I think we covered that."

"Yes, you're right. You said the mayor helped you get in contact with the don. Can you tell us something about the interview?"

"No."

"You don't want to tell us? Why not? Are you in fear for your life?"

"Miss Necklace, if that is your real name, I am not afraid of anything. I have used the time of my captivity to get to know me, to find my inner self, to touch the newsman within me, and I discovered I am really happy in my skin."

"Good for you, Larry, but what about the interview with Don Marcasi?"

"I cannot talk about Don Marcasi now because I am planning a major mafia television exposé. I, Larry Lincoln, Hero Held Hostage, have the complete interview with that criminal mastermind, Don Victorio 'The Brain' Marcasi of Monte Castella, Sicily, child of the mafia and godfather."

Lincoln's voice rose with volume and strength as he became caught up in his own oration. "I have it all on tape, and I will be showing this dynamite exclusive that I alone have exclusively and will telecast it to the American people, who have the right to know, according to the first amendment of the Constitution of the United States."

The Polucci brothers were so overwhelmed with the speech they began to clap. Tanner threw his hands to his face and dropped into a chair.

Baywatch jumped in. "Larry Lincoln will present the story first on his evening news show each night for a week, and he will follow that with a one-hour mafia television documentary that will blow viewers' minds and the lid off of crime in American."

Once again Dauber spoke to this cameraman. "Better swing over to Baywatch, Billy. I don't know why, but let's go with the flow."

Seeing the camera on him, Baywatch continued. "In fact, a mini-series is not out of the question. This is something that must not and cannot be held back, something never seen before on television, an important and historic breakthrough of enormous significance and with far-reaching implications."

"That must be one fantastic interview, Mr. and Mrs. America," Necklace shouted with excitement over the noise, "and it's one that YOURchannel's outstanding anchorman Larry Lincoln will be bringing to you soon. Good job, Larry. We'll pause now for commercials and come back with questions from our viewers."

New York

ide by side, Saxton and Handleman ran down the YOURCHANNEL hallway, shoving employees out of the way and jostling each other in the rush to be the first to burst into Ingersoll's office.

"Did you hear that idiot ranting about some insane special?" Saxton shouted. "Where the hell does he come off announcing a show that we know nothing about? What was he doing over there in the first place? The man has gone completely around the bend. This interview is a total disaster."

Handleman followed up. "I certainly didn't have anything to do with this. It's that damn Pearl Necklace. It was her idea, like … like … crossing her legs. This is an embarrassment to the news and entertainment business. I knew this was going to happen if we let Miss July have her way. Back to centerfolds for her. This is exactly what I said in the memo I wrote right after our last meeting. Everyone will find my position in their email and on my Facebook page."

Ingersoll remained seated, watching the commercials appearing on the eight-foot television screen mounted on the wall under his company theme. "I think it's the greatest news entertainment show YOURchannel has ever telecast," he said calmly, almost in reverence. "That balding oaf will get ratings we've only dreamed about. This is show business, you blathering idiots. This could be television journalism's finest hour. This will be compared with the McCarthy hearings, the moon landing. Now shut up. I don't want to miss a single moment of this."

Saxton slumped into a chair. He was sure beyond any doubt the Lincoln interview was a terrible mistake and the greatest disaster ever conceived and executed on television. Now he realized he had made a crucial error. Never before had he taken a firm stand on anything without first knowing the position of his superior. The success of his entire career was based on that moral principle. It was not his life that flashed before his eyes, it was his résumé. *I guess I'll just have to destroy Ingersoll to keep my record clean*, he thought.

In the meantime, Handleman wheeled and rushed out of the office to see if he could stop his secretary from sending his memo. In a panic he ran as fast as he could through the hallway, slamming people against the walls and over desks, intermittently screaming to his secretary not to hit the send key.

Ingersoll smiled and turned his attention back to the screen as the commercials faded to black and a beaming Larry Lincoln appeared once again.

Necklace opened: "Yes, we are back again, people, with YOURchannel anchor Larry Lincoln and the *Hero Held Hostage* show. Larry, we have just heard from New York, and they tell us that this newscast is creating a stir across the country. The American people are caught up with your sensational mafia story, your reporter's dedication to truth, and now your current dangerous dilemma in the hands of these ruthless, threatening criminals. But your fans are at your back, Larry. In fact, we have some of them on the line now, and we're going to let them talk to you directly. First, we have Marilyn from Millsboro,

Delaware, a twenty-something winner in our Talk to Our Hero contest. Go ahead with your question, Marilyn."

"Hi, Larry, Marilyn here. Right now, I'm shaking to be talking to you at this moment. I do have my question ready, but I must tell you first I think that beret is so cool. Well, that said, I'll ask my question, Mr. Anchorman, but first I must be up front about something. I don't watch your regular news show or any TV news, actually. Sorry about that but, you know, TV news is so … you know … so eighties. But I have to tell you this thing you're doing now is beyond awesome. I mean, all tied up and wondering if you'll ever get out alive."

"And your question for Larry, Marilyn?" Necklace broke in.

"Oh, yes. Larry, you said you were going to Italy on a vacation. My question is, after what you have gone through, would you still recommend taking a vacation in Italy?"

Lincoln hesitated momentarily and Mayor Vocino answered, "Before he was kidnapped, he was having a wonderful time in Monte Castella. He definitely would recommend what we call our Eden of Sicily. Right, Larry?"

"Right, Mayor Vocino," Lincoln answered.

"Who was that, Larry?"

"That was the mayor of Monte Castella, and he is also a hostage."

"Oh, my God, this is incredible. I have to ask another question, Larry. Are you allowed to tweet? I'll follow you if you do. We can mix it up. That would be great fun."

"I tweet," shouted Carlo. "@carlo_black …"

Necklace quickly interrupted. "That was one of the kidnappers, who just received a head slap," she added.

"This keeps getting better," Marilyn responded. "Tell him I'll be following him, too, if he would repeat the Twitter info. This is exciting. This is so today! Larry, you must absolutely do some selfies with each of the kidnappers or as a group and post them."

"They took my phone."

"Oh, my God, Larry, how could they do that?"

Tanner gave Necklace a cut sign. "Next, we have Jack from Chicago, Illinois. What is your question, Jack?"

"Am I really on television? Great! Say, Larry, I want to tell you how much I've enjoyed *Hero Held Hostage*, and now we have *Pearl in Peril*. So, you know, like keep it going, YOURchannel! Now my question. But first, a confession. Sorry, Larry, but like the last caller, I don't catch television news either. I mean, all those drug commercials. It's like watching a nursing home. But I haven't missed a day since your kidnapping and since that babe took over. Talk about hot, man."

"Thank you," Necklace responded sharply. "Do you have a question?"

"Oh, did I touch a button there? Oh, yeah, Larry, when will your Italian tell-all show be on? I'm planning a mafia party at the local pub to watch it. We're going to do this right. Suits out of the thirties, weapons, gangster videos, music from Berlin, Gershwin, Porter, the works. I'll post it on YouTube."

"I'll take that one," Baywatch interrupted. "Thank you, Jack. You can expect the special to be announced the day Larry is released. Our freedom negotiations are well underway, and Larry will soon be back in front of the camera, anchoring away as always. Stay with YOURchannel television for details."

"What about Pearl? Who was that?" the viewer asked.

"Okay, Jack, thank you," Necklace cut in. "We now have Sarah from Oak Ridge, Tennessee. Go ahead Sarah."

"My name is Baywatch, agent to the stars," Baywatch shouted.

"What was that?" Sarah asked.

"Go ahead, Sarah. We had a little unwanted interruption," Necklace answered.

Sarah responded. "Larry, you cannot imagine how angry I am. I'm boiling over. I watch your show every night, sometimes with the ladies from our bridge club, and I want to tell you, we've got your back on this unspeakable crime. This is an attack not only against you but against all newsmen, and I'm not going to sit back and take it. Our club has already started a fund for the erection of the Tomb of the Unknown Anchor. I hope to have it placed right there on the DC Basin. We'll dedicate it to you. God bless you, Larry, and may He bring you back alive, but if not, there's the tomb. That's all I have to say."

"That's a great idea," Lincoln answered.

Necklace followed up. "Yes, that's terrific, Sarah, and thank you. That's a marvelous plan you have. Go for it. We'll pause now for a commercial. Much more to come, America, so stay with us."

Steve Tanner took his hands from his face, rose, and moved quietly out of the room. During the last commercial, he had taken a phone call from YOURchannel informing him of the vast audience that was tuned in. "I have to get some air," he whispered to Pearl. "I need to look at the stars."

He walked out onto the driveway, pulled a cigar butt from his pocket, which he had snuffed out earlier, and lit it with a trembling hand. The evening and countryside were black, and he had no difficulty in finding the Big Dipper, his favorite constellation. He followed the star line to the North Star, on which he had always focused whenever he needed to regain his equilibrium. "It's not even a question any longer," he said aloud. "It was held in check at one time, but it started seeping in under the door like smoke preceding a fire. Then suddenly it blew the door away." He sent a puff of cigar smoke toward the star.

"Where do you think you're going?" asked Gianni, shattering the silence. He had followed Tanner out of the house and was now standing directly behind him, pressing a gun into his back. "No one is to leave here, by order of Don Paolo."

Tanner turned and looked at the Mickey Mouse face for a few moments. The moon cast a light on the mask, transforming Mickey's smile into a grotesque sneer. "No more," he said and pushing the gun aside, he slammed his fist into Mickey's nose, sending Gianni tumbling backward, tripping and falling to the ground. "Mickey, you'll never know how much better that makes me feel." He stepped over the fallen kidnapper and returned to the interview.

"You broke my Mickey nose," Gianni screamed.

"We're going back on," Dauber warned. "Counting down. Three, two, one. You're on, Pearl."

"Welcome back, America, to the *Hero Held Hostage* show and more conversations with YOURchannel's star newsman. Larry, can you tell us how you were kidnapped a second time?"

"That's a silly question. Of course, I can. After the interview with the don, the mayor was driving us back to Palermo, and a truck slammed into us and we were surrounded by a dozen men with Uzis. We were unarmed and could not fight back. We were brought here, and then I was forced to listen to despicable, unbelievable ransom calls from my ..."

"You've been through some terrible experiences," Necklace interrupted, "all in pursuit of a story. No wonder you have such a loyal audience at YOURchannel. Larry, we now have on the line that famous television star and celebrity interviewer, Kingmaker, calling from Miami. I'm sure he ..."

"No intro needed for me," he interrupted. "Lincoln, you're a sensation, and I must have you on my show. You're the man right now. Not near the top yet, but you're climbing, celebrity-wise. What I want to do now, in front of the millions who are watching, is invite you to appear on my show the minute you get back. Here's my question. Do I have a commit? My show first."

"You've got it!" shouted Baywatch.

"That was my agent, Burt Baywatch," Lincoln followed. "I guess we just committed."

"Good man! I'll send you my ratings to give you an idea of my power. It'll show what a smart move you've made. You might think about preparing some kind of political announcement when you're with me. Remember my power in recent elections."

"We're way ahead of you, Kingmaker," answered Baywatch.

Ingersoll leaped out of his chair. "What the hell is he doing? He can't commit to being on some show without our approval. We own that bald eagle. Who's the goddamn ventriloquist who keeps answering the questions?" He pressed the intercom. "Janet, get Legal in here right now and tell him to bring Lincoln's contract."

"Larry, we have your mother on the phone," Necklace cut in. "Go ahead, Mrs. Lincoln. Your son is waiting to hear from you."

"The name is Pendal, Miss Show-It-All. Larry, you've been putting on a little weight. All that kidnapping has done wonders for you. I know there are millions watching, but tell me, have they hurt you, son?"

"No, Mom. I'm fine."

"That's good but I do worry. Especially when you don't call. Who is Nina?"

"You don't have to worry about me, Mom, but you have to understand I've been held in captivity and I do not have a phone. I'm the Hero Held Hostage. Remember?"

"Oh, that's right. I'm sorry, dear. I realize it is difficult to call your mother. The Italians don't have phones, I suppose. What about Nina? I suppose you call her."

"She's a wonderful girl, Mom. How is Dad taking this? I hope he's not worried."

"He's fine, dear. He said to say hello and give his best to that Pearl Necklace."

"Mom, I must say goodbye now. They want me to take other calls. I'll phone as soon as possible."

"Whenever you can, dear. I understand."

"Larry, we have another famous television talk show host, Dianiana, waiting to talk to you. You're really a hot item."

"Hello, Mr. Celebrity. I heard you telling Kingmaker you might be on his show. Put that on hold. He's cable! You must come on my show, *News As Entertainment*. Larry, with me you get network broadcasting and ratings that guy wouldn't get if he had Dr. Phil doing a strip. Don't forget, Mr. Hot News, I've got the ratings. Here's my question. Can I put you on my schedule?"

"You've got it, Dianiana!" Baywatch said. "Slot us in, but it has to be for no less than twenty minutes. And we're not sharing time with some serial killer."

"I'll agree to that, but I have to tell you, serial killers bring great ratings and mine are …"

Necklace interrupted. "Isn't anyone screening these calls? Okay, we're back with YOURchannel viewers, and it's Henry from Dallas, Larry."

"Mr. Lincoln, I just graduated from high school and I want to be a television newsman. I hear you guys really get the babes. Is that true?"

"You'll have to work hard if you want to be in this business, Henry. Be sure to take all the right journalism courses: diction, voice and emotion projection, facial expressions, grooming. What college are you planning to attend, Henry?"

"Harvard."

"Good school, Henry. Nothing wrong with that choice if you want to be a funds manager. For a career in journalism …"

"Don't take that advice too seriously, Henry," Pearl said, breaking in. "Larry, we now have Representative Johnny Ray Jamison, chairman of the Foreign Relations Committee. You're really scoring with the heavy hitters. Go ahead, Congressman."

"Larry Lincoln, I am shocked and outraged by this whole

situation, but I'm not surprised. I've been warning this country about Cuba for a long time now. They're not getting away with this. This is a slap in the face of every American."

"Senator, I'm in Sicily."

"I'm going for an embargo. It'll be a lesson to the world that you don't go kidnapping an American anchorman. Hang in there, Larry. I'll get you out."

"Okay, Larry, one last question. We've got George on the line from Houston, Texas. Larry is ready for you, George."

"Hey, Larry, great show, but I'm a little disappointed."

"What's the problem, George?"

"I was expecting to see some pain. You know, maybe a little electricity or a fist into your face. Like with blood splattering. All the ads promised brutality."

"I can do that," Carlo said and started to walk toward Lincoln, but Paolo grabbed him.

"George, all of the torture has been psychological except for the gash where they cut my hair."

"Can you show us that?"

Necklace cut in. "Just time for one more call, Larry. We have Mr. Informed Sources himself on the line."

"Larry, this is Frank of *Guess What?* magazine. Right now I'm looking at a mock-up of next week's cover and it's all you. Before we go with it, we have to be guaranteed an exclusive. We'll give you six pages, I promise. We already have your mom and dad locked up. We have every picture they ever took of you. Same with your boyhood friends, girlfriends, and fellow employees. But like I said, we need an exclusive."

"That's all the time we have now," said Necklace before Baywatch could answer. "The kidnappers are telling us to shut down the interview."

"Wait a minute," shouted Mayor Vocino. "I have something to say about the kidnappers."

Necklace turned to Tanner for an answer.

"Why not? We seem to be doing everything right."

"We have been given permission to interview one of the other hostages here," Necklace said. "He is Tomaso Vocino, mayor of the town of Monte Castella. He is the man responsible for bringing together Larry Lincoln and Don Victorio 'The Brain' Marcasi. Mayor Vocino, why did these men kidnap you?"

"For twenty-five years I have been mayor of the beautiful town of Monte Castella, a town that has become a mecca for tourists, located in the center of the wine country, a town that offers a delightful mixture of the past and present, grand splendor, simple charm, and safe streets.

"The most famous man to come to our town was General George Patton. He chose to stay here before resuming the campaign to take Palermo in 1943. Before that we had the Vikings, Phoenicians, Greeks, Carthaginians, Romans, Arabs, and French, each adding their unique touch of romance and historic wonders. Tourists can enjoy all of this plus a trip to the home of the boss of bosses in Sicily, that most famous mafia celebrity, Don Carmine Marcasi. They can also take selfies with Don Marcasi."

"And meet members of the Black Hand Mob," shouted Paolo.

"Can you tell us about the infamous Black Hand Mob, Mayor?" Necklace asked.

"They are a ragtag bunch whom the don will soon wipe out. This kidnapping of Mr. Lincoln and us is their last criminal act. After that, no more kidnappings. Unless, of course, travel agents want to include that as part of their tour packages. Everything can be arranged by the Monte Castella Tourist Council. You can follow us on Facebook, Twitter, and soon …"

"Thank you, Mayor Vocino."

"I might add one last thing," the mayor continued. "We are expecting a Hollywood movie to be made right here in Monte Castella in the very near future. The film script is on the desk of the most famous American film director right now just waiting for his approval."

"Thank you, Mayor Vocino," Necklace shouted. "That wraps up our interview with our Hero Held Hostage, Larry Lincoln, live from Sicily. We'll now switch you back to our regular programming."

Ingersoll turned the television off. "That was fantastic," he said. "We have a mega hit on our hands."

Sanford, the president of Legal Affairs, was standing at the desk, holding Lincoln's contract. "We'll have no problem, George. We have him completely locked up. He can't do anything without our approval."

"Good. Now, first things first. Find out about that movie script that the mayor just mentioned. I want it. YOURchannel is going Hollywood. It will be our movie and available only through YOURchannel. If my guess is right, we have a star on our hands. And see if you can get that Don The Brain guy under contract."

"I'll look into it right away."

Later that night, after finishing dinner and a good number of drinks at his club, William Saxton returned to his office. He had enjoyed the evening primarily because he had used every minute planning the destruction of CEO Ingersoll and advancing his own future. There was no way he was going to allow one tactical error blemish his otherwise spotless career. He felt what he was about to do could very well find its way into a business school textbook as a classic lesson to be learned in advancing an executive's career.

He marched down the empty hallway to his office, switched on the lights, and went directly to his computer to bring up what he considered his masterpiece letter to Arnold Schumbeck, CEO of the conglomerate that owns YOURchannel. He read it over once, added a few more incendiary paragraphs, and hit the print key. Picking up the finished document, he moved quickly to LaRue's office. He slid his hands into surgical gloves and typed the memo into LaRue's computer. After a final reading, editing, and spellcheck, he added LaRue's name and emailed the letter to Schumbeck. Then he filed the letter into several folders.

With a sardonic chuckle, he brought up a clean screen and started pounding in the final nail.

Dear Mrs. Ingersoll:

It is with a heavy heart that I write this letter, a letter that will shock you and cause great disappointment and pain. It concerns your husband's behavior away from home. I bring this to your attention only because I have always admired you not only for being faithful to your husband but also for the way you sacrificed your career in Hollywood and Las Vegas to devote your life to serving and supporting him throughout the long two years of your marriage.

I find it difficult knowing where to start, aware of the hurt this will cause due to your innocence and sensitivity. Should I begin with the mistresses he is keeping in Chicago and New York? Or mention his dalliances in Europe and an unspeakable escapade in Japan in January? No, those sordid stories would only serve to pierce your heart. Nor will I go into his reputation among the actresses, secretaries, waitresses, and sales girls in this city. Besides, too much detail would only move this man's sexual activities beyond belief.

No longer can I sit back and allow you to be so injured. It simply breaks my heart and probably yours,

too. There is much more but I cannot go on. I am sure
you have heard enough.

I hope you will not think me presumptuous when I
suggest the law firm of Lewis, Hartfield, and Strang.
You will find them sensitive, caring and successful.

Thinking of your welfare only, I remain a friend.

Alex LaRue

Saxton emailed and faxed the letter to Ingersoll's home and
sent a copy to Schumbeck. Then he printed several copies, which
he tore up and threw into the wastepaper basket. After hitting
the save key and filing the letter in the same folders holding the
Schumbeck letter, he shut down the computer, slipped on his
jacket, and with a skip to his step, walked out of the office.

Monte Castella

"Let's wrap this thing up and get out of here," Tanner said as he walked across the room and began to untie Lincoln.

"Not so fast," said Paolo. "He stays here."

"What are you talking about? The deal was to release him once the interview was over. You've been paid."

"He's right," said Lincoln. "I'm not spending another minute here."

"I make the rules here. I work only with Mr. LaRossi. He made the deal, and the deal was to keep him until he says to let him go. He's the money man, and I deal only with the money man."

"Then call the son of a bitch!" shouted Lincoln. "He'll tell you to release me. You have the money."

Paolo walked up to Lincoln and grabbed him by his collar. "You are dealing with the Black Hand Mob, and you don't give orders to Don Paolo, leader of the Black Hand Mob. That could be dangerous. If I decide to call him, I will decide to call him." He paused to look at his watch. "I have decided to call him. But in private." Paolo began to leave, then stopped and turned to his brothers. "Make sure the hostages remain tied. The rest of you must leave."

Paolo walked to another guest room and dialed LaRue's

number. "Mr. LaRossi, how did you like the show? Did you see us on television?"

"I certainly did, Paolo. You were fantastic. Great outfit. Which one was you?"

"President Reagan. But enough of that. I have business to discuss. They want to take Lincoln with them. Is that what you want? Should I request more ransom money from them?"

"No more money, Paolo! Remember our deal. I can't give you an answer on releasing Lincoln. I must talk to the chief about that. He may want to see the ratings first. Better hold him for another day. No more money, though."

"What about the television people?"

"Talk to Steve Tanner, he is the one in charge. Tell him to call George Ingersoll as soon as possible. He'll let them know what to do. By the way, who the hell is Mayor Vocino, and what is he doing there?"

"That is our thing. None of your business."

"Whatever you say, pal. Ciao!"

Tanner and his crew were packing up the van when Paolo approached them. "Lincoln and the other guy stay here one more day. The mayor and his brother can leave if they agree to pay the ransom. That is between us. One more thing. You are to call Mr. Big for instructions right away. Mr. LaRossi said to tell you he liked the show." Without waiting for a response, he turned and walked toward the barn.

"I have a bad feeling why Ingersoll wants to talk to me, a bad feeling about everything. I think we've been taken. The whole interview came off as a ruse. I'm beginning to wonder if the kidnapping was faked. I can't quite figure that part out. Larry isn't bright enough to pull off something this big. It's beyond him. And who is this Don Marcasi? Maybe Baywatch dreamed everything up, but I never thought he was that smart."

"The kidnapping had to have been real," Dauber said. "Larry would never have allowed them to cut his hair."

"They certainly were a happy group of hostages," Necklace added. "Did you notice how loosely they were tied? As for the interview, good God, if it weren't on television, no one in the world would have believed it. And that Black Hand Mob! They couldn't kidnap each other."

"How did you like the mayor with his travelogue?" laughed Dauber. "The entire thing has an odor to it. However, we have to stay with the story at this point."

"You say it stinks and you still want us to continue taking part in this charade," snapped Tanner. "Try to remember we're news people!"

"It's only television, Steve," Necklace answered. "Don't take it so seriously. Alright, the interview may have been a bit of a sham, but he really was kidnapped, and he really was held for ransom. So what if our interview came after the ransom was paid? We're covered. Don't blow it now. Let's play it out and see where it goes. We're building an audience. We always have the option of exposing it later. Along with all the things you've been complaining about."

"I don't know. I'll have to think about it. I understand what you're saying, but I don't really feel good. It's always a means to an end. This isn't what I set out to do in the beginning." Tanner lit his cigar and walked slowly away from the group. As he reached the van, he stopped suddenly and broke out in a laugh.

"What's so funny?" Dauber asked.

"Well, here I was contemplating the ethical considerations of continuing this charade, which we all think smells to high heaven, and guess what popped into my mind? I couldn't help myself. I began to think about the ratings! I'm wondering how good the ratings for the show are, how far our reach. There it is! This is what we do. Let's get to a phone. Ingersoll wants me to call him, and I'm sure it will be about the ratings."

"First, let's go somewhere to eat," Dauber said. "We can call for the numbers later. Any ideas?"

"Not back to Palermo; it's too far. How about Monte Castella? President Reagan said the mayor is free to go if he pays the ransom. He can guide us. You heard him say there's no better hotel and restaurant in all Sicily than the Grand Hotel Vocino."

After leaving the television crew, Paolo climbed the stairs to the loft, straightened his shoulders, and jauntily strolled into the room doing a good imitation of James Cagney. With his confidence surging, he was ready to shake down Mayor and Angelo Vocino, having in mind an interest in their hotel and restaurants. *We must break out from just kidnapping*," he thought. *A good mob has many sources of income, and the protection racket is a good place to start.*

His thoughts changed instantly when he entered the room and saw Carlo and Gianni tied to the chairs with socks stuffed in their mouths. He wheeled around and headed for the stairway but ran into the door that Angelo had quietly closed behind him.

"Have a seat, Paolo," Mayor Vocino said calmly. "It is time we have a little talk, a discussion about money." He grabbed Paolo, pulled him to a chair, and shoved him down hard. Paolo's bravado started to ebb as he looked up at the four men staring down at him. However, he tried not to show any signs of weakness.

Angelo was the first to speak. "Mr. Lincoln, you see before you the Black Hand Mob. They're the don's bodyguards! They were to protect you and the don. Instead, they turned on both of you. You can't trust anyone these days. If Don Marcasi allows these three fools to live, they can look forward to spending the remainder of their lives in jail."

Carlo and Gianni shook their heads violently while releasing garbled sounds of protest.

"You are not treating us with respect," Paolo said. "We are men of honor. After tonight, we are also celebrities. We have been on television."

"Let me read him his rights," said Baywatch.

Mayor Vocino said, "He has only one right, the right to talk about the ransom money. I must ask you not to lie. For your sake, don't lie. Now, without hesitation, tell us how much money you have collected from the American television company."

Paolo again released a Sidney Greenstreet laugh, which he had enjoyed so much listening to in *The Maltese Falcon*. Imitating it had always worked to build up his courage. "You'll never get Don Paolo Gaetano 'The Boss' Polucci to talk."

Angelo Vocino raised his open hand. "Which side of his head do you want me to smash in?" He did not wait for an answer, but instead, initiated the blow. Paolo lurched back in anticipation and stumbled backward over the chair and onto the floor. From that position he looked up at the two Vocino brothers glaring down at him.

"Okay, okay. It wasn't really a lot of money. We collected a million dollars from Mr. Lincoln plus another five hundred thousand from the television people. Mr. Lincoln will tell you, they are very cheap people. Even when we threatened to cut off his ear, they wouldn't pay."

Without saying a word Angelo put his foot on Paolo's chest, initiating a quick response.

"Maybe it was a little higher." Angelo applied weight.

"Two and a half million," Paolo screamed.

There was a moment of silence; then Baywatch whistled and Angelo silently removed his foot from Paolo's chest.

Lincoln was the first to speak. "Are you saying they paid you two and a half million dollars to kidnap me a second time and interview me after they refused pay a dime to get me free in the first place? Even though they had my hair? How is it possible? How could they do that? My company, my co-workers, my friends."

"You think I should have held out for more?" Paolo asked.

"No, Paolo, you did just fine," Baywatch answered. "This is just what we need. Now it's time to talk about who gets what and make plans for the future."

"That's our money," Paolo said. "It is the property of the Black Hand Mob. It's in our bank. We earned it."

"Listen, you fool," Angelo Vocino snapped, "you are facing a hundred years in jail for kidnapping, assault, blackmail, and ridiculing a president of the United States. Don't even consider holding on to that money."

"Gentlemen," said Baywatch, "my mind is bursting with new ideas. With that money and the interview, the doors are going to swing open. What I talked about before is just the beginning. Larry. What do you think about the name Ahab Whaleslayer? Biblical but modern. I could dress like Gregory Peck in that whale movie—long coat, high hat. Would that be cool or what?"

"Right now I want to talk about my million-dollar dinner."

Mayor Vocino turned to Lincoln and smiled. "Excellent idea, Mr. Lincoln. I will call my restaurant and have dinner brought here to the Black Hand Inn. I suggest a light meal of minestra di ceci, gnocchi di patate alla montano, filetti di sogliole, and with our espresso, torta di mele. Along with the finest wine we can find in the cellar. We must celebrate ... and split the spoils.

"Mr. LaRossi said you and the mayor are free to go," Paolo said to Angelo, happy to change the discussion about money. "They are probably waiting for you."

"That's good, also," Tomaso answered. "We will still have the food delivered here, and we can dine with your people in town and tell them more about Monte Castella. Let's go, Angelo. The money discussion will have to wait."

"Hold on a minute," said Baywatch. "Tie up Larry again in the chair. I need to get a few photos for the autobiography."

"What autobiography?" Lincoln screamed.

"Not to worry. You'll love it. I wish I could have taken some of you with Pearl Necklace. What a book jacket cover she would make. God, she's beautiful!"

"I didn't think she looked that good. What book jacket?" Lincoln answered sharply. "Another thing—the way she handled my interview was amateurish. Luckily, I was able to cover for her inexperience."

"We should be in the pictures, too," said Paolo. "All three of us standing behind him."

After registering at the mayor's Grand Hotel Vocino, the YOURchannel crew separated and went to their rooms, agreeing to meet in an hour for dinner. An exhausted Steve Tanner threw himself across the bed and stared at the ceiling. He wasn't sure whether it was jet lag or the events of the past week that were making him feel so unstable. His mind drifted back to when he first decided to risk his job by throwing a spotlight on television news reporting, and suddenly here he was, lying on a bed in a small town in Sicily, preparing to phone his office to discover what the ratings were on an absurd interview involving cartoon criminals. This is not what he planned. Somehow he had lost control of events after the first broadcast, and the events were in charge.

Now I know what whitewatering on the Colorado feels like, he thought. Deciding it was not the time to get out of the raft, he rolled to the side of the bed and picked up the phone.

"Steve, I've been waiting for your call," Ingersoll responded. "The show was a hit. More than that, a damn smash. Pearl's idea of an interview was inspirational. The phone lines have been jumping from the minute the screen faded to black. Everything positive. If our instant survey is correct, we have scored a ratings sensation."

Tanner felt pleasure and guilt at the same time. "It didn't come off as being staged? I was worried about the Black Hand Mob thing. And the mayor and his brother."

"Are you kidding? They were great. Especially the mob guys with those wonderful masks and outlandish outfits. A lot of the calls coming in are asking about them. That's what I want to talk to you about."

Tanner slumped back across the bed. He knew instantly where this conversation was heading and he didn't feel good about it. "Not another interview."

"Hell, yes, another interview. This story is just beginning to boil, and from the Twitter feeds we're getting we need more exposure of the Black Hand Mob. I get the feeling they touched a nerve with the viewers. I'd like to see that Don what's-his-name. Could you get him on the show for a few minutes. I don't want to lose the audience just interviewing Lincoln. Who the hell is Don anyway, and how did Lincoln get hooked up with him?"

"Wait a minute. Another interview would be nothing but an obviously staged show—a sham, a farce, deception."

"So?"

"I know the first one was staged, but we walked into that, and it couldn't be helped. But another one would be pushing it too far. It would be show business, pure entertainment."

"So?"

"I mean, this was definitely a news story, remember? Our anchor was really kidnapped and really held for ransom. It was a news event. We covered it on our evening news."

"So?"

"We're turning basic news coverage into a prime time mini-series … or a reality show."

"Now you've got it, Steve. For a minute there I thought we lost you. Must be jet lag. I'm glad you're back on board. But first things first. Tell me more about this Don Cassidy."

"It's Don Marcasi."

"Whatever. Don't get technical on me."

"It seems that Larry wasn't coming here for a vacation at all. Somehow he—or his agent—had arranged a meeting with Don Marcasi to do a taped interview. He is alleged to be a mafia chief here and in the United States. The interview was supposed to be an exposé of organized crime. That's about all I know at this time. Larry has the whole interview on record."

"Wait a moment, Steve. Don't play games with me. You want me to understand that our Larry Lincoln, the one who wants larger type and smaller words on the prompter, set up an exclusive interview with a member of the underworld to expose the mob? All on his own? The same Larry Lincoln who got punched when he tried to talk to people on the street? And he has it all recorded?"

"That's our Larry. Don't ask me to explain it. However, I think we have to credit much of this to his agent."

"Miracle of miracles. Remind me to buy that new prompter. Anyway, forget that for now. First things first. Set up another interview and get the Black Hand guys to play a bigger role. Try some new masks. We must not let this thing get stale. Don't forget about Don."

"Don is his title, not his name."

"There you go again."

"Wait a minute, George. From what I hear, the Black Hand Mob is part of a gang that's trying to get rid of the don. They're enemies. We were told the don wants to kill them and now you want me to somehow get Don Marcasi and the Black Hand Mob together on the same show?"

"You say he wants to kill them? Fantastic! Any chance he might do it during the show? If you pull that off, I'll give you the biggest bonus this company has ever thought about plus a month vacation."

Ingersoll jumped up from his chair and climbed onto his desk. "Steve, I'm vibrating over this thing. Can you feel it? I'm standing on top of my Jefferson solid walnut desk and I'm tap dancing. Listen. Can you hear the taps? Got to get off the phone now. My phone lines are blinking like a Christmas tree. You're doing a terrific job. Hey, I almost forgot. I heard another network is sending their anchor to Sicily to cover this story. They've dropped everything for this. We're hot, Steve. Blistering, boiling hot! I have to hang up. A herd of reporters just came in. They're screaming for a chance to interview Lincoln. So go, go, go. This is giving us unbelievable television, newspaper, magazine, Internet, and social media coverage. Oh, don't forget to tell Lincoln about his new prompter. Can you hear me dancing, Steve? Can you just hear the sound of happy feet? Ciao!"

Tanner pulled the phone away from his ear but he could still hear the tapping of leather heels pounding against the desk. He closed his eyes, hoping a few minutes of rest would clear his mind and have everything that was happening make sense.

While waiting for the dinner to be delivered, Baywatch borrowed a pad and pen from Paolo and started making notes. "So much to do," he muttered to himself. "Got to get my ideas down and organized." He filled a good number of pages, then stood up and moved to the door. "Gentlemen, I need to make a number of contacts to get things rolling back in the States, and for that I need a little privacy. Can't waste a minute."

"If you make a run for it, Lincoln suffers," Paolo warned.

Baywatch crossed his heart, walked to another room and called one of his former clients. "Hello, Karl," he shouted, assuming that transatlantic calls would make hearing difficult. "Burt Baywatch here. Long time no see. How's my favorite writer doing?"

"Fine, but why are you screaming?"

"Sorry about that. Listen, I have no time for chitchat. I've got something big for you. You're still writing, aren't you?"

"Of course, you must know I've been quite successful since I hired a new agent."

"I'll ignore that. Like I said, this is a big one, Karl. This one will make you famous. Top of the heap, I guarantee, but you have to drop whatever crap you're working on. I need an autobiography like tomorrow. About a hundred and fifty pages. Nothing thicker. Around $29.95 with loads of pictures. Should be no more than a three-hour read for someone with dyslexia."

"Do I need to know whose autobiography it is?"

"I don't need a smartass right now. I need a writer with flair, pizzazz, humor, fun. You're the man!"

"I really hate that line, Burt. I really do."

"I'll never use it again. Listen, Karl, be sure to punch in some of the old Horatio Alger stuff. You know, boy rises from the suburbs, upper middle class childhood, to become the top dog in his field. Stay away from anything controversial. No politics, no religious stuff, but get God in and faith and mankind. You can steam up a few chapters with sex. You know a few actresses who will let you use their names."

"Okay, I know the formula, but who the hell am I writing about?"

"Larry Lincoln, the hottest merchandise in the country right now. That's why I must have this within a week—no later. Got to move while the fire's blazing. The title will be *Hero Held Hostage*."

"Talk to me about money and percentages."

"You should be talking to me about the chance of a lifetime."

"That was when you were my agent. I'm asking a hundred thousand up front plus expenses and ten percent royalty against a guarantee of two hundred thousand. I'm holding it down because you're an old friend."

"I can remember a time when you would have taken this on for a good dinner. You were nobody when I first met you."

"I was still a nobody when I fired you."

"There's no reason to get nasty. I'll wire the money as soon as I get back to the States. Fifty thousand up front, five percent royalty, and a guarantee of one hundred and fifty thousand. Can you promise it to me in eight days? I guaranteed the publishers it would be ready. They're holding the presses."

"No problem. I'll go half way: fifty front, ten percent royalty and still the guarantee of two hundred and fifty. Are you going to give me any facts or leave the whole thing up to me?"

"I'll outline him for you. Larry was born in Los Angeles,

went to high school there, college at UCLA, supporting himself as a model. After that, modeling full time and then work in local television in a number of cities around the country for a few years, doing everything from weather to sports to news reading. Made the big time with YOURchannel. You can fill in the rest. Make up some hard-hitting reporter stuff."

"Like the time he was punched trying a simple man-on-the-street interview? As I remember, it went big on YouTube."

"You can skip that. Contact his parents for some puff and pictures. Contact Alex LaRue at YOURchannel for photos. Nothing too current, though. You know ... the hair problem. Tell him Steve Tanner gave the approval. They have a ton on Larry with celebrities and politicians. Really go heavy on the celebrity angle. Loads of pictures and quotes about what a great anchorman they think Larry is. They'll let you quote them all you want as long as you use their photos."

"Don't tell me my business, Burt. I'll start today, but if I don't have the money in seven days, I stop and turn it into my own authorized biography. A deal?"

"I feel like I'm talking to a banker. Yes, it's a deal. You'll get the money. Money is not a problem. Hey, I hate to cut you off, but I've got a zillion things to do, and this call is costly. I'm in Sicily."

"I know. I saw that ridiculous interview on television. Larry looks like he put on some weight and lost some hair. I bet that beret was your idea."

"You're right, and I'm going to make that beret famous. I have beaucoup photos that I've taken here. Leave room for them."

"Make sure you get some with Pearl Necklace. That leg crossing would be sensational."

"I can't get that, and I wouldn't dare ask her to duplicate the pose. She'd deck me. By the way, the story should end with a triumphal return at JFK. Arrange to have a photographer there to get complete coverage. That's it for now. Do a good job on this and I'll have another Lincoln book ready for you as soon as I return.

Some self-help stuff. Have to cut it off now, Karl. They're waiting for me. I almost forgot. Don't be bashful about playing heavily on my part in his success. Ciao!"

Baywatch hung up and immediately made another call, this time to a newspaper gossip columnist.

"Telly Tattle here," she answered. "Telly's the name, tattle's my game."

"Telly, baby, this is Burt Baywatch. Long time no see. Are you still sugar and spice and everything nice?"

"Burtie, dear, great to hear from you. I saw you on the show, and it was sensational. You've struck the mother lode. What can you give me and only me? No used material or I'll cut you in little pieces."

"Telly, you're the first person I've called. You're getting virgin publicity material, but you must promise to give us the lead-in story in your column. Larry's name in bold type whenever you use it. Not just once."

"Don't tell me how to write, Burt, just give me something juicy."

"Okay, here it is, and you're the only person to know this. Larry Lincoln, Hero Held Hostage, will have his autobiography in the book stores within a month."

"That's it! You call that juicy? Come on, Burt. That's fluff. It's too obvious. Besides, I never plug in the first paragraph. It's one of the ethics I live by. I'll give it paragraph three, and that's all it deserves. I won't give it anything if that's all there is. I need something personal for an insider story lead and headline."

"Okay, but this is something Larry wanted to keep a lid on, and he'll wring my neck when he finds out I leaked it."

"Now you're talking my game," Telly Tattle answered, warming up to the prospect of a hot celebrity column.

Baywatch paused a moment to think of a story line. "Are you ready? Here it is. While in captivity, Larry met and fell head over heels in love with this Italian beauty. Her name is Nina, and she's a knockout, a stunning Latin beauty. I'm talkin' Sophia and Gina rolled into one, Telly. Here's the real story. She was actually instrumental in saving his life. She practically threw herself on top of him. You can take that any way you want. Give it the Pocahontas and John what's-his-name angle. You can't say where you got this."

"I never do, sweetheart. This is good. I'll fill in the details. It'll be four paragraphs. Do you have a quote from Larry I can use?"

Baywatch told her what Lincoln had said about finding and liking himself. "Don't forget the autobiography. It will be a tell-all. Lots of Hollywood and New York celebrity-and-sex stuff. The works."

"Who's doing the writing?"

"Karl Kasper. You know him?"

"Of course I know Karl. He's one of the best autobiographical writers around today. I've plugged several of his books. By the way, do you have anything on Pearl Necklace? She's hot news. Like is she banging anyone?"

"I don't know. I just met her, but we're talking agent contract already. You know me. No grass under a rolling stone. Listen, I would love to talk on, but things are popping fast over here. I'll stay in touch. Ciao!"

No sooner had Baywatch signed off when his phone rang. "When you're hot, you're hot," he said to himself. "Baywatch here."

"This is Perkie Perky of the *Glorious Good Morning* television show. You're Larry Lincoln's agent, right? I was expecting a call from you. Let's get to it. Tell me when you're coming back, and I'll clear fifteen minutes if Lincoln appears on my show before any of the other morning trash. Don't ask for pay because we don't play that game. Maybe some healthy expense coverage. What do you say? Do we deal?"

"You're on. I'll call you the minute we hit New York."

"Good. If you mess me up on this, you and any client you

might have over the next twenty-five years will never be allowed in the lobby of this network. Got that? I'm in the middle of a multi-million-dollar contract renewal, and I don't need any dead-beats fouling me up right now. Do you read me?"

"I got the message. You don't have a thing to …" He heard the phone slam down. "So that's Perkie Perky."

Baywatch signed off and turned to look in the mirror. "Everything's falling into place," he said, speaking to his image. "I knew it was only a matter of time, you genius. It was my fate, my kismet, my Minerva. Who could have predicted my big score would come with Larry Lincoln? Maybe I should have told Karl to begin writing my own book. Ahab Whaleslayer, *The Art of the Agent*. That's good, that's really good."

Never had Baywatch felt so happy, so sure of himself and his future. Before he could continue his conversation and self-con-gratulations, his phone rang again. "Excuse me a moment, Ahab, my audience awaits."

"Ciao, baby, talk to me."

"Things have taken a bad turn, Mr. Baywatch," a frantic Angelo Vocino answered. "Things have gone crazy here. The lobby is loaded with paparazzi. They want pictures of Mr. Lincoln. In fact, they want him."

"Fantastic! We'll hold a first news conference. Tomorrow he'll be on the front page of every American newspaper. This is won-derful, Angelo. We couldn't ask for anything better."

"No, no, You have forgotten, we are prisoners. They also want pictures of Don Marcasi. And something else: Those interview people are staying here. They're in their rooms right now. This thing has taken a bad turn. We will be exposed."

"What are you talking about … exposed? What's to expose? Expose is good. Expose is my business. That's what I do. Listen, Larry Lincoln, the famous American anchor, was kidnapped while doing an interview with the notorious mafia godfather,

Don Marcasi. Ransom paid, he's free. That's the plain truth. So what's to expose?"

Baywatch's joy began fading away. He detected something in Angelo's voice he had not heard before. "You sound so nervous, Angelo. What's the matter? Is there something you're not telling me?" He waited for an answer but all he heard was a click.

At the restaurant entrance, Steve Tanner and his team came to a sudden stop. There was Nina, moving about in the center of the room, laughing and posing, surrounded by a crowd of photographers, whose cameras were flashing as they followed her, capturing her every movement. He grabbed Pearl's arm and swung around.

"Let's get the hell out of here. Let's go to the Vocino restaurant down the street." As they moved away from the chaos, they heard Nina shout with delight, "I didn't say he was my lover. I said we were just good friends."

New York

America awoke to a news media blitz covering the Lincoln television interview. It was the story of the day. No newspaper, talk radio host, or television program dared to be left out, and it went immediately to the Internet and social media, achieving numbers rarely matched by a news story. The fear of not being on top of this event coupled with the spreading recognition of Lincoln as the new fifteen-minute celebrity kept opposing news staffs working in a frenzy throughout the night developing logos, graphics, story themes, and exclusive story lines.

In a state of panic, reporters were assembled, formed into teams with assignments, and immediately dispatched. Television and radio talk shows had their bookers frantically working the phones to get anyone personally or remotely connected with Lincoln or organized crime or any Hollywood producer, director, or actor who had ever been involved in crime movies to appear on their shows. Computer links spit out names of historians, sociologists, psychologists, psychiatrists, and criminologists who could be called upon to talk on any given subject at any time, providing the shows on which they appeared an aura of depth and scholarship.

Reality shows hurried not to be left out of the news cycle, and all were directed to have conversations, opinions, arguments, and vitriol centered upon the Lincoln interview in order to retain currency and unrehearsed human interest.

Since YOURchannel had a copyright on Hero Held Hostage, the other networks and cable shows had to develop their own show titles and logos. The *Perkie Perky Glorious Morning Show* came up with Anchor Anchored. Other titles and logos included Lincoln the Lionhearted, Anchor in Agony, and Freedom Frayed. The graphics on the Freedom Frayed logo would later win an award at the prestigious News as Entertainment recognition banquet. It featured barbed wire wrapped around a television prompter.

The *Perkie Perky Glorious Morning Show* got the jump on the other networks by starting an hour earlier than normal. This action surprised and angered the producers of the competing morning shows to the extent that they appealed to the FTC for an injunction.

For her crafty maneuver, Perkie Perky's bookers rounded up experts in torture, nutrition, psychic phenomenon, and sex therapy, who were presented in a round table discussion set up on a stage at Forty-Second and Broadway. To add star value, the network had arranged to have two pop divas perform. Its premiere news commentator, Twilight Tim, came straight from his celebrated *Early-Early Morning News and Thoughts* program to join her in analyzing the Lincoln interview and question the famous guests.

When the spotlights and camera red light flashed on, the large audience that had assembled to hear the music released a cheer on cue and held up signs the network had provided showing the Anchor Anchored logo. Camera one panned across the gallery of screaming spectators for a few moments, and then camera two opened on Perkie Perky, who appeared on the stage, smiling and shouting at the top of her lungs, "A glorious morning, America!" The crowd responded on cue, "A glorious morning to you, Perkie!"

"Wow, what a glorious group you are this morning, and what a glorious event we had last night. Wasn't that just one great show?" The audience cheered wildly for several minutes and then Perky continued. "Larry Lincoln was simply sensational … all tied up, bound to a chair, and wearing that adorable beret. How absolutely absolute!" The audience again burst out with wild applause and cheers.

"Alas, unhappily I must add, how terrible, how unforgivable the ordeal he's going through. What anxiety he expressed! What mental anguish, physical pain, emotional troubles, torment, and trauma he has been suffering! Please, someone stop me before I go sad."

"Stay perky, Perkie!" a crew member shouted.

"Stay perky, Perkie!" the audience repeated loudly.

"Thank you, all." She turned to another camera and changed to her serious expression. "Now let me ask all of you watching this show an important question. Do you remember where you were when you first heard the news that Larry Lincoln was kidnapped? I'll bet you do, and I'll bet you, like me, will remember years from now. Like the first time you heard Ronald Reagan say, 'There you go again.' Well, today we've assembled some of our country's leading doctors and specialists to delve into the mind of Larry Lincoln to better understand what effect his captivity is having on him."

She turned to yet another camera, changing to her happy face. "In addition, I'll be joined in this Anchor Anchored special by none other than our own famous Twilight Tim, the master of wisdom and words himself. Tim has been up all night communicating with his reliable contacts, and he is ready to bring you news you've never heard before about Larry Lincoln's social life. You certainly don't want to miss that. You'll hear it first on the *Perkie Perky Glorious Morning Show!*"

The audience erupted in cheers and applause.

"But first, let's find out what our glorious weatherman has in store for you this glorious morning. It's all yours, Happy."

"Thank you, Perkie. You're certainly full of pep and perk today."

"Thank you, Happy."
"You're welcome, Perkie."

Keeping her word to Baywatch, Telly Tattle opened her newspaper syndicated column with her usual quotation followed by three paragraphs on the Larry Lincoln story.

> *"I've used the time to find my inner self ... and I really like what I've found."*—**LARRY LINCOLN**

> *And well **LARRY LINCOLN** should! That great anchorman, the man who gives YOURchannel evening news real star value, last night showed the American people what courage is all about. There he was, handsome as ever, looking danger and the television camera right in the eye, and he never blinked.*

> *"Of course you already know that, but here's something you don't know. I have it exclusively from someone who should know that at one time during his captivity **LARRY LINCOLN** was at the executioner's doorstep, only to be saved by a young Italian beauty who literally laid down her body to rescue him. I can tell you something else—and remember, you heard it from me first—that dramatic life-or-death scene led directly to a torrid romance. **LARRY LINCOLN** has fallen madly in love with the woman who saved his life! How about that for a modern-day Pocahontas/ John Smith love story? Sorry about that, girls. It looks like our **LARRY LINCOLN** is out of circulation for a while.*

*You'll be able to learn about this relationship and
much more in the life of this celebrity when you read
LARRY LINCOLN'S autobiography, which my source,
the successful agent Bert Baywatch, tells me will be
published within three weeks. From what I've heard,
you are in for some real inside, low-down gossip on
celebrities. I mean, you'll find it hard to believe the
things they do. Remember, you heard Telly Tattle tell
it first.*

By ten o'clock, twenty-seven congressmen had already made
speeches on C-SPAN and hundreds of statements on CNN,
MSNBC, Fox News, and made Twitter postings claiming out-
rage over the kidnapping of Larry Lincoln. The representative
from Texas, Billy Bob Mullins, stepped up to the microphone at
the United States Capitol to deliver what many congressmen said
was the outstanding speech of the day. After clearing his throat
and looking into the camera, he placed a large illustration of a
bound and gagged Lincoln on an easel. Then he began speaking.

*Mr. Vice President, Mr. Speaker, my esteemed
and honored colleagues on both sides of the aisle, especially those on the Ethics Committee. God bless you all.*

*Last night, a night that will live in infamy, we
all saw a new low point in the moral history of this
republic. I was shocked, I was staggered, and I was
appalled by the sight of a low-life, despicable criminal
wearing a Mickey Mouse mask.*

*Maybe my twenty-six years in Congress and
as chairman of the Campaign Finance Reform
Committee have made me overly sensitive to human
suffering, but I am sure I was not the only one offended
by the spectacle of an American television anchorman,*

a man who has reached the pinnacle of journalistic success, the throne of the news kingdom, you might say, shackled to a chair in a foreign country.

The kidnapping of Larry Lincoln—a TV anchorman, for God's sake—is a direct result of the failure of this august body to act upon my proposed constitutional amendment to demand a federal balanced budget.

And I must add, would he be suffering as he is at this very moment if we had passed my congressional legislative act to erect a statue of Ayn Rand in the Capitol? The answer is again a resounding no!

The last demand brought an eruption of cheers, whistles, a standing ovation, and a chanting of "Impeach the president" from one side of the aisle.

Representative Mullins continued after his colleagues resumed their seats.

God bless you all. We must not continue in this current mode of business as usual. The time has come to get off the pot and protect our television anchormen. We must act and act now. Within two days I will have before you a proposed constitutional amendment that would make harming an anchorman punishable by a practice far too long out of vogue. I'm talking dismemberment! Thank you and God bless you out there watching this speech. And God bless this august assembly and God bless this wonderful country. And black anchormen, too.

On the *Lincoln the Lionhearted* talk show special, an interview between celebrity host Jennifer Johnson and her guest, Lincoln's

cleaning woman, was interrupted for a special announcement
by evening news anchorman Clark Smart. He appeared on the
television screen without his jacket, his shirt sleeves rolled up, his
suspenders off his shoulders, and his tie and shirt collar loosened.
He ran his hands through his hair, cleared his throat, wrinkled
his brow, threw his cigarette into his coffee cup, and stared grimly
into the camera. He began his announcement with his standard
evening news opening.

"Bulletin! Bulletin! Bulletin by Smart! We have just learned
from a dependable source that anchorman Larry Lincoln was on
a CIA assignment and that his kidnappers have been under CIA
watch for the past year." He paused to allow his statement to take
effect. "We have checked this story with several other sources,
and though none could confirm it, they all said it could be true.
There you have it. Larry Lincoln is really a CIA agent posing as
an anchorman. Details at six. As always, you heard it from me
first. This is Clark Smart, America's beloved anchor and author,
signing off as I always do: Bulletin! Bulletin! Bulletin by Smart!"

As he does every evening at the end of his news show, Clark
Smart flashed his famous toothy smile and held up two fingers of
each hand in a V-for-victory sign, something he had learned as a
child watching Presidents Eisenhower and Nixon on television.

As the day wore on, avalanches of news announcements were
made confirming and expanding the Larry Lincoln CIA story.
A few revealed that Larry Lincoln had been involved in covert
operations in the Middle East, Central and South America, and
Canada.

CEO George Ingersoll was leaning back in his chair with
his feet on his desk, reading through several press releases
about Larry Lincoln that had been created by Carl Macon,

YOURchannel's Public Relations president. His wife's raging voice was bursting from the speaker phone.

"This is the final straw, George," she screamed. "You will never again humiliate me, you damn whoremonger! Waitresses, secretaries, sales girls! No more, I tell you, no more. This time I've got you good! Do you hear me, George? George! Do you hear me?"

Ingersoll answered without looking up from the press release about the contract the mafia has on Larry Lincoln. "Yes, dear, I'm listening. You've got me good."

He put the phone on hold to cut her off and looked at Macon sitting across the desk. "I think the mafia contract price on Lincoln of five hundred thousand dollars is in this release is too high. Make it a hundred thousand. We're talking about a contract on an anchorman, not the president."

"You've got it, George," said Macon, editing the change on his copy of the press release.

Ingersoll released the phone's hold key and turned to another press release covering the torture Larry Lincoln had endured while in captivity. His wife continued shouting. "A mistress in every city! No wonder you're a deadbeat when you get home. To think I gave up my movie career to marry you. I could have been a top star by now, interviewed on the red carpet, appearing on the cover of every magazine. I gave up all of that to marry you. Well, this time I'm going for the divorce. I'm leaving to meet my attorney right now, George. This time I have a tell-all letter and email and a witness. Prepare to go broke, you slimeball. This will cost you like no other divorce you've ever been through. This is jackpot time for me, George. Am I getting through? I'm on my way. You'll read about it in Telly Tattle's column tomorrow. I just got off the phone with her, and I gave her the story and the figure I'm shooting for. She guaranteed me three paragraphs. Goodbye, I'm on my way."

While continuing to read the press release, Ingersoll answered.

"Be sure to take the pre-nuptial agreement with you, dear. Your attorney will want to read that. Love you. Bye."

He hung up the phone and finished reading. "This is a little tame, Carl. No wire service would bother to send it out. They've all heard about the hair stuff. Get some violence into it. Build up the fight when they grabbed him on the highway. Make it look like he put up one helluva battle. A lot of judo face kicking, knives, guns, the works."

"That's good, George. I like that."

"Then get these going immediately. What about the build-up for tonight's show?"

"Everything's underway, George. We're pumping up a gusher."

"I want ratings like this network has never seen before. I want us to shoot for the British royal wedding ratings. Hey, wouldn't that make a sensational headline on page one? Lincoln's Lockup Tops Kate's Clambake!"

"I love that," Macon responded while jotting down the potential headline. "I really love that. We're going all out for it, George. Two promos every ten minutes, flooding social media, a press conference every hour. We've got our people on every television talk show in America, and we have a bank of people pretending to be listeners dialing the radio talk shows. We're running ads, contests, and interviews with movie stars, and we're bombarding the top twenty markets."

"That's good. What about the arrangements for Lincoln's return at JFK and the parade?" Before Macon could answer, the phone rang again. "No calls now, Janet."

"It's Mr. Schumbeck on the phone, Mr. Ingersoll," Janet answered. "I think you should take it immediately. He sounds angry. Very, very angry."

Macon jumped to his feet and raced out of the room as Ingersoll grabbed the phone to speak to his boss.

"Hello, Arnold. I guess you've heard about the ratings.

Sensational aren't they? Advertising spiking up, too. Everything is up, up, up."

"Everything except your zipper!" screamed Arnold Schumbeck, CEO of the conglomerate that owns YOURchannel. "Now don't waste my time telling me you don't know what I'm talking about. I just finished reading this damn email from someone named LaRue, and if half of it is true, you should be in some medical journal."

Ingersoll jerked his feet from the desk and stood up. "I don't know what you mean, Arnold."

"I think I just told you not to waste my time. According to this email, which reads like a biology report, you've been screwing everything that moves—including me."

"Email? What email? There must be ..."

"Now shut up and listen. I bought YOURchannel to make money and gain influence. Since the money has been coming in, you still have a job. What I don't need is a messy feminist class action lawsuit and bad publicity. I don't like publicity, Ingersoll, good or bad. What I really hate are courtrooms. One courtroom can lead to another. Let one lawyer make headlines and a hundred more will be after us. Now get this, Ingersoll, from now on no more girlfriends, no more love apartments, no more love boats, junkets, tournaments, and no more fictitious expense accounts. You're going to be an Eagle Scout from now on. One hint of bad publicity and there won't be a place on this earth you'll be able to hide from me. Let's get one more thing out of the way. From now on the only picture of you in the newspapers or on television that I see had better include your wife."

"Yes sir, my wife."

"This hostage thing is saving your job, Ingersoll. You had better keep it going. If it doesn't, I'll fire you, and don't even think of a golden parachute. I've got enough on you to put you in jail. Ratings, higher ratings, and profits. That's all I want you to think about. That or suicide. Understand?"

"Yes, sir."

"Good. Now, one last but very important matter to handle. You had better shut up this LaRue guy. Give him a raise, a promotion, or whatever you have to do to keep him quiet and out of sight. Anything short of murder. Whatever it takes, Ingersoll, do it!" He hung up before he could get a response.

Without hesitating a second, Ingersoll hit the intercom button. "Janet, get my wife on the phone. Immediately! Get her on the damn phone before she leaves the house. After that, get LaRue in here."

Ingersoll slammed both fists against his desk. "Damn, damn, damn it all! Just when everything was going my way. I can't believe it! I'm blindsided! I just cannot, cannot believe it. I cannot believe it was LaRue. That little pipsqueak! Who could have known? Blindsided by LaRue of all people!"

Monte Castella

Baywatch, Lincoln, and the Polucci brothers were having an early lunch the day after Baywatch received the upsetting phone call from Angelo Vocino. Baywatch was seated at the table but not eating. He was bent over, holding his head with both hands. The previous night had not been a good one. Not only had he been upset by Angelo's frantic phone call and unexplained panic to avoid the paparazzi, but sleeping turned out to be nearly impossible.

Gianni and Carlo decided watching *The Godfather* movies would be an excellent way to spend the evening and entertain their guests, even though Baywatch objected vehemently.

The situation deteriorated when Carlo occasionally turned off the sound and he and Gianni took on the various roles, speaking in synch with the actors' lips. Baywatch tried to ignore the video but could not block out the sound of their voices. Occasionally his anger erupted with a loud protest, much to the annoyance of the Poluccis, who answered with threats of a gag. Lincoln, on the other hand, was quite impressed with their performances and would join in at times, taking on some minor roles when he could remember the lines.

Now, as Baywatch watched the Poluccis and Lincoln consumed the enormous lunch his captors had prepared, his anxiety increased, and he was unable to take anything other than coffee and cigarettes. The euphoria he so enjoyed the previous evening was gone and replaced with a feeling of impending disaster. Emotional equilibrium was not in his makeup, and his depressed state was worsened by watching Lincoln gorge himself.

Shortly after lunch, Tomaso and Angelo Vocino returned from Monte Castella. Both appeared to be in a pleasant mood, greeting Lincoln and Baywatch with affectionate words and hugs. "I hope you had a restful night's sleep," Angelo said. Seeing the stack of videos on top of the television, he added, "I see you were well entertained?"

"Yes, thank you," Baywatch answered, "We were able to watch *The Godfather*, starring the don's famous bodyguards. You missed it. Forget about that. Explain why you told me we had to avoid the paparazzi last night and why you were so troubled. That phone call ruined a perfectly beautiful high I was on."

"Nothing to worry about, my friend, nothing to worry about at all," answered Mayor Vocino, smiling and waving his hands. "Angelo was upset last night only because he was concerned that the paparazzi might use you two in order to track down the don. That would not have made him happy. He does not like report-ers, and we were afraid that kind of exposure might cause him to change his mind about your interview and demand that you return the tapes." He shoved Carlo out of his chair and sat down.

"So what happened at the hotel after the call?"

"We handled everything," Angelo answered. He yanked Gianni's chair from under him and sat down. "We told the pho-tographers you were already on your way to Palermo, and that's all it took. They were in their cars and on the chase instantly."

"So we can leave now?" Lincoln asked.

"Not yet. We have some good news for you. There is going to be another interview."

"That's good news?" Lincoln shouted, leaping out of his chair. "No, that's not good news. Good news is sitting in a comfortable first-class seat with a drink in each hand, feeling the plane leave the ground and hearing the wheels retracting. That's good news and that's what going to happen. This is it. I'm out of here and that's final."

Angelo was not disturbed by Lincoln's outburst. He had learned how to control the newsman. "Mr. Lincoln, you are a sensation. We were told your ratings for yesterday's show broke all your company's records. You are definitely your country's hero."

Lincoln sat down again. "My interview got ratings that high? How do you know?"

"We talked to Mr. Tanner, and he had just talked to your top man in New York," Angelo said. "We met your friends after they returned to my hotel. Everything went very well. We explained that we had paid our ransom and were released."

"They bought that story?" asked Baywatch.

"I don't believe so, but they didn't seem to care. I think they had quite a bit of wine with their dinner. We all sat down and continued to drink and talk for quite some time. It turned out to be quite an enjoyable evening."

"An evening with that woman could not be anything but enjoyable," added Mayor Vocino. "My legs would start to shake like a young man's whenever she looked at me. What a woman! What an imagination."

"What do you mean by that?" asked Lincoln.

Mayor Vocino noticed his brother glaring at him. "Nothing important. I was simply fascinated by her beauty and intelligence. Anyway, we have much to discuss. First of all, your Mr. Ingersoll insisted that there be another interview. To do that your people will join us later. You are to be the star again. They want the entire show to be questions from the United States viewers. A lot of people want to talk to you. You have become quite a celebrity, Mr. Lincoln."

"I have always been a celebrity," snapped Lincoln. "I have a great following."

"That's true," said Angelo Vocino, not wanting Lincoln to

become upset again. "My brother only meant that you are bigger than ever. More famous than all the other newsmen combined. That's what they told us."

"They said that?" asked Lincoln, breaking out in a wide smile. "It's good to know I'm getting the recognition I deserve. I have a vast following?"

"Absolutely," answered Mayor Vocino, joining his brother in playing upon Lincoln's vanity. "In fact, most of the evening's conversation was devoted to discussing your abilities. They have a great regard for your talents."

"It's about time. I bring in millions of dollars in advertising revenue. I have that kind of audience. When it comes to the news, I know how to deliver. I don't need hair reaching my eyebrows like Clark Smart. I don't need his phony bulletin, bulletin, bulletin crap either."

Baywatch was beginning to feel uneasy with the conversation. There was something in the Vocinos' attitude that bothered him. He detected a conspiracy of some kind, and he didn't like being left out it. He put aside his questions in order to move to an important matter. "Okay, let's get on with the business at hand—the money."

"What money?" broke in Paolo.

"Yes," said Mayor Vocino. "That is the first order of business." He reached into his pockets for a pen and a small pad and pulled his chair to the table. He was joined immediately by Angelo, Baywatch, Lincoln, and Paolo.

"The first order of business is my million dollars," said Lincoln. "I'm the only one here who is personally out."

"Of course, you get your money back first. Now for the other two and a half million, may I suggest that we give Don Marcasi fifty thousand and we split the rest equally."

"We only get one third?" asked Paolo.

Mayor Vocino continued. "Our half will cover the town's

current expenditures and help set up a tourist center and public relations agency."

Paolo sandwiched his head between his hands. "We get nothing? After all of our work."

"What about our truck repairs, the traffic fine, our clothes?" Gianni added.

"I don't wish to be disagreeable, Mr. Mayor," said Baywatch, "but a million and a quarter to set up a travel agency does seem to be a little excessive. Let's be fair here. There would have been nothing without Lincoln being kidnapped."

"That's right," Paolo broke in. "We started everything. Thank you, Mr. Baywatch. You're absolutely right. It was our thing. Without us ..."

"I think sixty, forty would be a bit more equitable," continued Baywatch. "We will need a lot of front money to set up the books, the licensing deals, the promotions and the movie."

"We're back to nothing!" Paolo screamed.

Gianni stopped converting the dollars into euros. He walked behind Paolo and whispered to him.

Paolo listened, then leaped up, grabbed his brother and kissed him on both cheeks. "That's brilliant, Gianni. You are truly the financial genius of the family." He then leaned close to Angelo and passed along Gianni's idea.

Angelo stood and glared at Paolo. "One moment, gentlemen. I must have a word in private with the don's bodyguards." He grabbed Paolo by the arm and dragged him out of the room. Carlo and Gianni followed. Once out in the hallway, he shoved Paolo against the wall. "Before I choke the life out of you, tell me I misunderstood what you just said to me in there."

"I don't think you misunderstood. I said it would be too bad if Mr. Lincoln found out that Don Marcasi is really Giuseppe Palazzolo, the cobbler."

"Are you trying to blackmail us?"

"That is our thing, too," answered Gianni. "Besides, it is not blackmail. It is called hush money. I saw it in *The Big Sleep* with Robert Mitchum."

"No, no, Gianni," Carlo broke in. "I'm sure it was Denzel Washington in *American Gangster.*"

Angelo spun around but Carlo leaped out of striking distance. "Alright, how much do you want?" Mayor Vocino asked, returning his angry glare toward Paolo. "Remember, I can always put you all in jail and throw away the key."

"We will give you an offer you can't refuse," Paolo answered, flicking at his mustache as he had seen Marlon Brando do the previous evening.

"An offer you can't refuse," Carlo echoed.

"How much, imbecile?"

"We want half," Paolo answered, quickly stepping back.

"How will you ever be able to spend that much money while you rot in a cell for twenty years?" Mayor Vocino asked.

"One third?"

"Let's see if you can refuse this offer," Mayor Vocino countered. "Two hundred and fifty thousand euros and a suspended sentence."

Paolo looked at his two brothers, who were nodding furiously. "It is not fair, but we accept."

"Good. Now that we have that settled let me tell you about tonight's interview. If you follow my instructions and do exactly as I tell you, I might be able to find a bonus for you."

Late into the night, Dauber gathered the television crew to review in detail the second program plan. "We'll be using two cameras this time. It's important we maintain tight control in this small space. Billy will keep his camera directed at Lincoln at all times. Frank will cover anything else that comes up. Frank, be alert and be ready to go with events."

"What else can come up?" asked Baywatch, his conspiracy suspicions still nagging at him.

"We don't expect anything, but we must be ready. Remember, this is live television."

After two hours testing the cameras, checking the sound levels, microphone positions, lighting, the hookup with New York, and a long period of rehearsals and rest breaks, Dauber started the countdown.

"Ready, everyone. Four, three, two, one. Take it, Pearl."

The show opened up with a close-up of a smiling Pearl Necklace. Lincoln, Baywatch, and the Vocino brothers were once again bound to their chairs, and behind them stood the three members of the Black Hand Mob.

"Good evening, America. Pearl Necklace here reporting once again from Monte Castella, Sicily. It is now day two of live with Lincoln and answers from the anchor. In reaction to the overwhelming response to our interview with news anchor Larry Lincoln yesterday, we are bringing you another question and answer session with our Hero Held Hostage. We are going to take another close look at this crime and an outrageous assault against law and order and freedom of the press. It will be another great moment in television news history brought to you exclusively by YOURchannel and our sponsors."

She turned to face Lincoln. "How are you doing today, Larry Lincoln, YOURchannel news anchor and Hero Held Hostage?"

Just as camera one opened on Lincoln, Carlo, standing directly behind him, pulled out his revolver and began wiping it with his handkerchief.

"Just fine, Pearl. It has done me a world of good to know that there are so many people concerned about my captivity and my wellbeing and are watching this show. I am told we have received very high ratings. I thank you all."

"America is at your back, Mr. Anchorman. The country certainly cares about the man who delivers the news every evening.

Your fans have come to know you, and through watching you every night, they consider you a member of the family. To them, you're Larry, not just a newsman. For so many viewers, the evening doesn't begin without you. But before we continue, could I ask the kidnapper in the Mickey Mouse mask to put away his weapon?"

Paolo kicked his brother in the ankle, and Carlo quickly shoved the weapon into his jacket pocket.

Necklace continued. "Thank you. Larry, since we have so many people—famous and important ones—who want to talk to you, we're going right to the phone lines. First up is someone you compete with, a fellow anchorman, a man everyone knows: Clark Smart. What's your question, Clark?"

"Bulletin! Bulletin! Bulletin from Smart. Thank you, Pearl. Good evening, Larry. I'm flashing my victory sign for you, buddy. Both hands. Too bad about your haircut. Sorry I have to bring that up but there's no use …"

"Thank you, Clark," Necklace interrupted. "What's your question?"

"Hey, don't cut me off, Miss Legs. Okay, Larry, as you and my public well know, I'm an investigative reporter of the first order as well as America's number one anchorman. That's because I always tell my writers to go for the jugular. Get under the surface. Make the questions hard questions. I throw fastballs because that's the only way I know how to play."

"Who said you're number one?" Lincoln snapped.

"The ratings, that's who, and that's what we live by. I don't mean to cast aspersions, but we didn't go out and hire a flasher. No insult intended, Pearl."

"What's your question, Bozo?" Necklace responded.

"No need to get touchy. I tell it like it is. Okay, ready or not, let's get right to my first hard question. I hope you're prepared for this. How did you feel the moment they abducted you, the moment they tied you to that chair and cut your hair? I think your captors were attacking the very foundations of free speech, gnawing at the thread from which civilization dangles, taking us all to the edge of another dark age and silencing the voices of freedom and justice, creating darkness where once there was light, hunger where once there was plenty, cob where once there was corn. That's my opinion, that's what I think. What's your take? And make it short."

"Was that a question?" Lincoln asked.

"Am I going too hard on you?"

"Certainly not," Lincoln answered. "I was just wondering if there was a question somewhere in there. You always answer your own questions? As for my capture, I can tell you I was angry but never fearful. It took three men to …"

"I take it you are talking about those three short guys standing behind you? Okay, I'll accept that for an answer. Now let's get right to my latest investigative report and my next hard question. There have been leaks all over Washington that you are an undercover CIA agent. Information I have received from informed sources has sort of confirmed this. I have no idea how they came by this information, nor does it matter. The question is, are you CIA or newsman, spy or speaker, cloak or dagger? As I see it, my answer to this is …"

Necklace interrupted. "Do you ever let anyone answer your questions?"

"Don't try to change the subject on Clark Smart, Miss T-and-A. Lincoln, I was the first to break the CIA story, and I'm giving you a chance to come clean. Is it true that as a CIA agent you were trying to overthrow a government? Agent or not agent, that is the question."

"I don't know what you're talking about," Lincoln answered with confidence. "My agent is right here with me,"

"Don't play cover-up with me, Lincoln. You know what I'm talking about. CIA—Central Intelligence Agency—the covert cowboys, the spooks, the spies, the trench coats. Could this be a case of CIA intrusion into the journalism profession? Never mind. I am going to break the story on my *Caper in Castella* special tomorrow."

"Excuse me," Mayor Vocino interrupted. "It's *Monte* Castella, flower of the Mediterranean."

Smart answered quickly. "Tell your co-covert operator to clam up, Lincoln. I won't be sidetracked. Besides, if you include the word *Monte* in the logo, you break up the alliteration. That's basic journalism. Let's get back to my question. CIA—yes or no? That's a simple question and one that I will get answered. But before you answer, here's my take on it. It's yes. Why else would a television news show keep an anchor with a receding hairline? You might as well come in from the cold, Lincoln. You're a spook, right?"

"He can't talk about it," shouted Baywatch, sensing another publicity bombshell loaded with the potential of keeping Lincoln in the headlines for weeks.

"I can't talk about it," Lincoln repeated.

"That's the confirmation I was waiting for. I'm signing off now. Bulletin! Bulletin! Bulletin from Smart. Can you see my victory signs, Lincoln? By the way, I'll be on a plane soon, heading your way. I'm planning live interviews with everyone involved in this matter. It will be a typical example of the Clark Smart hard-hitting method of getting to the bottom. Look for me."

"We will," answered Mayor Vocino, "and we'll have rooms reserved for you at the Vocino Grand Hotel."

"Thank you, Mayor. I'll be in touch. A Mercedes will do. Good night, America. Watch my show tomorrow for new revelations on the undercover cover-up uncovered."

"That was Clark Smart," Pearl Necklace said. "Famous for his questions and his answers television program."

"That's sarcasm," Clark Smart shot back. "I know sarcasm when I hear it. At least I don't comb my hair forward like …"

"Next up is your mother again, Larry. Go ahead Mrs. Pendal."

"Hi, Larry. I can't stay on long, dear. The people from *Insider*

Gossip magazine are due here in an hour. Can you believe it? I'm going to be a cover story. They said you are the king of buzz right now, and they do buzz better than anyone. Everything is happening so fast. Today that nice Mr. Kasper was here for two hours telling me about your book."

"What book?"

"Your autobiography, dear. It should be out in a matter of weeks. I do hope you'll be free by then. It would be a shame to miss the book tour and signings. Don't fret now. Dad and I will be there."

"What tour? What are you signing?"

"I know Dad would love to talk to you, but he's in the den doing an interview with a fellow from *Heart2Heart* magazine. You never told us about being a CIA agent. We're both so proud of the work you and Nina are doing for our country."

"Nina's a CIA agent?"

"I know you can't say anything more, dear. I have to cut off now. Gloria Gourmet is waiting to do her show in our kitchen. She's going to instruct me and her audience on how to throw a party for a returning hero. So much to do. You look great, even with the extra pounds. Call first thing when you get back. I'm certainly happy to see that Pearl Necklace put on some clothes. Bye now."

"Your mother is very busy these days, Larry," Necklace said, "but it's now time to bring on one of the leading voices in the United States Senate for the past fifty-four years, the junior senator from South Carolina, Augustus Longstreet. Good evening, Senator."

"Good evening, Miss Necklace. Am I on the screen?"

"No, Senator. We're on Larry Lincoln."

"Well at the very least, I think I deserve a split screen. After all, I am a United States junior senator and, I should add, the chairman of the CIA Oversight Committee."

Necklace looked at Tanner and received a nod. "Yes, I just received word we can do that for you, Senator."

Before speaking again, Senator Longstreet waited until he saw his image on half of the screen monitor. "That's better. I always like people to see me so they know I'm still alive. Thank you kindly, young lady. First, Mr. Lincoln, I want to tell you how much I have enjoyed the *Hero Held Hostage* show."

"Thank you, Senator."

"Well, you're very welcome, son. I don't think I've seen you before, but then—well, maybe I just don't remember. You know, I make it my business to watch television news shows every night. Not only do they tell me what's happening in the Senate but also help me stay in touch with America. Just this morning, I was listening to *Twilight Tim's Early-Early* news show when I heard about your involvement with the CIA. Now you can imagine how that riled me up. I tell you, it was like stepping on a cat's tail. Well, I called the CIA director first thing to find out just how the hell he could allow one of his agents to be taken hostage by some tinhorn crooks."

"I resent that," shouted Paolo.

"Who the hell was that?" Senator Longstreet shouted back.

"That was one of the kidnappers, Senator. I think he was objecting to your use of the word *tinhorn*."

"Well, you let me talk to that damn dago."

Necklace motioned to camera two to zoom in on Paolo who was wearing a Spiderman mask. He was dressed in a black suit with a bright red handkerchief in his jacket pocket, a lavender vest, black silk shirt, red tie, and lavender gloves. When he saw the camera turn toward him, he folded his arms, striking a Mussolini pose.

"There you are, Senator. Face to face with one of the infamous Black Hand Mob."

"Listen, you low-life, as the eight-times-elected junior senator from the great state of South Carolina and chairman of three of the most powerful committees in the US Senate, including CIA Oversight, I hereby demand that you release news anchorman Larry Lincoln immediately."

"Hey, what about me, Senator?" Baywatch shouted. "How about demanding my release too? I'm an American citizen."

"Now who was that?" Senator Longstreet asked.

"That was Larry Lincoln's agent, Senator," Necklace answered, motioning for the camera to focus on Baywatch. "His name is Burt Baywatch, and he was kidnapped along with Lincoln."

"Hi, Senator. Good to meet you," Baywatch said. "Don't over-look freeing me."

"Are you with the CIA too? Is that your code name?"

"Sorry, senator, but I can't talk about it."

Mayor Vocino jumped in. "May I talk to Senator Augustus?" he asked. Camera one panned to the mayor and his brother.

"Who are those two?" Senator Longstreet asked.

"I am the mayor of Monte Castella, the flower of Sicily, nes-tled in the valley at the base of the world-famous Monte San Calogero. This is my brother, Angelo. You must come to visit us after we are freed from these kidnappers, Senator. Monte Castella is a town of classic Italian porticos, charming cobblestone streets, captivating fountains, and ancient Greek temples. In fact, our town was once dedicated to the fertility goddess Aphrodite."

"There's no reason to talk dirty," Longstreet snapped back. "Are you our CIA contact in Sicily?"

"Not at present, but we plan to have an American Express office opening here soon in addition to the General Patton Tourist Center, and we are developing our own website and Facebook page."

"That's very good, Mayor," Baywatch interrupted, now aware of what was happening. "The General Patton Tourist Center. I like it. Maybe a World War II tank out front plus a gift shop. The General Patton Tourist Center and Gift Shop."

"I don't understand what the hell is going on here," Senator

Longstreet continued. "If you're not with the CIA, why are the terrorists holding you hostage?"

"We are not terrorists," shouted Paolo. The camera swung back to him. "We are men of honor. At present, kidnapping is our thing. However, we are definitely planning to expand our operations. A little blackmail, some extortion, but certainly not terrorism." He let loose with another Sidney Greenstreet laugh.

Suddenly, the door to the room was kicked open and banged against the wall. The room went silent as Don 'The Brain' Marcasi, his arms folded across his chest, marched into the room, followed by two masked henchmen, each carrying a shotgun, which they quickly aimed at the Polucci brothers. Without hesitation, the cameraman spun around and adjusted for a wide-angle view to pick up the action of the entire room. Dauber dropped the split screen, eliminating Senator Longstreet from view but not the audio.

"Thank God, it's the don," shouted Mayor Vocino. "He has come to rescue us."

Don Marcasi looked at the Polucci brothers, slowly raised his arm, and pointed. "Drop your weapons, you traitors! Your days of deceit and disloyalty are over. No one can turn on Don Victorio Carmine 'Big Brain' Marcasi and live to tell about it." He turned toward the camera and worked his face into a sinister scowl. "I am Don Marcasi, the boss of bosses. There is a contract out on me." He made a sign of the cross.

Carlo jumped away from the don's henchmen and attempted to pull his revolver from his pocket to confront Marcasi, but it caught on his pocket lining. Desperate to pull out the gun and play out his role, he gripped the weapon tightly and yanked it violently. The gun fired, filling the room with an ear-deafening roar followed by total silence. Everyone stood motionless except for Lincoln, who let out a cry and tumbled over, still tied to his chair. The sound of the bullet whizzing past his head made him lurch sideways, tipping his chair over. On the way down, his head smashed against a table as he fell to the floor.

"What the hell is going on there?" Senator Longstreet shouted. "Is anyone dead? Who's the fat guy? Why am I off the screen?"

"It's Don Marcasi," Mayor Vocino exclaimed. "He's come to free us. Calm yourself, no one is hurt. The bullet went past Mr. Lincoln and into the wall."

"Don who?" asked the senator.

"Don Marcasi, Senator," Pearl Necklace said. "He is the head of the mafia in Sicily. He is the godfather around here."

"I'm a godfather too, but I don't go around shooting people. Is he with the CIA? Somebody there must be with the CIA. Twilight Tim told us that flat out on his television show, and Clark Smart has been talking about it all day. So has every other anchorman, reporter, talk show host, and disc jockey. It's on Faceback and all those other things I can't figure out. Damn it, I want some answers. As the chairman of the Senate CIA Oversight Committee, I have the right to know what the hell the CIA is doing. I'm almost sure of that."

"Hold on, Senator," said Pearl Necklace. "We'll free Larry Lincoln and he can interview the don. He knows him well."

"Change that," Tanner whispered to her. "Larry's out cold."

Pearl Necklace looked across the room to see an unconscious Lincoln on the floor. She reacted quickly.

"People, it looks like Larry Lincoln, Hero Held Hostage, has been hit. I repeat. Larry Lincoln, the famous YOURchannel anchorman, has been shot. He's bleeding, but it doesn't appear to be serious. Unfortunately for you viewers, we will have to delay the interview with Don Marcasi. I apologize for that. We'll work on reviving Larry." She nodded to the cameraman to focus on the don.

Don Marcasi saw that the camera was aimed at him again, and with a swagger as well as a limp, he walked up to face Paolo. "You have broken the code of honor, the code of trust. You have betrayed me, a made man, and our thing. For that you must pay. There must be rules. Without rules, we have nothing." With that he threw his arms around Paolo and kissed him full on his Spyderman lips.

"That's disgusting!" Senator Longstreet spit out. "That man had damn well better not be in the CIA."

"Oh, my God," Carlo cried out. "He has given the kiss of death. Just like Al Pacino in *The Godfather*. We are finished, done for." He crossed himself.

"I think it was *The Last Don*, starring Kirk Douglas," Gianni whispered to his brother.

"Is Al Pacino there?" asked Senator Longstreet. "Is he with the CIA? I thought he was an actor."

Don Marcasi took his arms from around Paolo and turned to Carlo and Gianni. He hesitated a moment trying to decide how to kiss their Mickey Mouse masks. Finally, he wrapped his arms around each in turn and kissed Mickey's nose.

"I hope there aren't too many kids watching this pervert," Senator Longstreet said. "What kind of a show is this?"

"This is television newscasting, Senator, at its finest!" Necklace shouted. "This is real and honest and live! This is the stuff a newsman dreams about … reporting news as it happens."

Don Marcasi gave the order. "Take them away. I never want to see them again."

The don's gunmen motioned for the Poluccis to leave. Paolo began to walk out, but stopped and turned again to Don Marcasi. "I want you to know, Don Marcasi, it was just business. Nothing personal. You must understand. Strictly business."

"That's right, Don Marcasi," Gianni repeated as he stepped behind his brother. "It was just business. Nothing personal. You must understand."

"That goes for me, Don Marcasi," Carlo said. "It was just business. Nothing personal." As he started to leave, he noticed his revolver on the floor and bent down to pick up it up.

"Leave it, stupid," Angelo Vocino shouted.

Don Marcasi turned his back to the departing Poluccis and put his hands on his hips. "I understand what they are saying, and I accept that. This is the life we have chosen. I do not take it personally, but they have broken the rules. Away with them!" The three Polucci brothers were marched out of the room followed by the don's accomplices.

"There you have it, ladies and gentlemen," Pearl Necklace whispered into the microphone. "Another fantastic news show from YOURchannel and a new milestone in the history of television news. You have witnessed on live television the mafia's famous kiss of death."

She turned to look at Lincoln. "Unfortunately, Larry Lincoln, Hero Held Hostage, is still unconscious, and we will be unable to continue the interview. It appears that he has a slight head wound from the gunshot. I think we can get a close-up of that."

Dauber ordered Billy to zoom in on Lincoln's head. A trickle of blood was coming from a cut a few inches above his ear, the result of hitting the table when he fell. The cameraman stepped over Lincoln's body to get a better angle.

Necklace continued speaking. "I think he will need several stitches, and that's really a shame. It will mean the doctors will insist on shaving the hair away from the wound." She turned her attention back to the don.

"Don Marcasi, before you leave, will you answer a few questions from our audience? Senator Augustus Longstreet is still with us, and I'm sure he would like to talk to you."

Senator Longstreet jumped in. "I want to ask him about his involvement with the damn CIA. If he is, he had better clean up his act. It was revolting to see him kissing those guys. I'm going to talk to the director about it the minute this show ends."

Don Marcasi held up his hand. "I don't talk to big shot politicians. Besides, I have said everything to Mr. Lincoln. You will have to wait for him to show you my interview. Everything is right there. My life, my father's life, the life of the mafia. The full story from the very beginning. I have broken the code of silence for which we are so famous, and for that I may not live too much longer. I will pay with my life. It is over for me. Over!" He made a slight bow toward the camera, turned and walked to the door. There he stopped and turned back again to make one last statement. "My life is now prime time television."

Dauber switched to camera one which had a tight focus on Pearl Necklace. "Everyone will be waiting to see those tapes, Don Marcasi, and speaking for all of the Larry Lincoln fans, I want to thank you for freeing him. I'm sure you never expected Larry to be wounded."

"Thank him for saving me, too," Baywatch interrupted. "You might mention that Larry Lincoln's autobiography will be in bookstores nationwide within two weeks."

"There you have it, Mr. and Mrs. America," Necklace continued. "You have witnessed one of the most exciting moments in television history. First, the interview with Larry Lincoln, Hero Held Hostage, and the freeing of Larry Lincoln by the chief of the Sicilian Mafia. Add to that the announcement of the history of the mafia to be revealed on YOURchannel exclusively and told by Don Victorio 'The Brain' Marcasi, who along with his father and grandfather were at the very epicenter of this infamous worldwide crime organization. The complete exposé is in the form of interviews with Don Marcasi by anchorman Larry Lincoln. Check your local listings for the date and time. It is something you will not want to miss. We must now conclude our newscast from Monte Castella, Italy."

"The paradise of the Mediterranean Sea," interrupted Mayor Vocino. "Rooms with a view now available."

Necklace continued her signoff. "Larry Lincoln will be home soon, following his recovery, which I'm sure will not take long. We hope you'll be at the airport to welcome him home. This is

Pearl Necklace for YOURchannel. Goodbye, good luck, and good viewing."

"That's a wrap," Dauber said.

"Awesome," Baywatch shouted. "Absolutely awesome! An Emmy! I absolutely guarantee it. Maybe two. One for newscasting and one for drama in a mini-series. If we can get the movie on the screens this year, an Oscar. That's never been done before. An Emmy and Oscar in two categories in the same year for the same story. Someone get these ropes off of me. I must get on my phone. So much to get underway!"

Angelo Vocino spoke to his brother. "This time I will strangle Carlo. He could not have missed Mr. Lincoln by more than a couple of inches. *Inches!* What if he had hit him? It would have ruined everything."

"All's well that ends well, Angelo," Baywatch answered, "and this certainly ended well."

Pearl Necklace gave a thumbs-up sign to Mayor Vocino, then turned to Tanner. "In spite of a little overacting by the don, I thought that went very well. We never planned on the gunshot, but it did add excitement, don't you think? We couldn't have planned it better."

"I'm thinking about what type of hat we can come up with to cover both sides of his head when he goes back on television."

"How about one of those things Valentino wore in *The Sheik*," Baywatch answered. "That would be sensational. Maybe start a hot new trend. I'll talk to someone in licensing. A Larry Lincoln–Valentino head thing. Italian silk, of course. A complete, high-quality line in a variety of colors. The logo on one side of that elastic band that holds down the scarf and the Larry Lincoln beret logo on the other side. Be a sensation in your gift shop, Angelo."

Pearl Necklace turned to Dauber, who had walked into the room. "Did we get a good shot of Larry as he was falling over? That would make a sensational promo shot for the build-up to the mafia program."

"We got the whole thing. Better yet, the microphone he was wearing picked up the thud of his head hitting the table and the floor. Combine that with the close-up of the blood flowing down the side of his face and you have twenty seconds of high drama."

"I love it!" Baywatch said. "We can get some stop-action shots of that sequence for the autobiography. This just gets better and better. Someone cut me loose! There's a fortune waiting to be made."

New York

The following morning, the *Twilight Tim Early-Early News and Thought Show* began at 5:00 a.m., its usual time. The deep-thinking news commentator had planned to use this particular show to announce changing his name to Twilight2Tim in an attempt to appeal to a younger market, a segment of his viewer base that had almost disappeared. However, the Lincoln hostage show of the previous night was too dramatic to ignore.

His program opened as it always did with a logo that included the show's name and an image of Rodin's famous statue *The Thinker*. The screen faded to black and then subdued lighting appeared, outlining the figure of Twilight Tim sitting on a stool in the middle of a stark television stage in his standard opening position mimicking the statue: his right elbow on his knee, his chin resting on his fist, and his feet resting on a rung of the stool. He held the pose until a spotlight directly above him turned on. Slowly he raised his head. As the camera moved in for a close-up, he looked directly into the lens with an expression of deeply felt compassion.

"It is over," he whispered.

After a long pause to allow his opening words to grab his audience, he continued. "Yes, Larry Lincoln is safe. However, I pose this thoughtful question. In the future is no anchorman safe?"

He paused again. "Does America look weak?" Another pause. "Can an anchorman also be a CIA agent and give both jobs the full attention each deserves? Could there possibly be a conflict of interest? Or on an even broader scale, could the CIA not know Larry Lincoln was one of its own?"

Twilight Tim straightened up from his pose. "For the answers to these questions that must be on the minds of all Americans, I have asked someone with close connections to the CIA's director to join us tonight. He is an informed source and a former CIA shadow whom I will address as Mr. Source to keep his identity undisclosed. Through an interplay of brilliant, probing questions from me and hopefully honest answers from my source, we will endeavor to unscramble the events of the past week and put into perspective the facts as we know them to be true and varifiable while clarifying the unclear, separating the chaff from the wheat, the grape from the vine, and the bulb from the socket without dwelling on the obvious in order to devote every minute of this complex and thought-provoking news and commentary show to lifting the fog engulfing the Lincoln affair, striving constantly toward that ever-elusive goal we in the news and entertainment industry call *truth*. That is what we will endeavor to accomplish tonight and what we will pursue in the future as long as the *Twilight Tim Early-Early Morning News and Thought Show* generates good ratings.

"Now for my remarkably succinct questions—questions that no other anchorman, reporter, commentator, talk show host, editor, columnist, pundit, or blogger has had the insight to ask, I introduce you to Mr. Source." He turned to face a large screen on which a man whose eyes were closed appeared.

"Hello! Hello, Mr. Source," Twilight Tim shouted. "Hello, there!

The man awoke with a start and blinked his eyes beneath the bright television lights. "Would you repeat that question?"

"I have not asked one yet, but I will now. Let's begin with a question about the Shah."

"Which Shah?"

"The Shah of Iran, of course."

"He's dead. Died a long time ago, and I can verify that."

"Yes, he is, but wasn't agent Lincoln's mission somehow connected to bringing the Shah back to Iran?"

"Bringing him back from where? I think we just agreed the Shah is dead. Make up your mind there, pilgrim."

"I'm talking about bringing back the institution, not the man. Am I going too fast? That often happens with my guests. My mind is always racing ahead, galloping, if I may extend the metaphor, at full speed for the finish line, which I call the truth line. Now tell me if you can, was anchorman Larry Lincoln working on a covert plan to reinstall the Persian throne?"

"I don't think so."

"That sounds somewhat evasive, ambiguous, obscure and wooly. Am I stepping too close to a national security issue with my questions? I have been known to do that as a result of my penetrating mind and my unstoppable quest for news behind the news. That's what separates me from those six-foot evening television news guys with their perfect profiles, toothy smiles, and great hair and also those adorable television news women with their long, flowing blonde hair, outrageously gorgeous, mouth-wateringly luscious, stunning, ravishing beauties who make me want to …"

"You said a mouthful there, pilgrim. Like that well-bred filly Pearl Necklace. I mean, when I watch her … whoa, Nelly, dismount and close the gate."

"Thank you. You illustrate my point perfectly. They're good people, mind you, and Lord knows, highly paid. Except for Lincoln, of course. But look at his hair. It does make you wonder sometimes. Is that all there is? Forgive me for philosophizing. I have a tendency to do that. I have always pursued truth rather than just the facts. Let's proceed with further questions."

"Is this show always on this early?" Mr. Source responded.

The next morning Telly Tattle's gossip column appeared with the headline

Monte Castella Is In, Aspen Is Out

When I talked to my friend Mayor Vocino of Monte Castella, he would not name the celebrities who have been making that beautiful Italian paradise the latest and trendiest watering hole for the rich and famous, but I am not one to be denied. Working with the man close to the action, Burt Baywatch, I found out who they are, and now you're going to know. Remember, you heard it from me first—as usual.

I was able to obtain the mayor's highly guarded booking journal and learned that in just three weeks a who's who party is planned at the Grand Imperial Hotel Vocino. Those attending this gala affair will include famous A-list celebrities from Europe, Washington, and Hollywood.

My source also tells me that real estate in and around Monte Castella is being scooped up by everybody who's anybody, and prices are soaring. Does this mean Martha's Vineyard is obsolete, Jackson Hole hollowed, Aspen ashes? Wow! I would say the movers and shakers better move fast if they plan to make this scene.

Throughout the day every network reacted to Pearl Necklace and the *Answers from the Anchor Two* show with follow-up programs on the Lincoln story, which had now reached the highest levels of ratings power, the platinum standard in quality television news reporting.

The *Perkie Perky Glorious Morning Show* produced the day's highest viewership numbers, and would later capture the industry's Creativity in Entertaining News award, the NEWT. She staged her program in the lobby of Rockefeller Center and featured a panel of news reporters carefully selected for their television exposure and registered celebrity status. They were seated around an oval table, the top of which was covered entirely with a three-dimensional map of Sicily. Enormous baskets of flowers surrounded the guests seated at the table. Behind the flowers, risers were placed to accommodate the audience of New York tourists.

The drop-dead revealing wardrobe worn by Pearl Necklace on all her evening news shows had an immediate influence on newscasting, and that became apparent when the camera's red light turned on Perkie Perky as she walked onto the set, wearing a trench coat that extended only to her thighs, dark sunglasses, and a wide-brimmed fedora. She moved to center stage, turned slowly around on her spiked heels, and came to a stop facing the camera. Quickly she dropped her coat, flicked off the glasses, and sailed her hat into the audience.

"A glorious good morning, America!" she shouted, throwing her arms out wide.

"A glorious good morning to you, Perkie Perky!" the audience responded, followed by whistles, screams, and applause in appreciation of her tight-fitting mini-dress, which featured a neckline plunging to her navel and very little covering her back, an outfit competing with anything seen at the Grammy Awards show. Members of the panel raised cards showing the number ten.

TV

Clark Smart opened his evening news show with his standard bulletin, bulletin, bulletin introduction and went directly to the Larry Lincoln story.

> *Tonight I am going to leave the story-telling to the readers on other networks and instead will bring you a show unprecedented in television.*

He paused for dramatic effect, allowing the cameraman time to zoom in for a tight close-up of his face.

> *Tonight I'm going to do away with the usual snow and tornado reports, loyal dog and cute kitten stories, and feel-good sagas from YouTube. Tonight I am going to reveal that the avalanche of news you have been hearing about Larry Lincoln is just so much bunk. Tonight I am giving you actual news, and the news is this: The Larry Lincoln kidnapping is pure fiction. Tonight, I will be on my way to Sicily to destroy that myth and bring you the truth.*

The reception for Larry Lincoln at the JFK terminal went as planned by the YOURchannel public relations staff. The theme and logo created for the occasion was Crisis Crunched—Lincoln Liberated! A large section of the runway adjacent to the terminal had been cordoned off for the members of Congress, the press, show business celebrities, four high school bands, and two National Football League cheerleader teams. Rows of bleachers were set up for the public, plus a stage for an assortment of rock groups and stand-up comedians to entertain the crowd and the television audience waiting for Lincoln's arrival.

When the plane taxied into position, a red, white, and blue carpet was rolled out, leading to the speakers' stand. Lincoln was the first to emerge from the plane, wearing a Cossack hat pulled down to his ears. He paused to wave to the crowd then bounded down the stairs to shake hands with Senators, Congressmen, movie stars, and highly rated celebrities.

Lincoln paused with each person long enough for the photographer to take photos for inclusion in the autobiography. Meanwhile, his autobiography writer Karl Kasper was working the audience of celebrities for their thoughts about the Lincoln kidnapping and any wild parties they thought he might have attended, whom he would subsequently quote in the book.

Following the handshaking, the cheerleaders surrounded Lincoln and accompanied him to the stage where they performed their victory dance routine and led the crowd in a series of welcome-home cheers.

Speeches by members of Congress followed. Senator Jamison spoke out angrily against his Senate colleagues for their failure to back his proposed embargo of Sicily. Senator Longstreet praised the CIA and their agent Donald Marcasi for the covert rescue operation. Congressman Billy Ray Mullins used the occasion to propose a new monument in Washington dedicated to the Dallas Cowboys Cheerleaders. Perkie Perky, wearing a fishnet mini-dress that triggered an explosive ovation when she dropped her coat, gave Lincoln the *Inside Talk* magazine Buzz of the Month award. George Ingersoll presented Lincoln with a new teleprompter.

Everyone sat as Lincoln stepped up to the microphone. He thanked the country for standing behind him and then described in a few words the thrill of being back in America. When he paused to pull his prepared speech from his jacket pocket, everyone on the stage stood, applauded, and raced to the stairs. George Ingersoll walked up to Lincoln and told him to be in his office at eleven the next morning for a staff meeting. "We have quite an agenda to cover. Be prompt."

The following morning Steve Tanner, Pearl Necklace, Larry Lincoln, Bill Saxton, Henry Handleman, Carl Macon, and Phil Sanford sat quietly around the table, waiting for George Ingersoll to finish a telephone conversation with his wife.

"Sharon Harlow?" he questioned. "That's a wonderful stage name, darling, but let's talk about it later. I have a large group here right now waiting for—yes definitely, Diana-Kate is not only much better but also more timely. That name is you, believe me. Diana-Kate, yes, I love it. Have to go now. Kiss, kiss. Love, love."

He hung up and walked around his desk to the conference table. "First things first," he stated quickly and sharply. He remained standing and continued without hesitation. "I have a series of announcements to make. I have given our operation at YOURchannel a great deal of thought since Lincoln's kidnapping, and I saw the need to make some major changes in our management team. I feel these changes will go a long way to maintaining the ratings momentum we have recently achieved."

"You fired Alex LaRue," Lincoln interrupted.

"No, Larry, we did not fire Alex, though I can understand your consternation. This is not the order I was going to follow but since you mentioned Alex, I might as well begin with him. Alex LaRue is now president of the News division at YOURchannel."

In unison everyone except Pearl Necklace leaped up from their chairs. "You're joking," Tanner shouted. "Not LaRue! Not the head of the news division! That can't be."

Saxton joined in, flashing his business card. "*I'm* the news president," "You can't have two news presidents."

"You're right. Bill. Now everyone sit down and stay calm. First things first. I've had my eye on Alex for a long time now, and I think the time is right to reward him for his dedication and accomplishments at YOURchannel. Not to mention his email writing skills."

"What accomplishments?" Saxton demanded. "He's a gofer."

"That's what I thought until I read a couple of his recent

dispatches. I realized how badly I had misjudged him. He's a very clever and creative little son of a bitch. I can't help but admire that in a person. Even Arnold Schumbeck was impressed. As was my wife, I'm sorry to say."

Saxton grabbed his head with both hands and fell back into his chair with such force it tipped over, carrying him with it. He remained there on the floor staring at the ceiling.

"Besides," Ingersoll continued, "I don't think I have to remind everyone how instrumental he was in handling Larry's kidnapping and release."

"He had nothing to do with my release!" Lincoln snapped. "If it had been up to him, I would still be tied to a chair in Sicily. I'll never forgive the treacherous bastard."

"I agree with your description, Larry," Ingersoll said, "but sometimes a quality like that must be respected and rewarded. Anyway, Alex will not be seeking your forgiveness any time soon. From now on he will be working in France. Specifically, in our Cannes news bureau."

"We don't have a news bureau in Cannes," Tanner said. "We don't even have a telephone in Cannes."

"Alex is there now, setting one up." Ingersoll answered. "I've always felt we had a weakness in that part of the world. From there he can provide us with full coverage of the Cannes Film Festival and the Monte Carlo royalty. I will be unable to attend this year, and as you will see in a few minutes, it is important that we will be represented there."

Saxton regained his composure, stood up, and tried another attack. "I don't know of a single corporation that has two presidents of one division. A corporation can have lots of presidents but not two in the same division. It's not done."

"Is that true, Phil?" Ingersoll asked Sanford, president of Legal Affairs.

"It would be confusing on business cards," he answered, "but you could designate them geographically."

"Splendid idea. Saxton, you are now news president of tele-phone area code 313. That means Detroit if I'm not mistaken. LaRue will be news president of Cannes."

"George, if I can break in here," interrupted Henry Handleman, "I want you to know that's a brilliant move. I've always admired LaRue. That young man is razor sharp, and we're lucky to have him with us. He's going places … as we have just witnessed. No question, he'll make a real statement in Cannes."

Saxton raised his hand. "Could I be senior president of News? We don't have a senior president."

"I don't think we can do that, Bill," Ingersoll answered and turned to the president of Legal Affairs, "Phil can correct me if I'm wrong, but we can only have one senior president. Never mind, we're jumping ahead again. First things first. I'm merging news and entertainment into one division. I should have done this long ago. There's way too much duplication around here. From now on we will have only one division operating under the office of the senior president of News and Entertainment Enterprises. Of course, we'll have to reduce the staffs to eliminate the duplica-tion of efforts I spoke about. We must start paying more attention to profits."

The room went silent for a few moments while everyone took in the last announcement. Handleman was the first to speak. "Another brilliant idea, George. I've always had great admiration for whomever you have chosen, and I look forward to working with him. I assume I will retain my role as president of Entertainment."

"Certainly, but it will be president of Entertainment in area code 212. Unless you've missed something here, this is really a demotion for you and Saxton. Naturally, that means a drastic reduction in salary for both of you. Lean and mean, that's what we're going to be at YOURchannel."

He looked to the wall carrying the company slogan about YOURchannel being a team network. "Saxton, make a note. I want this team crap painted over. I want the new company slogan to be YOURchannel Is a Lean and Mean Channel. God, that's good. I want it up there by tomorrow. Schumbeck will love that. Have it done in gold to color coordinate with the sofa."

Saxton lifted his chair into its correct position and sat down slowly. "I've been demoted, lost my title, had my income reduced, and been humiliated in front of my peers, all in the course of fifteen minutes. Now I'm told to have a wall painted. This will be all over the Hamptons by noon."

"That reminds me," Ingersoll added, "no more company cars, second homes, or club memberships. That's straight from Schumbeck himself. Sorry about that, Saxton, but it's best to get the bad news behind us. Done and done, as my father used to say. Now, let's move on to something cheery."

He looked toward Lincoln, who quickly interrupted. "You're going to give me a weekly news magazine show?"

"Don't be foolish, Larry. Speaking of foolish, would you mind removing that hat? No, I'm not going to waste you on a project like that. You're a celebrity, a hot celebrity. We must strike while the celebrity's hot."

He walked around the table and stood behind Lincoln, placing his hands on his shoulders. He glanced down at Lincoln's hair and rolled his eyes.

"What we have sitting right here is Mr. News himself. Look at this face. It's on every television morning show, talk show, quiz show, news show, entertainment show, Internet link, Facebook, Twitter, YouTube, Instagram, on page one of every newspaper and junk tabloid, and on the cover of every sleazy and serious magazine in the country. There isn't a radio talk jock who isn't mentioning his name every fifteen minutes. So what does he want to do with that exposure? Blow it on a damn weekly television news show."

He paused to pat Lincoln's shoulders. "No, Larry, you're too big for that. This is not the time for another television news weekly exposing nothing. This is cash-in time. First we're going to air your Don Marcasi interview show, *Larry Lincoln, Mano a Mano with the Mafia*. This will keep our ratings at their current high level. Following that—here comes my next announcement—I'm giving you a three-month leave from your duties here to star in the making of ... are you all ready for this? ... do I hear a drum roll? ... the making of the new YOURchannel Film Company's first television movie, *Lawrence of Sicily*."

Lincoln tried to stand, but Ingersoll clamped down on his shoulders, making it impossible for him to move. All he could do was tilt his head back and look up at Ingersoll's chin.

"I don't know about that, Mr. Ingersoll," Lincoln interrupted. "You'll have to talk to my agent. He already has a movie in the works."

George Ingersoll bent over and whispered in Lincoln's ear. "I spent an hour over the phone with your Mr. Baywatch this morning, reviewing your contract with YOURchannel. He turned out to be very agreeable once I read a few important paragraphs. In fact, the movie title was his. I suggest you meet with him immediately after our little meeting."

He straightened up, released his grip on Lincoln's shoulders, and walked behind Pearl Necklace. He started to place his hands on her shoulders but thought better of it and buried them in his pockets.

"Now for my next announcement. First let me back up a bit. A very short time ago, the YOURchannel News Division and the Entertainment Division were languishing at the bottom of the ratings barrel and looking down. Then with two strokes of unmitigated genius, Steve Tanner turned the ratings chart upside down and our advertising revenues downside up. The first stroke was to change the format. More than that, he changed the entire concept of the evening news readings. I knew instantly he was on to something. The second stroke was hiring Pearl Necklace, a move that elevated him to the level of nirvana. That is why

Steve is now the senior president of YOURchannel's News and Entertainment Enterprises."

"Hear! Hear!" shouted Handleman, slapping the table with the palms of his hands. He quickly stopped when he saw Ingersoll glaring at him.

"Changing the concept of the news program would not have been enough in itself to bring about the success we have enjoyed. It took Pearl, with her imagination, insight, and intelligence to give it life, aided of course by, excuse me, Pearl, her goddamn earth-moving beauty, and a body that makes me shake."

He paused to look across the table at Saxton and Handleman.

"While I'm thinking about it, I expect you two to leave your recording devices on my desk on your way out. To continue, not only did she display her talents on the show, but her idea of the Lincoln interviews and the astonishing concept of the rescue finale were simply mind-boggling."

Lincoln's jaw dropped. "You mean to tell me it was her idea to have me shot?"

"That was an accident, Larry," Necklace answered. "I'm sorry about that. There was never to be any gunplay."

"I came within an inch of having my head blown off!"

Ingersoll stepped in. "Let's not get bogged down in dramatics, Larry. It's important to keep our priorities in order. First things first, as I sometimes say. Besides, I'm increasing your salary considerably."

Ingersoll walked back to his position at the head of the table. "Let's get on with this. For my final announcement, I am appointing Pearl to the newly created office of president of YOURchannel Programming. In this position, she will be in charge of producing everything that goes on the air here. Now you can applaud, Handleman."

As the group walked out of Ingersoll's office, Lincoln broke into a run and headed toward the elevators. "This time I'm really going to kill him!" he shouted. "They'll never convict me. I'll be a hero to anyone who has ever had an agent!"

Tanner took hold of Pearl Necklace's arm and pulled her aside, leaning forward to kiss her cheek. "Congratulations, Ms. President of YOURchannel Programming.

"Congratulations to you, Mr. In-charge-of-it-all. This is what you wanted, isn't it? To be in a position to make the big decisions?"

"I think so. I'm not sure. The past weeks have left me somewhat confused. This isn't the final act I had in mind, but I guess it's not all bad. I think."

They began walking down the hallway and Necklace asked, "You haven't changed your mind about the *Washington Brothel Show*, have you?"

"Not in the least. I can't wait to get started. How about a celebration lunch?" Tanner asked.

"Tom has already asked me, but I'm sure he wouldn't mind if you joined us."

"I think he would. Can we all get together tonight? I'll get Larry, Baywatch, and the film crew. We'll make it a party."

"I'd love it. I'll meet you at right after the broadcast. Right now I have to run. Tom is waiting, and later I have an appointment with Arnold Schumbeck in his office."

Baywatch had his feet up on his new desk and his phone pressed against his ear. "So I can expect a first draft in a week. That's great. The check's in the mail. Love you. Bye. Ahab Whaleslayer signing off." He hung up the phone and reached for the journal in which he was maintaining an agenda he had set up for Lincoln. He marked the date when he would be receiving the movie script for *Lawrence of Sicily* and then turned back the journal's pages for a review.

Wednesday:

9:00 a.m.—Live interview on Perkie Perky show. Bring Larry's hat.

10:30 a.m.—Tape a segment to be used in the soap opera, Let's Play Doctor. Wear bandages.

12:00 p.m.—Lunch with Telly. Develop some quotable lines.

2:00 to 4:00 p.m.—Do remote with eight talk radio interviews.

8:00 p.m.—Live on Dianiana show. Bring rope and gun for re-enactment.

Thursday:

9:00 a.m.—Photo session for the cover jacket of Larry's autobiography followed by review of pics selected for same. Ask Pearl Necklace to attend. Ha!

12:00 p.m.—Lunch with chairman of New York's Democratic party to discuss Larry's future.

3:00 p.m.—Call Angelo Vocino to discuss concept of the Black Hand Film Festival in Monte Castella. Also discuss the Lincoln Monte Castella Cook Book by Don Marcasi.

11:30 a.m.—Live interview on the Twilight Ted Early-Early News Show. Bring the Bible.

Friday:

9:00 a.m.—Conduct auction for magazine rights to Larry and Nina love story.

11:00 a.m.—Talk to Senator Longstreet about Larry's speech to Congress.

12:00 p.m.—Lunch with autobiography publisher to set up book tour and discuss the new book: Lincoln's Weight Loss Without Exercise.

4:00 p.m.—Meet with New York's Republican party chairman to discuss Larry's political plans.

6:00 p.m.—Talk to DizzyWorld about Hero Held Hostage ride.

Monday:

9:00 a.m.—Meet with lawyers to set up licensing operation and commercials. Discuss clothing line, toiletries, toys, appliances, hair rejuvenation, first aid kits, etc.

12:00 p.m.—Lunch with Larry to inform him that Nina is flying in this afternoon to help hype books, movie, etc.

2:00 p.m.—Pick up Nina at airport.

He stopped reading when he heard the door open and looked up to see a wide-eyed Lincoln approaching his desk with a gun in his hand.

"Oh, my God. Larry, what the hell is that for? What are you doing?"

"You rotten backstabber! First, you tell me the mafia interview would be so easy. Just watch, you said. And what was the result? I go through hell, that's what. I'm thrown in a pile of cow dung, tied up for days, scalped by halfwits, I lose my evening news show, I'm turned into a sideshow freak on national television, shot at, have my skull crushed, scalped a second time, and now this. You give away my movie rights without even so much as a word to me."

"Is that all that's bothering you?"

"I was just pausing for air."

"Larry, put the gun down. Don't do something crazy. Listen to me. I'm this far away from a deal for a Broadway musical." He held up his hand with his thumb and forefinger close together.

Lincoln lifted his arm and aimed the gun at his agent's forehead. "I'm going to give it a surprise ending."

Baywatch turned his calendar book around and pushed it toward Lincoln. "Look at this agenda, Larry. It's right there. Read it. You're the man. The phone keeps jumping. We want Larry Lincoln! We want Larry Lincoln! The media can't get enough of you. Don't screw it all up now. We're just getting started."

"It's you I'm going to screw up."

Lincoln looked down at the calendar and Baywatch took advantage of the distraction and dove for cover under his desk.

"You coward. That's just like you. Stand up and take it like a man."

"I don't do man stuff, Larry. No Nathan Hale, no Joan of Arc. That's not me."

Lincoln aimed the gun at the desktop. "This is a Magnum something, and with this weapon I can shoot right through the desk. I'm going to make my day."

"Don't do it, Larry. I just had it delivered this morning. Solid walnut."

Lincoln paused for a few moments, and then pulled the trigger. An ear-shattering blast filled the room, then complete silence. Lincoln dropped the gun on the desk.

"You can come out now. The gun is on the desk."

"Damn you!" Baywatch screamed while remaining under the desk. "You scared the piss out of me. I can't believe you actually tried to kill me. What did you hit?"

"I wanted to, and Lord knows I have the right to, but I can't shoot you."

"I knew you would come to your senses," Baywatch answered.

"It has nothing to do with my senses. The gun isn't real. I took it from the prop room." He shoved the weapon off the desk.

Baywatch picked up the gun and peeked over the desk to make sure Lincoln did not have another weapon. "You son of a bitch. If that was your idea of a joke, it wasn't funny."

"I wasn't joking. I had to do something. I felt like the whole world was pissing on me. Like I'm everyone's stooge. The movie thing was the last straw. How could you have done that to me? Without a word."

"You did it to yourself, for crying out loud. Did you ever take the time to read your contract? You signed your life over to YOURchannel." He ran his hand across the desk to see if the gun had scratched it. "I tried to phone, but you were already in the meeting. There was absolutely nothing I could do about the movie rights. I was happy just to get you the raise and the bonus."

"What bonus?"

"The two-million-dollar bonus to drop the suit we were planning."

"I'm getting two million?"

"Two million, baby, plus five percent net on the movie less my percentage."

"Ingersoll never mentioned any of that. That's fantastic." He rushed around the desk to pick up his agent and throw his arms around him.

"You're damn right it's fantastic. And you almost shot me. What's happened to trust in this world?"

"I still have my news show?"

"Sort of. You have to share it with Necklace." Lincoln drew

back. "Larry, let's face reality here. I saw the ratings since she took your place. Having her do the show is like another bonus. Go with the flow. You'll still be reading some of the news, and you'll have the best ratings in the business. It will be different but it will work out well for you."

Lincoln looked into his agent's eyes. After a long silence, he smiled. "She really is beautiful. What the hell. Let's get out of here. I'll buy lunch. Two million plus seven per cent of the movie."

"Five per cent. Less my percentage." Baywatch added. "That's only the beginning. We can review your agenda while we lunch."

Lincoln threw his arm around his agent's shoulder as they walked toward the door.

"Who's playing the female role in the movie?" Lincoln asked.

"Ingersoll insisted on someone named Sharon Harlow or Diana-Kate. I've never heard of her, but he claims she's a sensational actress. I'm going to be her agent. By the way, can you sing?"

"I'm tone deaf."

"Not a problem. I have a deal going teaming you up with this rock group I represent. Remember Albert Einstein, the rock, blues, gospel, whatever group? They're interested in cutting an album with you. We were thinking along the lines of a Larry Lincoln Christmas carol collection."

Palermo

A phalanx of handsomely outfitted Italian policemen escorted anchorman Clark Smart through customs at the Palermo airport and into the lobby where he was surrounded by the paparazzi, American tourists, and curious Italian travelers. He was wearing his new khaki adventurer ensemble, which had been tailored in Britain for the occasion, plus his designer Italian silk cravat and Italian hiking boots. Before stepping up to the microphones that his network had arranged, he sent his staff off to claim his six-piece luggage collection and locate the white Mercedes sedan that Mayor Vocino had promised would be waiting.

"Gentlemen, I will accommodate you with all the photos you wish, but first I must tell you and the American people that I am here to do the hard reporting for which I am so famous. I plan to get to the bottom of Larry Lincoln's kidnapping and his connection with the Central Intelligence Agency. There was something wrong with that interview special, and I intend to bottom-fish it. My thorough investigation in Monte Castella and the disclosure of what I uncover will be aired on a television news special we will call *Anchorgate*.

"Can you give us your famous victory sign?" shouted one of his staff who had quietly slipped into the crowd of photographers.

Anchorman Smart responded with a toothy smile and raised

his hands with the victory signs. Cameras clicked repeatedly as he turned in several directions, holding the pose to give everyone an opportunity for photographs.

"That's all for now. My assistants will provide each of you with a brief bio of my life in television news and a list of awards, books, and my salary. Now I have a hard-hitting reporter's work to do, so if you will excuse me …"

Continuing to smile, he put on his designer sunglasses and made his way through the crowd to the terminal doors. As he stepped out into the bright sunlight, he felt someone grab his arm. Smart turned to face a man wearing an Italian World War I uniform, an officer's gold-braided hat and a body-length officer's cape draped across his shoulders. Large mirrored sunglasses, a walrus mustache, and a black beard covered much of his face.

"Quick, Mr. Anchorman Smart, put your arms around me and kiss me on both cheeks. We must appear to be old friends."

"Kiss you?" Smart looked at the man's face in an attempt to figure out who he was but saw only his own puzzled image in the sunglasses. Before he could say anything further, the officer threw his arms around him and pulled him close in a bear hug.

"I am Verdi of the Italian secret police," he whispered into Smart's ear. "We are working with the CIA to protect you. Your life is in peril. They have sent the Hungarians. Do not hesitate. Remember the pope. Move with me quickly."

The officer kissed Smart on both cheeks and pulled back without releasing his grip on his arms. "My dear friend," he shouted loudly. "How long it has been. It is so good to see you again. Come, your car is waiting."

He turned and began walking rapidly, dragging the startled anchorman along with him. "They are following us. We must make a break for it. Run, run for your life."

"My luggage!" Gable called out, desperately struggling to keep from falling as he was being hauled at running speed toward a new Mercedes van parked along the curb. Another man dressed as an Orthodox priest with a beard extending to his chest stood by the van's open rear door, frantically waving them on.

The moment Smart reached the van, the officer and the priest picked him up and threw him into the rear. The priest followed instantly, leaping on top of him, while a third man stuffed a sock into his mouth. The army officer slammed the door then turned and saluted the crowd, which had stopped to watch the activity. Clicking his heels and doing a military about face, he moved quickly to the van's front door and jumped in. He looked in every direction three times and then pressed down hard on the accelerator. With a shriek of the tires, the van sped off without incident toward the highway to Monte Castella.

After a few minutes, when he saw he was not being followed, Paolo looked at himself in the mirror and smiled.

"Al Pacino, eat your heart out."

Printed in the United States
By Bookmasters